SINS OF THE ANGEL

WAYNE J. HARRIS

authorHOUSE®

AuthorHouse™ UK Ltd.
500 Avebury Boulevard
Central Milton Keynes, MK9 2BE
www.authorhouse.co.uk
Phone: 08001974150

First published by AuthorHouse 7/29/2009

ISBN: 978-1-4389-9469-7 (sc)

Printed in the United States of America
Bloomington, Indiana

This book is printed on acid-free paper.

This book is dedicated to two of the angels in my life,
Jackie and Daniel.

I would like to thank Rev. Dr. Jonathan Pye for his sermon on angels which sowed the first seed that grew into this book.

IN THE BEGINNING

Every body exists in time and space. Everything in the temporal universe must have a start.

A PATH OPENS

1 Timothy 2:12
But I suffer not a woman to teach, nor to usurp authority over the man, but to be in silence.

'Angels and demons walk among us!' bellowed Doctor Gideon Matthews, lay preacher. 'We are surrounded by demons. Real demons from Hell. Disguised as people.' He sniffed the air for brimstone and sulphur, but, for the moment, he could only smell the musty church. 'Have you seen the depraved, deplorable actions of so-called celebrities? I have been told of disgusting things, truly repellent sexual exhibitions on the television. These are the acts of demons!' A shudder of revulsion passed through his thin shoulders at the very thought of these acts. 'I tell you, some demons have even taken over the Church and we must all be ready for the good fight.'

He paused for breath, reviewing the congregation to judge the reaction of his listeners.

They were rapt.

'As Revelations predicted,' he boomed out, 'the Apocalypse is almost upon us and God has allowed the Devil dominion over the earth.' He could feel the power of

God's wrath energising his body. 'The Evil One tricks and confuses us all. He wants every soul to come under His dominion in Hell. It is only by constant attention that we see through the deception and avoid the steel trap of sin.'

He grimaced to show his distaste and then softened his voice to draw them in closer to his quintessential belief. 'And that is why women cannot be allowed to hold High Office.'

Several of the faithful nodded slightly. It was a good crowd of maybe fifty people.

Yes, he thought in exultation, *these are the people who understand.*

'Women are by their very nature lustful,' he shouted. 'They cannot help it.' He shook his head in sorrow at the plight of these poor women. 'They will do anything they can to satisfy their carnal desires.' The wooden lectern was hard against his hands as he pounded it in rhythm with his words. 'They say they want to have a child, but it is only their base animal urges that drive them to these filthy activities. As it says in Proverbs "For a whore is a deep ditch; and a strange woman is a narrow pit. She also lieth in wait as for a prey, and increaseth the transgressors among men."'

He paused to scan for nay sayers, for this was the most contentious part of his sermon. There may have been some difficult people present. One man glared up at him. *I know you – you're a liberal* he thought in disgust. Near him was a woman whose face was totally without expression, almost as if she was not even present. Another man held a strange mad smile. Many shared his outrage.

'Women can only get into heaven by God's grace when He forgives them their sins.' Again he thumped the lectern on every word as he continued, 'and women will lead the Church, this Church, the Bride of Jesus, to ruin. We must stop this madness and save God's holy creation. We must stop these succubae.'

He softened his voice and leaned forward, strengthening the conspiracy with the best of these good people. 'And that is why I ask you all to follow me as we renew the church, tear it down and start again without the weak minded, without the ineffectual and without those who are dancing with the devil in one of his most common guises – a beautiful woman!'

He stood tall and proud once again but he kept his voice gentle. 'So read your Bible, and watch for the holy sign.' He pointed upwards. 'The sign from Our Lord and Saviour Jesus Christ,' his hand held the imaginary power of the church as he raised his voice in glory to God. 'When I am able to grasp the power from under the noses of the weak and the liberal!'

His hand formed a fist at his chest, pride swelling his heart. 'Many people are on our side. A bishop is with us. I can't say who yet, but be assured we are getting the support we need from high and low.' He pointed up the road to the Anglican Church, 'the vicar of this parish is with us.' He pointed in the opposite direction, towards the Evangelical Church, 'and others are with us, too. Many of us can't say anything yet, but our time will come. Listen to me all of you. We *will* have the church back, we *will* cast out these demons and we *will* be saved in the days to come when the unbelievers, sinners and liars will go to Hell to suffer at the hands of God's appointed tormentors for eternity.'

He paused again, exhausted but pleased at the steely looks of agreement from most of the congregation. 'And now a hymn.' He glanced at his notes and couldn't see which he had chosen. The organist started the music without waiting for a signal, playing the popular version of Amazing Grace.

It was too late now. He couldn't stop it. He hated it when hymns were set to modern melodies.

Doctor Matthews marched triumphantly to the entranceway as the hymn was rumbled, moaned, trilled and warbled by the worshippers. All this singing was a distraction. True worship to God could only occur through prayer and fasting. He waited for the noises to unwind down to their eventual end.

In front of the open doors, framed by the hay-sweet evening light of an English village in late spring he declaimed the benediction. 'May God go with you all, and may His Judgement strike the sinners dumbfounded as He guides us to His glory through the Church He will create through us all.'

The congregation stood and trailed out past him. He acknowledged the farewells and praise from the righteous and he ignored the approbation from the weak and liberal.

The blank faced woman walked past him still in a trance, not acknowledging his presence at all.

The liberal shook his pathetic head.

The mad smiler stopped, blocking the remaining few behind him. 'That was marvellous, sir,' he said staring into Doctor Matthew's eyes.

Something in this man's manner made the preacher feel uncomfortable. 'It's good to have another to share the burden,' he answered.

'I think you should be a saint.' The eyes were too bright, the smile just a bit too wide.

He had heard it all before at many of his sermons and so he gave his stock answer. 'Only the dead can be saints.'

The man nodded wildly. 'Yes. Yes. And martyrs.'

His heart sank in despair. Another useless idiot, he thought to himself. 'Thank you,' he said in curt dismissal.

The man nodded once again and walked down the stairs without looking back. The last few waiting behind him filed past with an exchange of vaguely polite comments.

At peace in the silent church, Doctor Matthews tidied up the pews, locked the doors and stalked out into the adjacent alley.

Yet again he rehearsed his life, his plans and his work as he strode along the hedged path. All peoples must hear God's Word and follow God's Way so that all may come to Him and not suffer eternal damnation. And women priests were the greatest threat. And now those damned liberals were even talking of women bishops. It must not be allowed!

His back ached and his legs hurt. He touched his cross as it hung from his neck to remind him of the sacrifices that Jesus made for him and that he in turn must make for everyone else. He withdrew his Bible from his pocket and opened it at random to see the message it had for him. There on the page was his favourite quote, yet again.

Matthew 26:41. 'Watch and pray, that ye enter not into temptation: the spirit indeed is willing, but the flesh is weak.'

Glory be to God. Even though he opened to a random page, time and time again it was always that page and that quote. It spoke directly to him, judging him also, for his flesh had been weak once.

If only I hadn't married her, he thought. *But for her I could now be a priest, pure and holy, free of fleshly temptation. And all the fasting and praying was not enough to overcome this one time of weakness. If only.*

But he was married and that event was undeniable and could not be undone for it had occurred in the full view of God.

Lord, why did you create so many distractions from your holy word? Why have you given us gross bodies to distract us with their messy needs? Why have You created hunger, greed, lust, and all disgusting aberrations separating us from your perfection?

So many who could hear ignored him. Some even lampooned him! The papers wrote the most appalling things. Lies! Slander!

He marched more quickly, stamping his feet, holding the lip tightening anger within the rigid muscles of his slim body.

He never saw his murderer.

God's will be done, he always thought, but apparently God's Will was not done in the way that Doctor Matthews expected.

God did not intervene as the knife penetrated to Doctor Matthews' kidneys. The knife separated that which should not be separated. The knife damaged that which should not be damaged. God did not intervene to stop the blood from abandoning his body.

As Doctor Matthews lay in pain and dizziness he became aware that his life was ebbing away onto the filthy lane. He called out, demanding a miracle to enable him to continue. *He had so much to do before his life could end. So very much to do. God needed him. God must rescue him.*

God is usually parsimonious with miracles so as not to make our world incomprehensible but this time there was a miracle. Although it was not the miracle that Doctor Matthews expected.

Manifestation

1 Corinthians 12:7
But the manifestation of the Spirit is given to every man to profit withal.

I looked down at the body I had been given. It was covered by a sheet. My brain remembered that word. Sheet.

The left arm was visible.

My arm.

...

Was visible.

...

I was connecting with the body, its memories appearing as needed. I looked around.

Looked.

...

I had done it twice now. I looked again.

Three times now.

...

There were beds and medical equipment. I was in a hospital and that tube in my arm meant that I was ill.

Hospital.

III.

…

I was fully integrated with a body now.

Integrated.

Body.

…

My body wanted to tell me something. Something important.

…

I had been murdered!

A country lane. A pain in the back. Stumbling forward. Falling. More pain. The blood. Coughing and spitting. When? The past, the present or the future?

AWARENESS

1 Corinthians 15:44
It is sown a natural body; it is raised a spiritual body. There is a natural body, and there is a spiritual body.

I was awake.
I looked around.
A female nurse was present.
How did I know that she was a nurse?
It was her uniform.
My connection to this body was much stronger now and so was the pain – a pain that I had to learn to bear in some way.
'Good morning,' she said. She brushed a grey hair from her plump face. 'How are you feeling?'
I stared at her. I needed to do something. Talk? Yes talk. But how? Just do it? Say something. What? Just do it?
She looked at my face, felt my ... arm? No, wrist. The body thought that naming these precise parts was important somehow. As if the choice of body part mattered. Signifying

something. My body knew what. She was feeling my pulse. It was a medical procedure, a monitoring process.

'Can you speak?' she asked.

The body shook its head. How did it know to do that? Was that my mouth that was dry and sore? My body also noted small details, perfume, the touch of sheets against my body, a clattering sound.

'You can understand me, then?'

I nodded. Yes. We nodded, body and me. One consciousness. One body. Together.

My side hurt. It must have been where I was hit.

'Do you know where you are?'

I looked around at the clues I had already identified. The beds, huge and forbidding with metal sides. Wires and tubes leading from my body to machines. Complex wall sockets. Gas bottles. Why was she asking me stupid questions?

Hospital. It was a hospital. This was a hospital. 'Hospital,' I snapped at her.

She nodded, pleased. 'You gave everyone quite a scare, you know?'

Was she still speaking? She was watching me. She fiddled with the tube from my arm. Feeling my wrist. Or did she do that earlier?

'We all thought you were dead, you know? It's a miracle that you're alive. The doctors were so pleased that they were able to save you, Doctor Matthews.'

Miracle. Yes. The body knew the word. I knew the concept. Miracle. A holy word. He was dead, too. The one they were talking to. He had gone. And now I was here.

Gone to where?

Something was wrong. I was alone. The body and I cried in pain and anger. All these sensations were too great. I surrendered myself to non-awareness.

INTEGRATION

Job 10:20
Are not my days few? Cease then, and let me alone, that I may take comfort a little.

I could hear a woman's voice.

'Hello,' I said, but my voice croaked, dry and incomprehensible.

She touched my arm. I opened my eyes. Her face was close, staring into my eyes, only a few inches away, round and white, edged with grey hair and laugh lines. Her thin lips were covered by light pink lipstick. Her faith was strong.

'So, you're awake again, Doctor Matthews.' She was Irish.

'Yes.' My voice was clearer.

'How are you feeling?'

A good question. How was I feeling? I concentrated on my body. There was a pain in my back, but it was easily bearable. My throat was dry and my stomach felt odd. 'Can I have some water?'

'Yes, of course.'

The smile on her face raised a hallelujah chorus of joy in my body. I had to please her again just to see that beautiful smile once more.

I recognised her uniform. She was a nurse. She poured some water and passed it to me as I monitored her with the sharp focus of a helpless man, waiting while someone else must meet his bodily needs. She was so very slow.

I sipped at the water.

'Good,' she said. 'Not too fast. You're looking much better than last time I talked to you. You seem to be on the mend, now.' She took the glass from me and placed it on a bedside table. 'I'm afraid that the police want to come and talk to you, later on. Do you think you're ready?'

I nodded. I felt a need to talk, but I didn't know what to say. There was a cross hanging on a chain from her neck. I knew what that meant. I knew other things, too.

'I'm a Doctor of Theology, aren't I?' I croaked.

'Yes, Doctor Matthews. And a very good man you are. I've been to one of your sermons. I think it's wonderful the way you stand up for what is good. Why didn't you become a priest?' She waited patiently for an answer, head cocked to the side, hands folded in front of her.

I lay in silence, too confused to speak but enjoying the praise.

She continued after a pause of a few seconds. 'There is so much sin these days and there you are, telling everyone to be good and to put aside their sins. We need to keep to the old ways. It's so wonderful to see you recovering.' The smile warmed my soul. 'It's been a few weeks, you know? You need to get up and about. Strengthen yourself and get back to your good work.' She was watching me carefully all the time, talking for both of us. 'Did you know you were actually dead when you arrived?'

I nodded.

'The doctors were amazed. Your heart started beating again. On its own. Without any intervention. There was just enough blood left in you to keep you alive. They didn't understand, but I did. It was a miracle.'

I smiled. Her faith had guided her to the truth.

She touched the cross at her neck. 'They were all puzzled. They think they have to do everything. Doctors can be so arrogant. But I understood. You've come back to continue your good works haven't you? God sent you back.'

She was wrong in so many ways but at the heart of her meaning there was a truth. Why *was* I here? Why should a being like me be needed here?

'Yes,' I said, just to please her and perhaps to get another smile.

She touched my hand and leaned toward me. 'Did you have a near death experience? Did you go to heaven? Did you meet God?'

I didn't want to talk about it. I wasn't ready. Instead I nodded weakly.

'What's heaven like?' she pleaded. 'I know what it says in the Bible and the priests talk of it, but what's it like to be there? To really feel God?'

I couldn't bear it. My body reacted angrily. 'Leave me alone,' I shouted.

'I'm sorry, Doctor Matthews. You're tired. I didn't mean to upset you. We can talk again later.' She paused as she stared at me. 'If you want,' she added. She turned and left.

I was alone again and it hurt more than ever. A body with pain and thirst and hunger demanding I pay attention to it. This was not right. I could not accept this. Eventually I calmed down and my awareness was transformed into the subtle state of dream filled sleep.

I Am Not That Man

Psalm 107:26
They mount up to the heaven, they go down again to the depths: their soul is melted because of trouble.

'What's heaven like, Doctor Matthews? Do you feel privileged that God resurrected you with a miracle? When are you going back to your good work?'

It was the Irish nurse. She had been absent for a few days but now she was back and asking more questions than ever. I was still annoyed with her and her stupid questions.

'Heaven is nothing like here,' I grumped at her.

'Do we all look the same as here?'

'No. How can we? It's Heaven.'

'Then what do we look like?'

'We don't look like anything. We don't have bodies.'

'But surely we must have bodies. How will I recognise my loved ones?' She frowned. It was clear that she had never really thought about the afterlife before.

I was getting exasperated. 'Have you ever been bored?' I shouted. 'Have you ever had day after day after day of nothing ever really changing?'

She placed her hands on her hips. 'There's no need to be so rude about it,' she said. She was offended.

I felt a bit guilty. 'I'm sorry, but it's hard to explain. You have to let go of your old ideas.'

She shook her head – too rapidly. She wasn't ready to let go of anything.

I tried again. 'You must understand,' I said. 'If there is time, then things must change. They can change in a loop, or in a cycle with constant repetition, or they can change in new ways. Every way there are problems. Repetition is a dead end with no meaning left to it. Changes enable us to become something new and different, like the difference between being young and old.'

'You have forgotten your scripture and your belief,' she judged.

'No, it's just that Heaven is timeless.'

'I hope you haven't lost your faith, Doctor Matthews. What would become of your work in the church? You need to stop women becoming bishops.'

My anger took over. 'I am no longer Doctor Matthews,' I shouted. 'I am not that man. I reject everything he said and did. I do not want my own church and I don't care if there is an army of women in all parts of the church. I'd even like a female pope!'

She dropped her voice to a low, barely controlled whisper. I could see the muscles stand out on her jaw as she tightened her lips and clenched her teeth. 'So you've become a heathen. You're letting a lot of people down, you contemptible little man. You shouldn't be allowed to live.' She marched away.

Now I had made an enemy but I couldn't be Doctor Matthews anymore. I didn't have enough hate in me.

WRATH

Psalm 37:8
Cease from Anger, and forsake wrath: fret not thyself
in any wise to do evil.

Each blow was delivered with a steady rhythm. 'You
will not sin. Sin will bring your eternal damnation.'

She cried out softly, trying her best to control herself.

Her first sin had been wrath. Like so many children she
did not get her own way and became angry. She was too
young to understand the full meaning of her father's actions
but she soon learnt not to show any anger. Virtually every
day of her young life had been shaped with these beatings,
at first only when actual sin was identified but now, ever
since she had learnt to hide her sin, the beatings were given
regularly "on account of her being a sinner".

She managed to control her sobs and patiently withstood
the pain, waiting for the final Bible passage to be quoted at
her when the stress of the experience would enhance her
memory. It was only a matter of time before this beating
would become just another memory.

At last the blows ceased and the benediction was
announced.

'James 1:20. For the wrath of man worketh not the righteousness of God.'

She prayed to God to help her to control her anger before she was doomed to burn in Hell for an eternity.

As an adult she was grateful to her parents for they had taught her the importance of the soul. It was the body that always caused one to sin and so it must be controlled. A few minutes or hours of suffering were nothing when compared to the eternity of separation from God. From God's point of view – outside of time – all suffering has already ended. God sees the lesser importance of the transient against the eternal.

But so many people did not understand. So many people ignored their souls by indulging in sins – anger, gluttony, greed, envy. All short term and worthless. The sinners must be helped. They must be saved, like her, before they damned themselves to an eternity of Godlessness.

She needed to do the greatest good for the most people. Her scientific training taught her the value of being methodical and so she thoroughly researched every person near and far in order to identify the most evil people. She would save their souls whatever the cost.

Salvation

2 Peter 2:21
*For it had been better for them not to have known the
way of righteousness, than, after they have known it, to
turn from the holy commandment delivered unto them.*

A monk enveloped in robes and cowl kneels over an
unconscious man lying on a carpeted floor. Nothing is
visible of the person within the robes. A beautiful, naked
angel in perfect human form except for the smooth lack of
any sexual or excretory organs stands behind the monk,
whispering instructions.

**'Bind him hand and foot and cast him into the
outer darkness. In that place there will be weeping and
gnashing of teeth,' whispers the angel.**

'I know that quote. Matthew 22:13.'

The helpless one is bound hand and foot with strong
cords of hemp.

'What's happening?'

The angel ignores the observer's question. More
instructions are whispered.

'Let the lying lips be put to silence.'

'That was Psalm 31:18 wasn't it?'

The man is roused by a shake. He looks around in puzzlement and a hint of fear appears in his eyes. The angel's strength increases and its body glows softly.

'Of how much sorer punishment, suppose ye, shall he be thought worthy, who hath trodden under foot the Son of God, and hath counted the blood of the covenant, wherewith he was sanctified, an unholy thing, and hath done despite unto the Spirit of grace?'

'Hebrews 10:29. Is this a holy court?'

'You have committed the ultimate sin,' the hooded one chants, high pitched.

The bound man looks around, confusion in his eyes. 'What?

The chant responds. 'You were a priest, a leader in the church of our Lord Jesus.'

'Is that what this is about?'

'You are leading others away from their true calling, from Jesus.'

The bound man becomes angry. 'No. It's the church. It's not needed, anymore. It does so much damage in the world. God doesn't exist or he would not have abandoned us. People have a choice. You should not have to believe in Jesus or God or Heaven.' At the last moment he recognises his anger and tries to become reassuring, calm and considered.

'Why then is this people of Jerusalem slidden back by a perpetual backsliding? They hold fast deceit, they refuse to turn,' said the angel.

'Jeremiah 8:5. You can't be a holy court. You're using the Old Testament. We are more knowledgeable now, the New Testament applies. Everyone must hear both sides to make a choice, good and evil. Otherwise only Good is present and we will simply be automatons or only Evil is present and we must

21

always commit evil to survive. This poor man is performing a holy duty by offering everyone a choice. Let him go.'

The angel and the monk ignore the sophistry of the observer. The victim is apparently unaware of the angel and the observer.

The chanting starts once again. 'Your backsliding has condemned you. You are turning away from God.'

The judged one snaps back, 'there is no such thing as a soul.'

The monks' hands rush to the head, holding the soft material of the cowl to his ears to exclude the terrible words.

'My people are destroyed for lack of knowledge: because thou have rejected knowledge, I will also reject thee, that thou shalt be no priest to me.'

'Hosea 4:6. Let him go. Please let him go.'

The angel finally acknowledges the observer with a smile.

Another high-pitched chant sounds from beneath the hood, 'God has rejected you.'

The man tries to bargain once more, barely controlled desperation starting to sound in his voice. 'That's okay. I don't think it matters, anyway.'

'Which hand do you write with?' is chanted

The man tries to hide his right hand, somehow anticipating what might yet happen.

'Wherefore if thou hand or foot offend thee, cut them off, and cast them from thee: it is better for thee to enter into life halt or maimed, rather than having two hands or two feet to be cast into everlasting fire.'

'Matthew 18:8. No! You can't. That's not an instruction. It's not right.'

As the accursed man watches, a knife is produced from under the robes. 'No,' he calls in desperation.

The binding cords on the offending right hand are moved to expose the wrist. The angel's obedient servant sings in a falsetto, 'and if your hand causes you to sin, cut it off and throw it away.'

As the man contorts his body in a desperate attempt to escape the pain and loss, the knife hacks into the wrist, removing the source of evil. He screams and bucks his body.

Finally he faints.

It is slow and difficult to cut away the hand, arteries pumping and blood splattering the robes. The bones prove particularly difficult but the judgement is executed with determination and patience.

'Stop it. Please. Do no more.'

An unnaturally long tongue whips out from the angel's mouth to lick at the blood. The stump is wrapped in a cloth to stop the flow of blood.

'See now that I, even I, am he, and there is no god with me; I kill, and I make alive: I wound, and I heal: neither is there any that can deliver out of my hand.'

'Deuteronomy 32:39. It's not happening.'

The victim is awakened.

The monk sings once more. 'Your eternal soul. You must come back to Jesus while there is still time.'

'What?' The man sobs, some faint hope at last. 'Whatever you want.' All the anger has left.

'Say that you love Jesus. That he is your only true saviour and that you forsake all others.'

'Yes. Yes!'

'Say it.'

'I love Jesus. He is my...'

'Your only true saviour.'

'My only true saviour.'

'And...'

'Oh God it hurts. It hurts. Please save me.'

'And you forsake all others.'

'Yes! Yes!' The words are barely comprehensible with the sobbing.

'Say it.'

'I forsake… I forsake all others.'

'For Jesus.'

'Yes, for Jesus. Please call me a doctor.'

'Good. We have saved your soul.'

The mouth is sealed with tape to prevent any further blasphemy that might undo the penitent words.

'Nevertheless the foundation of God standeth sure, having this seal, The Lord knoweth them that are his. And, let every one that nameth the name of Christ depart from iniquity.'

'2 Timothy 2:19. No, he is not saved. That was forced from him. Only a true choice is valid. By offering no alternative this man can make no moral choice. You are tricking the monk.'

'At the mouth of two witnesses, or three witnesses, shall be that is worthy of death be put to death,' the angel announces.

'Deuteronomy 17:6. No! What now? Am I your witness? There is only one of me. Where are the others? You can't put him to death on my witness alone.'

The angel looks up, smiles and points to itself.

'No!'

The tongue flies out from the angel's lips insinuating itself in spirals until its tip touches the mouth of the victim who seems unaware of the angel and its tongue.

A hand pinches the man's nostrils, which, with the mouth sealed, breaks his narrow link to life. The redeemed one thrashes about, but the tongue of the angel flicks down once more and he becomes motionless except for the tears.

Gradually, he turns blue and collapses yet still the nose is held closed.

The monotone chanting continues. 'And so you can sin no more, and thus your immortal soul has been saved through the suffering of this physical husk.'

From within the grey robes a handful of hairs and some skin and blood are thrown into the room.

The angel nods with great approval and casts a spell, integrating the deposited hair, skin and blood into the scene. It looks up hungrily and gestures-inviting the observer into its heart.

Am I to be judged one day in this unholy court?

The beautiful head nods, the beautiful face smiles and the eyes glow a deep red around the pupils. The tongue lifts up coming closer. The perfect arms rise and the fingers become talons.

I woke up screaming and sweating. The image of the severed hand was still in my mind's eye. The Irish nurse appeared within seconds.

'Are you all right Dr Matthews?'

I nodded, but only weakly. That poor man. It was too awful, too distracting. Why did I have such an awful dream? Was it something to do with Dr M.?

'What happened?' she asked.

'A dream. There was an angel. No, it couldn't have been. A man was tortured and killed.'

'Oh dear. Well you're safe now. Perhaps you heard another patient.'

'My Bible. I need my Bible.'

'Everything you had is in here.' Her hand touched the drawer and hesitated. 'We gave your wallet to your wife.'

I shook my head. 'My Bible. Can you look for it please?'

She opened the drawer and looked through it. 'I can see your handkerchief but nothing else. Are you sure you had it?'

'I don't know. I just thought...'

'You're confused. It must be a reaction to the trauma you've been through. I can get you another Bible. Or would you prefer a sedative?'

'Yes, please.' Oh yes, indeed. I needed something to help me cope with this hell.

'Which?' she said.

'The sedative.'

She returned with a tablet. I swallowed and waited to return to the gentle escape of non-awareness.

BODY AND SOUL

Humans are not perfect, for if they were they would have no choice but to obey God.

Investigations

Deuteronomy 19:18
And the judges shall make diligent inquisition.

I could feel the sheets of the bed, cold and cool. My eyes and nose assessed the room and the judgement was not good. It smelt of disinfectant. The dull green paint of the walls and ceiling was blistering. The bed, the walls, the furniture, everything was old and shabby, dull. It was as if the maintenance staff were waiting for the ward to heal itself. But there was no magical reconstruction here. Time was passing. Decay and old age were stealing the newness from everything.

'Doctor Matthews.'

I searched for the voice.

It was the Irish nurse again. She was standing close to the bed. I hoped she wasn't still angry with me.

'The police are here to talk to you.' She gestured, open-palmed, to a policewoman standing at the end of the bed.

I forced my body awake and inspected the policewoman. She was attractive with red hair, a round face, a slim feminine waist and curved hips, their shape visible despite the uniform.

'Do you feel up to an interview?' the nurse asked.

I nodded.

The nurse drew the curtains closed and helped me to sit up. The policewoman looked around, wandered out of sight for a second and came back with a chair. The nurse disappeared.

My interviewer sat, opened her case and took out a pen, a notebook and a small voice recorder. 'Doctor Matthews,' she said. I suppose she was announcing my name for the recorder.

'Yes?' I could see that she had little faith, almost no belief in eternal truths outside this world. It wasn't dormant – it was absent.

'I'm Sergeant Wright. I'd like to ask you some questions.'

'Okay.' Her perfume distracted me. I became very aware that I was lying in bed next to a beautiful woman. Some part of me decided that I needed to control myself.

'Do you know what happened to you?'

I nodded.

'Could you speak please?'

'Yes. Yes. I was hit. From behind.'

'Okay. You were stabbed, actually.'

And then the interview started. She wanted to know everything. Was there anyone who had a grudge against me? Of course not. Had I received any threatening letters? Yes, lots. Rebecca, my wife always burned them; they were only cranks, afraid of what I had to say. Could I identify who wrote them? No. Where did they come from? Everywhere. How did they know where I lived? They wrote to me via the University. Could I identify anything? Did I know why I was attacked? No and no and no again. Endlessly, the same questions again and again and again. I was storm-battered by their number and speed. I tried my best but I simply didn't know anything. I had some vague memories of a sermon just before I was stabbed but all these questions confused me and I couldn't be sure of what had happened.

I must admit that I also found it hard to concentrate on her words and not her appearance.

It was irrelevant now, anyway. After all, I wasn't him any more. Why should I care?

'Thank you,' she said, turning off the recorder. 'You've been very helpful. But I do wish you hadn't ignored those letters. If we could just see a few...' She closed her notepad.

'Have you talked to my wife?' I regretted having to mention Rebecca to her. It wouldn't improve my chances with this wonderful woman. My thoughts surprised and shocked me. What was causing this obsession?

'Yes.'

My body provided a memory. 'There may be some letters left. I received a few in the last few weeks that Rebecca might not have burnt yet. It's been too warm for a fire.'

'I see. Why didn't you say so before?' She was peeved.

'I only just remembered. You were on at me and I couldn't think.' Oh no. She was angry with me. I didn't want that. I wanted her to like me, to want me in the same way that I wanted her.

She smiled. 'Yes, of course. Why did you ask about your wife?'

'She knows all about the letters. Even the ones from work. I bring them home. She opens them, sorts them out and leaves them on my desk. I don't have time, you see.'

'She never said anything to me in her interview.'

This was odd; but then again, according to my memory, maybe not.

The policewoman interrupted before I could remember anything more. 'We're still investigating your case but I'm afraid there was a nasty murder on Thursday. It was rather gruesome and we want to catch the killer as soon as possible, so we've given it priority for the moment. We'll get back to you as soon as we can. Okay?'

I nodded. 'Please come and see me again,' I pleaded.

'Thank you once again, Doctor Matthews.' She left.

I rolled over, exhausted.

I was asleep in seconds.

Trouble

Job 3:26

I was not in safety, neither had I rest, neither was I quiet; yet trouble came.

A nurse walked over and sat by me, a bowl of food in her hand. She was attractive as the young always are; dark hair and face, slim. She might have been Indian. Her faith was weak, almost insubstantial.

'What is your name?' I asked.

She smiled and leaned forward towards me. 'Janet. It's good to see that you're all right. You'll be going home soon.'

'Home?' A surge of panic stopped my heart for a second. 'Why do I have to go home? Can't I stay here? I'm not well yet.'

'Your wife will be there.'

I stared at the sheets covering my body. I was miserable. Rebecca wouldn't care about me. She would make my life unbearable. I wanted to stay amongst all these pretty, young nurses.

'Anyway,' she added, 'you hardly need looking after now. Have you tried to feed yourself?' She placed a bowl and spoon on a table with wheels and rolled it to a position above my chest. 'Sit up now.' She slipped a hand down my back and helped me to sit. I was weak, but I thoroughly enjoyed her touch at my back. I looked into the bowl. The food was grey and unappetising, filled by unidentifiable food chunks and a thick, oily liquid. It stank of grease. I guessed it was some sort of stew. I was hungry. I reached for the spoon. 'Is there cheese in it?'

'Um, I don't think so.'

'I'd like some cheese. Any sort.'

'Perhaps later when you've eaten some of this.'

My hunger took control of my arm. I tried to get as much as possible on each spoonful, forcing it into my mouth and swallowing as quickly as possible. Despite its appearance it tasted good.

The nurse smiled at me. 'You seem to be fine. I'll be back in a while.'

I stared at her bottom as she walked away.

My stomach demanded my attention. It was rebelling at the way it was being treated, threatening to regurgitate its contents. I forced the food down anyway.

The ambulance crew left me in the living room with Rebecca. She was thin lipped and stern, as usual.

The house stank of cat's urine. This was normal, too. I looked at the white walls in our tiny living room. It was an old cottage sadly neglected because Doctor Matthews was using the money to create his alternative church, not even giving it to the poor and needy. The miserable old fool liked to suffer. I was so glad that I was no longer that man. The walls were in desperate need of a new of coat of paint to cover the damp stains. I sat on the sagging sofa and a cat came and jumped on my lap. As I pushed it away I saw Rebecca's frown deepen but even then she didn't break the aggressive silence she had held since she met me at the door. The house was always funeral hushed.

'Hello dear,' I offered. I felt awkward, but I was hopeful that she would respond and care for me. Some part of me decided that hope was a waste of time.

'Hello Doctor Matthews.' Her tone was flat, emotionless and unloving.

With those words I could feel the vitality drain from every last corner of my body. His memories seemed to indicate that this peculiar response was normal, even commonplace.

'Are you well?' she asked as if asking the butcher for a freshly killed side of lamb.

'I have just come out of hospital. I nearly died.' I suppose I was whining when I think back on it. I wanted her to look after me, to stop hating me. But I didn't know how. I had gone through too much.

'Yes, of course. God's will be done' – said in a rush as if it were one word – 'your role has been confirmed. I was surprised, but perhaps you are right. Perhaps He wanted to keep you alive for some strange reason.'

'Yes.' Did she know I was here for a reason? Did she know what it was? Did she know who I was now?

'At least *you* have a role,' she muttered in self-centred, bitterness.

Perhaps I could help her? My memories said it wasn't possible. She never responded with anything other than hate and coldness. 'Your life has worth,' I said hesitantly.

She dismissed my offer of peace with a grunt.

I didn't want this. I wanted her support, her love. Something within me added that I wanted her body also. I wanted to be cared for and coddled, caressed and touched. Especially caressed and touched. 'You didn't visit me in hospital,' I said, wishing I could avoid accusing her, but doing so anyway.

'No, it was too hard to get to without driving.'

'Ah.' Some experience of Dr Matthews indicated that there was no point in saying anything more about it. 'Do you have any food? Could you prepare something for me? Cheese?'

'What?'

'I'm very hungry.'

'I suppose I can do something for you.' She stood slowly, indifferent to my needs, but perhaps some semblance of duty remained in her heart.

'Do you love me?' I asked.

She stopped and turned her head minimally, just enough to see me but not enough for social interaction. 'You are my husband.'

'What's that suppose to mean.'

She looked away so that I could not see her face. 'I pledged to love you when we married.'

'Yes, but do you love me? Do you want to care for me? Do you want me as a man?'

She stared at me, full faced, sharp and uncaring. 'A tuna sandwich. But don't expect me to clean up after you.'

Not even any cheese. Life wasn't worth living. Why did it always have to be so difficult? I wished I could go back to the hospital.

A Husband's Rights

Psalm 88:18
Lover and friend hast thou put far from me, and mine acquaintance into darkness.

I was watching the news on TV about the war on terror. The President of the USA announced another attack on the terrorists. The opposing fanatics responded with defiance. Both sides were obsessed with fighting for the same religious reasons, each blaming the other.

My eyes were focussed on the beautiful, buxom and very sexy female presenter. My body kept fidgeting, my hand resting on my warm crotch, demanding something. I couldn't understand what was happening. When the programme finally finished, my thoughts focussed on the only woman in the house, Rebecca. I went searching for her.

She was in the bedroom wearing the same plain, white, neck to ankles dress that she always wore. She was very carefully folding my white underpants and placing them into a white drawer next to my white T-shirts. I hated this colourless house. Even the smell of the room was neutral and uninteresting. I needed colour and interest. I needed to experience an exciting world, not be dragged down by Doctor Matthews' boring and stunted life.

She stared at me. 'Did you hear the phone?' Her tone of voice was accusing.

I frowned but did not reply.

'You should have answered it, I was busy.'

'I hate answering the phone,' I said with a shrug. I wanted to protect myself from her anger.

'It was David. He wanted to know how you're feeling and when he'll see you again. We both thought that you would be eager to get back to work even at this time of year.'

I shrugged. College life was boring and irrelevant.

'You were going to give a seminar this week.' She stared at me intently. 'Have you forgotten it?'

'No,' I lied.

'They decided that you must be very ill, so they cancelled it.' I was being assessed for signs of recalcitrance. 'Aren't you well yet?'

Some part of me decided to make an offering to pacify her anger. 'You're a good wife.'

She frowned at me, slightly puzzled. 'What have I done? Surely I am allowed to talk to your employers?'

'Yes, of course. Why are you so angry all the time?'

'What do you care?'

'But I do. I love you. You are my wife.'

'Huh.'

I moved towards her. I had to touch her. 'Can you give me a kiss?'

'What?' She was incredulous.

'A kiss.'

She glared.

'Come, you are my wife. Surely I can kiss my wife?' I put my arms around her. She was stiff and uncomfortable.

I gave her a peck on the cheek. I could feel a need rising uncontrollably from within my body. My hand slipped onto her thigh and she froze. I gathered her dress with my fingers. I had to make close contact with her body. I forced my open mouth to her lips. She turned her head to the side and squirmed under my hands but I held her tight. My lips hunted hers as she dodged and weaved.

'What are you doing? Control yourself!'

I had to have her. 'Just a kiss. Let yourself go. Feel it. We could both enjoy it.' I had my hand on her bare thigh; my fingers were touching her panties. I could feel her soft skin over the hard muscles. I had to have more.

'Stop it!' she screamed in my face. 'Stop it, you animal!'

My hand was in her panties. It slid to the front. I could feel her pubic hairs. She pulled her hips back, making it difficult for me to reach her groin and still keep trying to kiss her.

'No,' she screamed. 'Stop it. You're hurting me!'

I stopped.

It was almost impossible but I stopped.

A part of me screamed in frustration.

'I just…' I couldn't finish the sentence. I forced myself to let go and step away.

The tears were running down her face. 'Why can't you … leave me alone? Please. I'm sorry. I can't. It's not my fault. I wanted…' She ran to the bathroom. I could hear the thud of the bolt locking the door, creating her place of refuge from my need.

Hardly aware of what I was doing I ran out the door, climbed into the car and drove off.

My Wife Doesn't Understand Me

Proverbs 6:25
Lust not after her beauty in thine heart; neither let her take thee with her eyelids.

This hotel room was the ideal escape from Rebecca and that house. It was all behind me now.

I inspected my surroundings. They were plush and colourful and smelt of flowers. Everything was wonderful compared to *her* fiefdom. I was sitting in front of a full cheese selection and a bottle of red wine. This was so right – a part of my pre-destined fate. My credit card had provided me with everything I ever wanted. Free at last! I could relax and enjoy myself.

I started with the cheese. My favourite was the Stilton. The cheddar was far too bland. I should have asked for something tastier. All too quickly there was nothing left. My stomach was stretched tight, straining the buttons of my shirt, but that didn't matter. Everything was great.

There was an old American movie on the television. It was set in one of those 1950's bars where everyone is having a good time. A man was complaining about his wife and, even though he was serving drinks, the guy behind the bar was giving great advice. Beautiful women surrounded them. That's what I needed! A bar tender's advice, a drink and some new friends!

I found the bar in a section near the main lobby. I was the only drinker present, sitting on a stool, leaning on the cold, hard surface and facing all those drinks. There was a vague smell of something sweet.

'What would you like, sir?' The barman was wearing some sort of uniform. He seemed very nice, but a bit young, about 30, perhaps. He had the name Garry on a badge. He had a little faith — perhaps it could have been developed.

I could hear a constant hum from the nearby lobby as people checked in and out and went about hotel business.

Dr M didn't seem to know anything about alcohol. I would just have to discover all about it for myself. Which one should I try first? Garry waited patiently.

'What's that one, there?' I asked.

He followed my pointing finger. 'Which one, sir?'

'The blue bottle.'

He held it up so I could see. 'Curaçao,' he said.

I read the label. 'Yep. I want some of that.'

He smiled gently. I liked him already.

'Perhaps you'd prefer it in a cocktail, sir? It's the usual way to drink it. It's called a Blue Lagoon. But it's a bit expensive.'

'Brilliant name. Yeah, I'll have one of them.'

He was a master of cocktails, selecting and pouring the different liquids so effortlessly. I loved watching him. Finally, a glass arrived in front of me, a paper umbrella shading a beautiful, blue liquid.

'That'll be five pounds, sir.'

I grabbed my wallet from my trousers.

'Are you a guest at the hotel?'

'Yes.'

'Ah. In that case you don't need any cash. What is your room number?'

'Um, I've forgotten.'

'Perhaps you have your key?'

'Of course! I pulled out my key and showed it to him.

'That'll be fine, sir.'

I remembered to sip the cocktail like everyone did in the movie. I looked around to see if there was anything worth seeing. A woman was sitting in the corner. It was odd that I never saw her come in. She must have been there all along, which was puzzling. Why hadn't I seen her earlier when I first arrived? She smiled at me and my heart started doing something strange.

'Would you like to come and sit next to me, Mister?' she called.

I nodded, and walked over taking a good look. She had an elfin face, boyish and slim cheeked but with bright red lips and big black eyelashes that demanded to be noticed. Her blonde hair was cut short in what Dr M would have called a Mia Farrow look. Her bare arms were muscular and her hands seemed to be large for such a small woman. Her red dress covered her up to her neck. I was puzzled because I couldn't tell whether her faith was strong or weak.

I tripped over a chair leg, and spilt my drink on another table.

'No problem, sir,' called the waiter from behind. He must have been watching me as I stumbled around. 'I'll sort that out. Would you like another drink?'

'Yes. Yes, please.' I was so embarrassed.

The woman pulled out a chair next to her. 'Come and sit down, Mister, before you hurt yourself.'

Now that I was closer to her I could feel it, strongly, from deep within my soul. There was something very important about this woman.

I sat down without any further falls, thank goodness. Another blue glass complete with umbrella appeared in front of me almost immediately. Her perfume was gentle and delicate, slightly sweet but not overpowering.

'Is that what you normally drink, Mister?' she asked. She reminded me of a cheeky kid in a movie. Her voice had a barely hidden laugh. I couldn't help wondering what she was smiling at.

'Umm, no. I don't normally have any alcohol at all. This is my first ever cocktail.'

'Yeah.' She nodded slightly, her smile sarcastic.

'No. Really. I used to be this real uptight bastard.'

'Don't tell me, your wife doesn't understand you either.'

'Yes! You're right!' What a woman! She could read my mind. And that smile had become the most glorious grin.

'Are you here on business?' She settled back into her chair.

'No. I just wanted to get away from my wife. Things aren't too good.'

'Okay, so, you've come to this hotel to get away from your wife and to have a drink?' She nodded to herself as she spoke.

'Yes! And some cheese.'

'Ah, of course. Cheese.'

'My wife won't let me have cheese!'

'No!' She was so concerned. She leaned forward and looked me in the eye. 'Did you know that cheese is the most common cause of marital breakdown?'

'Is it?' This was amazing news. 'How do you know so much about marriage?'

She sat back and frowned. 'Are you for real?'

'What do you mean?'

'Are you a cop?'

Her frown made me panic. 'What? Um? No. I'm a theologian. And I want to see the world. And I want to eat cheese. And I have a purpose for being here. I know lots of things. I'm here for a reason.' I wanted to tell her more. To tell her who I really was. Maybe she could help me, but in my soul I could feel there was something wrong. She was essential to my purpose but so complicated.

'What's your purpose then, mister? Are you here to help me? I have such a difficult life, you know.'

I reached out to her spirit again. At first I felt nothing but I tried once more and finally had a limited insight into her inner depths. 'Yes, I do know. Did you know that you hide your soul? Your life is difficult. You should think of other people's feelings and needs as well as your own. There's a part of you saying don't do this, it's wrong, but you haven't listened to it for a while have you? When did you last pray?'

She frowned and looked away blinking furiously. 'Fuck.' Her voice was shaking. And then she looked back at me, smiling with not even a hint of what had happened.

She stared at me, but the smile was forced now. 'Do you do that all the time?'

'What?'

'Tell people to pray?'

'It's not what I said.'

'Whatever.'

'I'm sorry. I didn't mean to upset you. Can't I make you smile again? I don't even know your name.'

She tipped her head from side to side, assessing me. Finally, she sat up, head back in a regal pose, her expression queenly. 'You could buy me a drink.'

I was to be forgiven! 'Of course! I'm so sorry. I should have realised earlier! Barman, a cocktail for the lady. Anything she wants'

The barman was already beside us. He was so amazingly efficient. She looked up at him.

'Another blue lagoon,' she said.

He nodded and left.

She smiled at me. 'That's made up for it. My name is Sarah.'

'What a wonderful name? Did you know it means princess in Hebrew?'

She stared at me and blinked several times as if slightly confused. 'It's good to see you appreciate my beauty,' she said after a while.

'What? When did I say that?'

'You offered the right drink.'

'What?'

She sat back, imperious. 'The drink you buy indicates our relative beauty.'

'Umm.'

'Can't you see it? The greater the difference between us, the more expensive the drink you have to buy me.' She pointed at me with an imposing index finger. 'So, you, being old and very ordinary, need to buy an expensive drink for me' – her hand gestured regally up her body to her face – 'young and beautiful.'

'Oh, I see. But what if I was young and beautiful and you were old and ugly?'

'Then I would be buying drinks for you. This is really important, you know? Rich men realise that they need to buy huge bottles of champagne or diamond necklaces because they are so old and ugly and the women are so beautiful. But so many men don't understand and don't get the right woman for them.'

'I see. I didn't know about all this. Should I be buying you a more expensive drink?'

'No, I'm also being very generous to you.' She didn't seem to know or care about the inconsistency that this implied, since she was obviously capable of conjuring her own compliments. Her drink arrived. She picked it up and sipped. 'Now, let's talk about your wife.' She leaned forward and whispered. 'Tell me what's gone wrong.'

I leaned forward, too. 'I don't know.' I was talking quietly, sharing my secrets with my new and dearest friend. 'She won't even give me a kiss. She's so stiff.'

'I'll bet you are too.'

'What?'

'Stiff.'

I felt my face go hot. 'I, ...'

'Oh you poor dear. You've never done any of this before have you?'

'Any of what?'

She put her hand on my knee. 'Had a drink, picked up a woman in a bar, had a good time?'

She gently brushed her fingers up my leg. 'When did you last have a good kiss?' She winked suggestively.

I didn't know what to say.

'Oh, no,' she said. 'You really are out of your depth. Well, you're very lucky, Mister. I can help you. I will take wonderful care of you. And all for just this one drink!'

'Really?' My stomach was forming uncomfortable knots.

'Yes. I like to look after hopeless men, and you are completely hopeless. It might be a lot of fun. Now finish your drink and take me to your room.'

I could feel deep within me that this might be wrong, but the woman was eager and she knew what she was doing.

How could it be wrong if she chose this path? If only Rebecca weren't so cold, I wouldn't be so easily seduced.

I downed my drink as quickly as I could, my hands shaking.

As I stood up, so did Sarah holding her glass. We crossed the lobby to the lifts. Everyone could see me with this woman. What would they say? Would they think she was my wife? That I was successful? Or would they realise that this was something more sordid?

I stared at Sarah while we waited for the lift. My stomach was becoming very uncomfortable. She sipped quietly and scanned her surroundings. After a few minutes she downed her drink, plonked it on a table, grabbed my hand and towed me to the stairs.

Three flights of stairs later, I was gasping desperately for breath outside my room. My hands shook so much I couldn't get the passkey into the lock. She gently took my hand and guided it in, rubbing her leg and chest against me.

'See,' she said, 'I'll help you get it in. I hope you're as stiff as this key.'

I was.

I opened the door. She walked around the room. 'This will do just nicely. Now, why don't you take your clothes off?'

'Okay.' I stripped off my trousers and shirt.

Before I could go further she grabbed my arm and led me to the bathroom door. 'Go and have a shower. I'll be in there in a minute to wash you down and get you properly started.'

Before I could even answer she bundled me into the bathroom and closed the door behind me.

'Make sure you're very clean for me,' she called.

I stopped and looked at myself in the mirror. My stomach was becoming painful and it looked huge. I sat down on the toilet wondering what to do. It was too much. Should I be doing this? Wasn't it wrong? I should go and stop her, ask her to leave. Explain I had made a mistake.

I heard a door close. I looked out into the room. My trousers were thrown on the floor and there was no sign of Sarah. I checked my trousers. My wallet was missing. I had been set up. I didn't even know her last name. I took a step towards the phone but the cramps in my stomach were so painful I fell to my knees.

How could this trickster woman be of use to me?

JUDGEMENT DAY

Numbers 32:23
But if ye will not do so, behold, ye have sinned against the LORD: and be sure your sin will find you out.

Rebecca slammed the newspaper down on the table in front of me.

'What in God's Realm did you think you were doing?' she screamed into my ear.

'I've got a headache.' All I could think of was the foul taste in my mouth.

'Yes, I don't wonder. Look at that headline.' She prodded the page violently.

The banner screamed, "HOLY ROLLER!!!"

'That's only a rag. You don't believe it do you?' I stared at the table, trying to avoid looking at the accusations in front of me. I had done so many immoral things in the last few days. I knew I was in the wrong and I wanted to hide from her.

'Look at what it says.' She snatched it back. 'Doctor Gideon Matthews. The greatest hypocrite in the world... Drunk... Gambling... You even sexually assaulted a woman.'

I looked up. 'That's unfair. I only tried to kiss her.'

'There's a picture.' The paper practically tore in her hands as she opened it to an inner page. She slammed it on the open page, displaying the evidence for the prosecution. The accusing finger thudded on the table. 'You have your hand on her breast. You're disgusting.'

'I don't feel very well.' A pain fired from my right temple to the left.

'I'm not surprised. It says here you were drinking! Drinking! You were drunk! When did you start drinking?' Her voice had become even more shrill, piercing right through my brain to amplify the ache.

'A week ago, when I was at that hotel,' I mumbled, raising my head and feeling it spin.

'And after that you went out again last night.' She paused for thought. 'That's another thing. How *did* you get your wallet stolen?' She leaned forward, her face inches from mine.

I laid my head on the table, desperately wishing it would all go away. 'It was because I got sick. Remember I told you?'

'Yes. And then you said it went away.'

'It did, when I went to the toilet.'

'So, this woman stole your wallet because you were constipated?'

'I don't know. She took advantage of me. I think you're enjoying this.' I could smell the wood of the table. I could also feel the contents of my stomach rising. 'Maybe I have cancer?'

'Enjoying it? Enjoying it?' She stood and threw her arms to the ceiling. 'I'm going to be so embarrassed. Everyone will blame me. They'll think it's my fault that, that, ... that you have become such an animal.'

'Well...' I looked up at her.

'Don't you dare say it.' I could see her clenched teeth. I was terrified of this small woman as she loomed over me, fists bunched.

My mouth had a thick foul taste. I tried conciliation, my head bowed, contrite. 'But all I wanted was what any husband wants.'

Her face went white. 'You know I can't … That's not my fault…'

'But I… I just wanted to feel what it was like. You know. Sex.'

'What?' She looked at me with disgust in her face and tears filling her eyes. 'How could you be so filthy? What has happened to you?' She quietened down, but it only made her words more focussed, more intense, more painful. 'You used to be a good man.' She held her head high. 'Upright and strong. Moral, courageous. Everything a good man should be. You used to speak out against just this sort of immorality.'

'I'm still a good man. Just not so uptight.'

'Oh, I see,' she declared. Her eyes narrowed. 'Is this another of your ways of getting at women? There are women vicars now and your campaign isn't working so you're getting at me in revenge. You really hate me, don't you?'

'What? What's that got to do with last night? It's not that. I'm not like that any more. It's since I was murdered.' There had to be something that would make her feel sorry for me. I wanted to throw up. I had a good idea. I looked up at her and pleaded. 'I was trying to find my murderer.'

'What?' She stared at me, puzzled. 'You weren't murdered. You're alive. And what made you think that your "murderer" was there?'

'It's where bad people go. You know, killers, thieves.' Her expression warned me off that topic. 'Well, Dr Matthews was murdered and now I'm scared that I'm going to be killed, too. Someone wants to kill me. I'm going to have to fight them and I don't know how. Someone supernatural, powerful. I'm scared. I'm trying to find them before they find me again. I was hoping that no one would notice that I was there last night…'

She had been silent, staring, mouth gaping. 'And who are you then if you're not Gideon Matthews? The Prime Minister perhaps?'

I decided not to tell her. She wouldn't believe me anyway.

She turned her back. 'You disgust me.' She spun around to face me again. I could see the hint of a smile. 'You never used to give me any trouble.' She stumbled as she said "trouble". 'Before, you could resist any temptation. Now look at you. You're pathetic.' She pointed a finger at me. 'You have to do a penance. Make it all right again.'

'No. I didn't do anything wrong.' Once again a pulse of agony united my temples in a common experience of pain.

'What? Drinking? Molesting women? Gambling? Of course they're wrong.'

I became defiant. 'Why? I didn't hurt anyone. The women were enjoying it.'

She shook her head at me. 'If you can't see why sin is wrong then you really have become a lesser man.'

I looked into her soul at last. I should have used my insights before. I could see the anger, the hurt. 'I'm sorry Rebecca. Perhaps you feel guilt, too?' I let the compassion in my voice speak out.

She looked at me puzzled, off centre. She was speechless at last.

Before she could attack me again I followed up my advantage. 'I'm sorry. I know that you've been hurt. But, it was Dr Matthews… Dr M…'

She looked at me astounded, perhaps ready to hear a message from me instead of Dr M.

'Look,' I said, 'he was a bastard. An uptight misogynist. You didn't deserve what he did to you. The way he treated you.'

She ignored me. 'Do you really hate women so much? Is that why you did this to me?' She gestured down to her body as if there was something to be seen, and yet she looked like any other forty-something woman.

I couldn't understand what was going on. The conversation kept changing too quickly. What had Dr M done to her appearance? 'Please, you must understand. I'm not ... I'm not the same person I used to be.'

'You *have* changed since that attack.' She sneered. 'You've become pathetic.'

'No. It's more important than that.'

'Okay, so what happened to you?' Tears were now flowing freely down her cheeks.

It was time to tell her everything, but I was a bit nervous. She was so angry. What would she do to me? How would she react? 'Dr M died,' I said. 'I came instead. I... I'm an angel.'

She slapped my face. 'How dare you!' She was genuinely shocked. 'How dare you say such a thing? Be a man. You've fallen to temptation. To lust. You've let your disgusting animal body control you and now you claim you're a heavenly creature. A perfect angel. Where's your halo? Where're your wings?'

I could feel my cheek burning. She had hit me. She had never done that before. 'Wings?' I said. 'Why should I have wings?'

'Don't change the subject, you filthy creature. Giving in to lust and depravity. Gambling.' She stopped and glared at me. 'How much money did you lose?'

'I don't know.'

She ran from the room. I decided to stay safely in the kitchen enduring the bad taste in my mouth and the pains in my head. I could hear her shuffling through my papers. She made a phone call to the bank and another to the credit card company. Finally, she stumbled into the kitchen and sat at the table next to me, staring into space.

It must have been bad.

'You've cleared out our bank account. And the credit card is at its limit. How will we survive?' Each phrase was numb, emotionless. 'We don't have any money. It will take years to repay it. We don't have any food. Thank goodness we kept the credit card limit so low. You would have spent even more, if you could, wouldn't you?'

I stared at my feet for ages. 'But I have a bigger purpose now. I've come here to this world for a very important reason. Money doesn't matter.'

She stared at the table. 'It matters. We have to live.' She looked at me. 'A purpose?' It was as if the words had taken all this time to register in her consciousness. 'What purpose? What could be so important?'

'I don't know. I just know that I have come to prevent a great evil.'

She shook her head and looked at me in despair.

'Really,' I said. 'I have a purpose. People are coming to me for spiritual advice. Last night one of the men working in the casino, he asked me about praying.'

'He probably recognised you from all those pronouncements you made in the church, you idiot! He was checking you out. He probably told the papers.'

'No. He wanted to know whether praying changed God's mind. That isn't checking me out.'

'And what did you say?'

'That there was no way of changing God's mind. He doesn't have a mind.'

'Oh, fantastic. You aren't even a theologian any more are you? Have you stopped believing in God?'

'No, it's not like that. I know about this. I really know about God and Heaven. I was there. God isn't a living being. He's not in this world. He's not a part of time.'

The contempt in her eyes said it all. She didn't need to speak.

'Anyway, a theologian doesn't have to believe in God. He studies religion.'

'So you don't even believe. What have you become?

'No. Please listen. You don't understand. I miss heaven.'

She lifted her hand to slap me once more but, as I flinched, the door bell rang. She glared at me and left. I laid my head on the table again, wondering whether I would feel better if I threw up.

It was only a few minutes later that Rebecca returned.

'Special Delivery for you,' she said as she slammed an envelope down in front of me. She stalked out of the room.

I opened the letter. It was to inform me that my car had been impounded because I had left it illegally parked. I had forgotten all about it.

Lust

Psalm 81:12
So I gave them up unto their own hearts' lust: and they walked in their own counsels.

Perhaps it was her sheltered life, but as a teenager she was not ready for the interests of men. Nor was she ready to identify and control her own awakening responses. Her first experiences were with fumbling boys who were still learning the arts of seduction, easily ignored and unlikely to incite a response.

And then she met Daddy.

'Come and see me,' he would say. 'We can study the Bible together. I will be your patriarch.'

So after school she would call at his house, still dressed in her school uniform ready for earnest study. She missed her father terribly for without him she had no guidance of any sort. Her foster parents had no idea of the proper mores and were horrified when she asked them to beat her after a terrible bout of gluttony. She did not ask again, not even when she detected a deadly sin. Thankfully, she had learned to chastise her body without the help of others.

'Come in my child,' called Daddy.

She liked it when Daddy let her be a child still. He was very old, perhaps fifty or even older.

'I have been naughty today,' she admitted.

'Ah, which sin this time?' Daddy was suitably grave in his manner.

'Cupidity' she answered. She watched as he licked his lips – they were always covered with spittle.

He shook his head. 'You must be punished.'

Her slim body shook with that strange combination of fear and anticipation.

'Come and lie on my knee.'

She obeyed, lying face down. Daddy would smack her buttocks where marks would not be seen by her confused foster parents. Their laxness would condemn her soul to an eternity of suffering. She prepared herself for the first slap. As always he placed his hand on her bottom to ensure that he had the right place.

'What exactly happened?' he asked her.

This was the essential moment. She must describe it exactly to be cleared of the guilt. 'Someone had a portable music player.' The first smack stung only lightly. 'It had music on it.' A second smack made her body shiver. 'I listened and I really liked it.' Smack. It was good. 'I wanted one, too.' A softer smack. What was wrong? 'And I would do anything to get it.' No smack came despite the outrageous sin. What was happening?

'I think you should be punished in a new way,' he said.

'What? Only pain will free me.'

'Like I said a new punishment.'

'Pain is enough. You must not damage my body for it is a temple.'

'There are other punishments. More sophisticated.' His hand still rested on her buttocks, moving back and forth.

'What about our Bible study?' His hand was very warm. There was a feeling she had only ever experienced once before in a terrible sinful dream.

'Did you know that humiliation can be as good as pain for punishment?' His hand kept slipping down between her legs, getting dangerously close to *there*.

'No. I prefer the pain.'

'If you were made to stand, naked as God intended, would not that humiliation be a good punishment?'

She felt a soft wetness between her legs. She tried to stand up but he held her to his legs, his hand now firm and holding.

'No,' she cried out, but it was half hearted. She wanted to enjoy this experience.

'You want this, my little girl,' he said. 'You are over sixteen, aren't you?'

She was puzzled. He knew it was her birthday just a few days ago. Why did it matter so much? His hand slipped inside her panties and touched something. It felt so good that for a moment she lost her awareness of the evil within.

His breathing was rapid and he was doing something to himself with his other hand. She looked at him. He was holding *that*. She drew back in revulsion. She did not want to be near *that*. He held her more tightly than ever. His eyes were open, starting at her, blazing with an inner light.

Fear of God's wrath overcame her body's desire.

'Let me go,' she shouted.

He let go of himself, grabbed her hand and pulled her towards *it*. She struggled but he was so strong and held her so easily. Would God punish her for not struggling enough?

'No,' she called.

'You can't stop now, you little tease,' he spat at her through clenched teeth. 'You know that you want this. Your body gives you away.'

She had to think fast. 'Yes,' she said.

He paused, and a dreadful over-eager smile distorted his face. 'Yes?'

'Let me turn around, properly. Then you can see my whole body in naked humiliation.'

'Yes.' He was practically drooling on her.

He loosened his grip on her so that she could roll over, but instead she rolled off his knee. Her body was athletic and flexible from self-chastisement, so she easily escaped before the old man could get up from his chair.

She ran from the room to the front door. How would she get out? He always double locked it. She needed his key. He was only a few steps behind her. She tried the door anyway in desperation.

It opened wide.

She heard a loud thud behind her.

She looked back. He was on the floor, his trousers around his ankles.

She grabbed her school bag and ran out. He must have forgotten to lock it! She left the door wide open for everyone to see him.

She ran to the park and found a bench isolated from all the others so that she could sob in solitude.

After many hours of crying she took her Bible from her bag and searched for the right quote. She read it aloud, just like her father always did.

'Mark 7:21 to 23. For from within, out of the heart of men, proceed evil thoughts, adulteries, fornications, murders, thefts, covetousness, wickedness, deceit, lasciviousness, an evil eye, blasphemy, pride, foolishness: All these things come from within, and defile the man.'

Her body would have betrayed her. She must never let that happen again, or her soul would surely be in Hell for eternity. Finally, she understood what the fumbling boys had wanted with their vague hints, groping hands and strange body postures. Every man was like this. No man could ever be allowed to do this to her or any other child ever again!

She checked the Bible to see if she was right. She opened it at a random page and read until she found the quote she needed.

'Ephesians 4:22. That ye put off concerning the former conversation the old man, which is corrupt according to the deceitful lusts.'

And now she understood for she had finally experienced that most adult of the deadly sins, lust.

JUSTICE

Matthew 18:6
But whoso shall offend one of these little ones which believe in me, it were better for him that a millstone were hanged around his neck, and that he were drowned in the depth of the sea.

The monk is not alone, for there are two others present as well as the terrible angel and the observer. All are hidden by cowls and kneeling in a line. An unconscious man lies on the ground before them.

The beautiful, sexless angel smiles at the observer - its tongue lifting, seeking, penetrating towards him.

'No. Leave me alone. Go away.'

The tongue flicks back into its mouth.

'Why do I have to watch this?'

The angel grins and opens its arms, inviting the observer to its love.

'Leave me alone. I am no threat to you.'

The angel shakes its body as if laughing but no sound comes out. It whispers to the waiting servants.

'Then said the king to the servants, Bind him hand and foot, and take him away and cast him into the outer darkness, there shall be weeping and gnashing of teeth.'

'Matthew 22:13. *You're worse than I thought. You think you're the king instructing this poor wretch.*'

The victim is gagged by the leader and bound hand and foot by the acolytes.

'Only with thine eyes shalt thou behold and see the reward of the wicked.'

'Psalm 91:8. *What gives you the right to declare who is wicked?*'

The tongue licks out to the accused and he awakens, terror immediately appearing in his eyes. The hooded trio await instructions.

'Then the high priest rent his clothes.'

'Matthew 26:65, *but that was about Jesus. And it was about blasphemy. This is a perversion. You can't make a story about Jesus apply to this man. Say the whole verse.*'

The angel sneers, the expression spoiling the beauty of its face.

The clothes are cut away, exposing the depraved body from chest to groin. The eyes of the sufferer transform into weary acceptance as if the removal of his clothes has told him of what is to come.

'Take heed that ye despise not one of these little ones.'

'Matthew 18:10. *Another partial quote. What has this man done?*'

The holy trinity chant in the strange falsetto, 'You are evil. Your actions are evil.' And then one voice chants, 'you have done terrible things to children.'

The judged man stares at the ground, unable to speak because of the gag, and perhaps uninterested in defending himself.

The gag is removed.

'Do you admit to what you have done?' chants the judge.

The response is flat, resigned. 'I only gave them love. I never meant to hurt them.'

'Do you repent?'

'Yes. Yes, of course. Whatever you want. I never meant to hurt them. I loved them.' He looks into the face hidden from the observer. Perhaps he sees some hope there for he adds, 'I was so scared.'

The angel speaks once more.

'Even so it is not the will of your Father which is in Heaven, that one of these little ones should perish.'

'Matthew 18:14. Exactly what has this man done?'

All the hooded ones chant in almost perfect unison. 'Even so it is not the will of your Father which is in Heaven, that one of these little ones should perish.'

The man nods in agreement. 'I *am* evil. Please, make it quick.' He shuts his eyes tight and a tear squeezes out at the side.

The chanting falters and resumes. 'Do you plead for God's Judgement?'

'No. You have already judged me, not God.'

The trio shift uncomfortably, concerned at these words.

The angel's tongue licks across the man's crotch. An obedient monk nods to show understanding and wields a knife to the man's crotch. The victim groans in agony and tears roll down his cheeks, while his knees give way from agony as his penis and testicles are hacked off. He collapses into unconsciousness. The whip like tongue staunches the blood flow before more instructions are given.

'And whosoever shall offend one of these little ones that believe in me, it is better for him that a millstone

were hanged about his neck, and he were cast into the sea.'

'Mark 9:42. *Thanks be to God that you're not near the sea. At least you can't do that to him.'*

The angel smiles once more to the observer. Its tongue flicks the paedophile's eyes waking him back to his personal hell. The head of the damaged one is lifted so that the consequences of the judgement can be observed but he can only moan in despair and agony. He starts to swoon yet again, but the tongue flicks the eyes to force him awake. His body is dragged to a kneeling position. He cannot maintain the position, so he is held in place by one of the anonymous trio.

A huge stone bowl appears and seawater is poured into it. The angel's faithful retainers wrap a huge chain attached to a millstone around the neck of the judged man so that he is forced to bow forward, his face held into the bowl.

'Oh no. *This is deplorable. How can you use the words of the Bible to justify this?'*

The depraved man coughs and splutters as his head is held beneath the water.

The angel's tongue glows bright as it laps at the liquid in the bowl.

After several minutes of struggle the drowned one finally collapses.

'Sufficient to such a man is this punishment, which was inflicted of many.'

'2 Corinthians 2:6. *What are you, really? You're not an angel. An angel wouldn't do this. Where are your wings?'*

The angel looks up and grins evilly once more as a pair of tiny, useless wings appears on its body. It glows holy and pure with a light so brilliant it hurts the eyes.

'Let me go. *Please.'*

The executioners stand and once again, hair, skin and blood are left as they depart. The angel casts its spell of hiding and distraction once more.

'Be ye afraid of the sword: for wrath bringeth the punishments of the sword, that ye may know there is a judgement.'

'Job 19:29. Is that my fate? Are you to kill me also? You do not have the right.'

The angel smiles a final time to the observer.

TEMPTATION

The ego is a body's guardian, but it will do absolutely anything to stay alive. Self deception is the ego's greatest weapon.

The Sins of the Flesh

James 4:4
Ye adulterers and adulteresses, know ye not that the friendship of the world is enmity with God? whosoever therefore will be a friend of the world is the enemy of God.

I had chosen her partly because of the tiny, tight shorts she was wearing but mostly because her blouse was undone virtually all the way to her navel, showing the smooth roundness of her breasts and barely hiding her nipples. She led me into a dark room with a single, weak red light bulb directly above the middle of a double bed. The room was only a few feet bigger than the bed. A sweet, musty smell invaded my senses and for a second I realised how tacky this was. I shouldn't sin like this, should I? But somehow I couldn't resist. I didn't want to think. I just wanted to enjoy it. All I cared about were the many delights to come.

'Over there,' she said, indicating a chair in the corner, away from the door.

I walked to my allotted place.

'Pay me first,' she demanded.

I couldn't understand why my hands were shaking as I drew my wallet from my trousers. My stomach convulsed. I tugged out a bank note and all my brand new credit cards fell onto the floor. She tutted and came towards me, bending down to pick them up.

'No!' I shouted pushing my open hand towards her. I may not know much but I had learnt enough to know that I wasn't going to get ripped off again.

She sneered at me and shook her head. I threw some notes on to the sheets and knelt down on the floor to pick up my cards. It was hard to see anything in the half-light. My stomach was too full as I had just eaten a huge meal at an all-you-can-eat Indian Restaurant.

'It's all right,' she muttered as she reached for the cash. 'I'm not a fucking thief.'

I stood up and slipped my wallet back into my pocket. I waited for her instructions.

'Okay,' she said, 'get your trousers off.'

'What?'

She raised her mascara eyes and looked to the ceiling for a second in exaggerated astonishment. 'Well you can't do it through your trousers, can you?'

'But...'

'Oh sorry. Maybe you do. Do you want me to rub you up inside your trousers?'

'No. No. I'm just a bit, you know, worried.'

'What?'

'I haven't done this before.' I stared at the floor. 'Can you take your clothes off, too? First. So I can be, you know...,' I could still stop myself. I wasn't an animal, like Rebecca said. I could change my mind, couldn't I?

'Okay. But if you can't get it up, you won't get your money back and I'm not going to do anything weird.'

'Please.'

She frowned. She undid the one button on her blouse and took it off. She wasn't wearing a bra. Her breasts were full, round and lovely, with brown areolas. I could see stretch marks around each smooth curve. 'You like them?' she asked.

I stared and nodded. My body took over. I had to have her. I had no choice now.

'Just as bloody well. They cost me a fortune. Still they've paid for themselves. I get lots of money, you know?' She sat down on the bed to remove her thigh length red boots.

Surely, she couldn't steal my money now? Anyway, I wasn't leaving the room this time, so I guessed I was safe. I undid my belt and let my trousers drop to my ankles. I could feel my penis growing full in my underpants. I watched her intently, waiting for her to reveal her pubic hair. Without looking away I bent down to take off my shoes and socks. I tripped forward. The bare wooden floor hurt my knees.

'What the fuck?' She shook her head, now naked. 'Just stay there, okay?' She came to me, knelt down, pushed me back onto my bottom and took off my shoes and socks. I felt like a baby. She pulled at my trousers.

'No.' I didn't panic this time. 'I'll just keep these over here.' I slid my trousers off, checked that everything valuable was still safely in them and put them on the chair.

'You been ripped off?' She didn't seem to care about my answer.

'Yes. Never again.'

'Do you want to take your shirt off?' I undid the buttons, my hands shaking.

She was fidgeting. 'Hurry up.'

'Okay.' I dropped my underpants. I was naked at last.

She lay on the bed and I stared at her body. Below her large breasts I could see every unnaturally skinny rib, the only support to her pasty skin. The bones on her hips stuck out forming a shallow bowl between her navel and thighs. When I saw the ugly wheals on her arms I looked away.

I climbed on to the bed.

'I have to look at your willy.'

'What? Does it get you going?'

She was always so angry. 'Fuck off. I want to see if you're clean.'

'What?'

'No little diseases?' She bent forward, head tilted as if she was talking to a child.

'Oh.'

Her inspection was thorough but so perfunctory that I could feel my hardness softening.

Apparently satisfied, she looked back at me. 'Okay, what do you want?'

'Umm. Everything. I want to know what it feels like.'

'Okay.' She took my hand and dumped it on her breast. 'Be gentle.'

I could feel the taut roundness of her breast and the softness of her nipple. I snatched my hand back. 'No. Sex.'

'Oh. Okay.' She rolled over to a bedside cabinet, opened a drawer and retrieved something. 'Put this on.' She was holding up a small square object.

'What?'

She sighed and shook her head. She ripped open the packet with her teeth and pulled out a round thing. I finally figured it out. It was a condom.

'Wait,' I said. 'Will it still feel the same?'

She grunted and sat back. 'Okay, another hundred.'

'What?'

She waved the condom. 'If you want it without this, it's another hundred.'

'What?'

'Look don't you get it? I'm at risk here. I need to have that made up to me.'

'What and the risk to your life is worth a hundred?'

'Fuck you,' she snapped. 'You don't know what my life is worth. Anyway, I'm taking the risk. What do you care?'

She was right. I was buying her body. I didn't really care about her at all, did I? Rebecca was right, I was a sinner, an animal. But I just had to do this, I had no choice. It was too long since this body felt a woman's softness enveloping its hardness. She was choosing to do this wasn't she? She wanted it. If it wasn't me it would be someone else. She wanted all the money she could get. No one was going to get hurt. Except me.

'I've not got any diseases,' I said. 'This is my first time remember? Won't I be more at risk from you?'

'I dunno. Look, have you got a hundred or not?'

'With the condom.'

She shrugged. 'Okay.' She grabbed my now flaccid penis and wrapped her fingers around the shaft. She pumped her hand up and down a few times. I could feel the pleasure flood through my body and my manhood responded immediately, growing full, ready to burst. She held the condom in her left hand and rubbed it against the glans. She rolled it down over my hardness. All this touching was too much for me and I felt an explosion starting inside me and rising through my shaft. She stopped touching me just as I was starting to come, making my orgasm empty and frustrating. It didn't have any of the pleasure I expected.

It should have been in her. I should have felt what it was really like.

'Okay.' she said. 'You needed that.' She was so perfunctory, so uncaring. She must have said it a thousand times before.

I lay there exhausted.

'Come on,' she said. 'Time to go, get dressed.'

'But you said half an hour.'

She scowled. 'What? You're finished. I can't wait for you to get it up again.'

As she climbed off the bed and turned to watch me I could really look at her soul, properly. Not from my need but from my heart. Her faith was weak, nascent. Present but suppressed. Why was she turning away from God?

She was too thin to be healthy. Her face was round, the eyes large and open. She could have been beautiful but the thick white face make up, black mascara and bright red lips were hiding her innermost self as well as her complexion. She had bags under her eyes and her pale thin skin, exaggerated the marks on her arms. Her legs and arms were too skinny, showing the shape of the bone underneath.

'Do you look after yourself?' I asked.

She was surprised by the question. 'Fuck off. That's my business. Just get dressed. I don't need a fucking social worker.'

I looked deeper into her soul. I already knew that she didn't value herself, otherwise she wouldn't be doing this, would she? But my insight showed how desperate she was for happiness. Desperate, also, to disappear from the pain she was feeling. 'Do you believe in Heaven?' I felt a genuine desire to help her to make up for what I and every other man were doing to her.

'Oh fuck!' she shouted. 'There's someone just the other side of this wall, you know. It's not my fault. You wanted to do this. It's you, not me. Don't you go calling me a Jezebel or anything.' She was backing away, terrified as she pointed at the wall. 'They can be here in a second. They can hear everything.'

'No, I don't want to hurt you. I just... Look, I'll put my trousers around my ankles. You know what that'll do to me.' I radiated every good feeling I could to her as I hobbled myself.

She smiled, weakly and uncertain but it was a smile, nevertheless. She was ready to respond. 'Are you...?'

'I can just see into you. I can see your soul. And I can see the hurt.'

She sighed. 'Yeah, yeah, yeah. That's an easy one. I'm a crack head. I'll be in heaven next time I get a fix.'

'No. Can't you see? It just makes the bad times worse.'

She peered at me eyes narrow. 'There's... There's something about you.' She stared at my face.

After a few seconds she shook her head. 'I haven't got time for this.'

The condom fell off the end of my shrinking organ onto the floor.

She moaned in frustration. 'Don't do that. This place is all I've got. It stinks enough as it is. Now I'll have a sticky floor.' She started to dress.

I retrieved the condom and then sat on the edge of the bed inspecting her little room. The floor was bare wood. The walls were grey and pocked with damp marks. There was a stained, brown blanket nailed over the window. It stank of mustiness – the smell of stale sex. I heard a woman crying out in either pain or an orgasm. If it was pleasure it was almost certain to be faked here. What a dreadful place.

And I was helping it to keep going. What had I done?

'Do you sleep here?'

She was pulling her boots on. 'No, of course not. You're not a fucking stalker are you?'

I shook my head.

She frowned at me. 'Look, I've got to go. I've got my work to do. Just hurry up and get dressed.'

'Just give me five minutes. While I'm getting dressed. To talk. That's all. After all I've paid for it.'

'Okay, but two things.' She sat on the edge of the bed, dressed and ready to run. 'You don't give your middle class male guilt trip to me and you don't try to change me.'

'Okay. Let's just talk.'

She sighed in resignation.

'What's your name?'

'Bethany.'

That fitted, it meant house of affliction in Hebrew. I picked up my shirt. 'What do you know about God?'

She looked at me carefully. 'Either you're a nut case or you're taking the piss.'

'No, really.' I watched her carefully, finding it difficult to put my arm in the sleeve because I was concentrating on her so closely.

'Okay, then. You want God, I'll give you God.' Her face was distorted into a sneer. 'He's a bastard. He created this world and he put me here. If I couldn't get high, I'd be really shit.'

'But you're miserable now. At this moment.' I took each button slowly. I didn't have much time. If only I could get to her, provide her with spiritual comfort and support. Perhaps I could make up for what I had done.

'That's because I'm straight. If you had paid me that hundred, you would have had more fun, and I'd have enough money.' She was defiant, sneering at me once again.

'Do you think that getting high is good enough to justify how you feel now?'

'Bullshit. I'll feel like crap no matter what happens.'

I dragged my sock over my foot, studying her every gesture and expression. 'But...'

'And it's God's fault.'

'Really. How do you figure that out?'

'He made my life shit. He made my mother get religion.'

'Isn't that a good thing?'

'Nuh. She wouldn't put out for her boyfriend anymore. She said they had to get married. Some preacher said that she should only have it off to have kids or it was ungodly.'

This was just the sort of thing Dr M. said. It could have been him. 'Where? Where was this?'

'Down in Torquay.'

That was nowhere near Dr M. It must have been someone else. 'What happened?'

'It was her shit of a boyfriend. They had a big fight. He decided if he couldn't get it from her, he'd get it from me.'

'He raped you? When?'

'Ages ago.'

'How old were you?'

She tilted her head to the side. 'Ten.'

'That was terrible.' I could see her pain, but this wasn't from one trauma. 'He kept doing it, too, didn't he? Why didn't you tell your mother?'

'Who do you fucking well think taught me the name Jezebel?' She stamped her foot. 'Oh fuck off. Your time's up.' She pulled the door open quickly using too much force. 'Just put your shoes on and go.'

'It wasn't because of God. It was her boyfriend. He had a choice and he raped you.'

'Look, you're so high and mighty. Look at what you've just done. Don't give me that crap. It's God's fault, and you're no better. God didn't stop you, did he?'

She was right. What I had done was wrong, as wrong as the man who raped her. Why wasn't I stopped? Why didn't I stop myself?

I walked out the door, my shoelaces undone. I turned back to her. 'Perhaps if you look inside yourself you can find a way out of this? You know you could be happy without the drugs. And it would be a happiness that would last. Forever. Even you. I could save you if you let me.' Something happened inside me. I don't know what but something intangible yet beautiful burst out from my body.

She stared at me, stunned. A tear appeared in her eye. 'No. You just… and …'

I touched her arm in love and she sank to her knees with one great sob.

She swallowed and I could sense the iron will within her take control, casting the feelings out. 'Look what you've done. I'll have to do my fucking eyes again. It'll take ages. Just go, will you. Please.' She stood up.

'You're so much stronger than you believe. I hope we can meet again one day. Without me doing…' I stepped out the door. Other people were in the corridor staring at us.

She followed me out of the room, locked the door behind her and tottered off down the corridor without looking back, each step making a tock sound. The others disappeared into rooms.

'If we meet again, I'll help you next time,' I called to her unresponsive back.

I walked down the stairs in despair, hearing the steps and voices of others behind and in front, all unseen as they avoided the nutcase. How could I save others if I couldn't help myself?

I needed something enjoyable to distract me. Perhaps cheese on toast would help.

The camera flash blinded me as I stepped onto the pavement. I tripped onto one knee.

'Doctor Matthews,' a man called in a dry, cracked voice. 'Could you tell me why you were in that building?'

I looked up and was blinded by more flashes.

'Have you been to see a prostitute? Isn't that a sin? I seem to remember that you were always quick to judge politicians. Are you ready to judge yourself?' The questioner wasn't interested in hearing answers.

I stood up, unsteady and uncertain. 'Who are you?'

'Joe Kayer. Blandshire Gazette. Don't you feel guilty at your behaviour?'

I could almost feel Rebecca's reaction already. 'Could you stop taking those photos? They're blinding me.'

'Isn't it a sin, visiting a prostitute?'

I had to find an excuse. 'Look, I was attacked.' I pulled up my shirt to show the scars. The flashes blinded me again. 'I've got to find my killer. Before he does it again. I was looking here. It's important. This is about good and evil.'

My eyes had recovered enough to make out the journalist's face. He was middle aged, tough and dry.

'Really? And what were you doing with a prostitute. Was it good or evil? Why did you have to see her in her room? Were you having sex with a prostitute?'

'No! I never had sex with that woman.' I turned and ran. He followed for a few hundred yards before I heard his footsteps stop.

I had to get home as fast as possible.

No Rest for the Wicked

Isiah 48:22
There is no peace, saith the Lord, unto the wicked.

A finger prodded me awake.

'What have you done now?' Rebecca demanded.

'What?'

She prodded me again. 'What have you done?'

'What's this?'

'There are reporters outside. They keep ringing the doorbell and asking to speak to you. They're asking me questions, too.'

'What are they saying?'

'You tell me.'

I rolled myself into the bedclothes so that only my nose and mouth were exposed. The dark warmth made me feel safer, more secure.

'One gave me a newspaper,' she said. 'It's got pictures. You were drunk again.'

Yet again I had been judged and found wanting.

I felt and heard something land on the bed, probably the paper. 'No I wasn't. The flash blinded me and I tripped.'

'So what did happen? Did you have sex with her?'

'No.'

'No one believes you.' I could hear the contempt she felt.

'Okay. I wanted to. You won't. So I wanted to. With her. But I didn't. Right?'

'You're disgusting.'

'Are you so perfect? Isn't it possible to make love without wanting a child?'

'How dare you?' She spoke in a barely controlled tense shout.

'I know I've been dreadful, but maybe you need to change, too?'

I poked my head out from under the duvet. She was standing with her fists at her hips.

'Rebecca, you're too controlled, too careful.'

'At least I'm not as bad as you are, Sinner,' she practically spat at me.

'Yes you are. It is only by the grace of God that you get into heaven. It's not by never sinning.'

'You...' She became speechless with rage.

I was only making her more angry. I tried a new approach. 'Perhaps you have a greater purpose, too? More than just having babies?'

She shook her head in angry denial.

I tried again. 'How do you know that you're barren?'

She took a step towards me, arm raised, ready to strike. I drew back into the bedclothes and she paused.

'Rebecca. Haven't you thought it might be Dr...? It might be me? We never made love. We only had sex two or three times. Maybe you need to make love to have a child.'

'What? Sex is for procreation. It's what you always said. You forced me to accept it. You b...' She stopped herself.

'Do you hate me? Because of what I've done?'

'Yes. No. I don't know.'

'Do I deserve to be hated?'

'Yes,' she shouted as she ran from the room.

I picked up the paper and stared at myself on the front page. I looked dreadful, pale faced and confused. They showed a picture of my side. The scar from the attack was ignored. Arrows pointed to how fat I was becoming with a label saying "gluttony".

I read the main article carefully. Most of it was made up. I couldn't believe that so many people could claim they knew all about what happened and still get it so wrong. Everyone thought I was a hypocrite, except maybe for Bethany, but that was only because she didn't talk to them.

I turned the page and my eye caught the inner headline, "Evil Meets Rough Justice". So evil could be overcome. A priest had been abused as a child and he had finally taken his revenge on his tormentor, although it seemed that the murder was a bit grisly. The paper avoided the details. Was I supposed to murder someone? To overcome evil with rough justice like the priest? I didn't think I could do that.

The phone rang in the hallway. I ignored it. After a few seconds Rebecca called. I put on my dressing gown and wandered out to her. She passed the handset, staring at me defiantly.

I took the phone, put it to my ear and turned my back to her. 'Hello?'

'Is that Dr Matthews?' came a faint female voice.

'Um. Yes.'

'Hello Mister. It's me, Sandy.' Her voice was easily recognisable.

'You said you were Sarah last time. What do you want?'

'Uh. Yeah. Sorry, Sandy is my middle name, and I've decided to use it now. Look, I just wanted to say how sorry I am. I hope you'll forgive me. It wasn't like it looked. I panicked. It was wrong. Sinning and all that. Sorry.'

'And in your panic you stole all my money?'

'Honest, mister, I was just checking to find out who you were. In case you were a murderer or someone. And when I saw that you were someone famous, I just ran, and I forgot that I had your wallet.'

'I see.'

'I want to give it back, but not at your house. Is that alright?'

I peeped out through the curtains. A reporter was wandering around at the back of the house. 'Yes. Definitely not here. Where?'

I glanced back at Rebecca. She was still glaring.

'At another hotel?'

'Okay,' I said.

'The Paradise? It's by the sea front. Just off the high street. Turn left at the bottom of the hill.'

'Yes, I think I can find that. When?'

'This afternoon? Three?'

'And you'll bring everything you stole, even my credit cards?'

'Yes.' The line went dead.

I hung up.

Perhaps she could help me find the angel from my dreams and together we could destroy it?

'What was that about?' demanded Rebecca as I turned towards her.

'Um. The woman who robbed me. She said it was an accident. She's going to return my wallet.'

She snorted. 'An accident? What sort of accident leaves you without your trousers? You'd better not be causing more trouble.'

'I'll need my car. Where are the keys?'

She sneered at me. 'Don't you remember?'

I shook my head.

She prodded a finger at my chest. 'You figure it out. It's not my problem.' As she walked away she shouted, 'and get rid of those reporters.'

While I was getting dressed I remembered that my car had been impounded.

My trousers and shirt were tight. The papers were right I was putting on weight. I went downstairs. The curtains in the living room were drawn. What was wrong with Rebecca? She always opened them. I parted them slightly and was blinded by an explosion of light. A photographer was right in the garden!

I went to the kitchen to get something to eat. I could see Rebecca sitting at the table, staring into space. It seemed almost a crime to sit in the dark in August.

'I'm starving. Do we have any cheese? I want some breakfast.'

'Cheese? What *is* wrong with you?'

'What?'

She stared at me, examining my face in detail. Eventually she shook her head. 'The doctors didn't say anything about losing your mind, but I suppose it was inevitable.'

'What?'

'You really don't remember?'

'No.'

'You're allergic to cheese. It makes you ill. You hate it because it gives you stomach ache.'

Were there no pleasures that I could have? 'I had some. At the hotel when that woman….'

'No wonder you were ill. Idiot.'

'See I am different.' I made myself some toast. I wanted a big, greasy breakfast, but there was nothing worth eating in the house. As I was waiting for the toaster I twitched a curtain to the side. A flash went off in my eyes. I slapped thick lumps of butter and peanut butter on the toast and wandered out of the kitchen.

'Don't walk around eating that,' she called.

'I'm going to the study. There aren't any windows there.'

There were three neat stacks of opened letters on my desk. As always Rebecca had reviewed each one and placed it on one of the piles, labelled "ordinary", "rubbish" or "important". I unfolded the letter at the top of the important heap. My Head of Department, David, wanted to know when we could re-arrange the cancelled seminar. He was going to have a long wait – at least until I understood my new purpose in life. Maybe I should tell him? No, I couldn't be bothered.

I had another reminder that my car had been impounded. I couldn't afford the fine, so how was I going to get to see Sarah without all those reporters following me?

I went to the front room and opened it up to the light, ignoring the clicking cameras. There were only two of the jackals out there. Was that a way of measuring how important you were, by counting how many reporters turn up if you did something wrong? So, a famous movie star is worth 20 paparazzi on the doorstep night and day, but an academic, who was also a minor member of the lay clergy, even with my profile, was only worth two local reporters during the day – or perhaps four if the others were still around out there.

I examined my jailors. I could see the bitterness etched into the lines on their faces, and in the harsh press of their lips. Tired hacks forced to doorstep people to make a living.

A plan presented itself.

'I'm going out,' I called to Rebecca.

She didn't answer.

I opened the door and stepped on to the path with the inevitable cacophony of screamed questions. I ignored them all.

The closest reporter and main cameraman was the reporter who had caught me a few days before, Joe Kayer. I felt a hidden faith within him.

'Hello, Joe,' I said.

He stepped closer. The lines around his cynical eyes sharpened as he focused his attention on me. He shoved his microphone into my face. 'Have you left the church?' he demanded.

Two more of the pack came loping around the corner of the house.

I took the initiative from Joe. 'You're hiding behind that mike. To keep your feelings from me. Why?'

'Dr Matthews, aren't you a sinner? You're doing what you used to condemn others for doing.'

I ignored his response and reached for his innermost feelings. 'You really hate this, don't you?'

The microphone dropped slightly and I could see his face clearly. I watched his eyes twitch as they alternated between my eyes and my mouth.

He was puzzled by what he saw, perhaps confused by my compassion and my challenge to his beliefs. 'I want to talk about you,' he said.

'You had such dreams,' I countered. 'Prizes, awards, fame. For your incisive and excellent pictures. You wanted to be more than this. They haven't worked out have they? I'm sorry.'

He blinked rapidly and glanced to the side. He pushed the microphone into my face once more. 'Do you think you'll be judged by God for what you're doing? Or don't you believe in God any more?'

'Joe, you didn't have to become a hack. You could change now. If you stopped the smoking and the drinking you could survive on much less money. Give up the job. Take a risk. It's not as if you have anyone who depends on you.'

He was baffled now. 'Stop that.' He looked around at his colleagues as they pressed forward. He was no longer leader of the pack and the rest were jostling for his position. 'What about your job?' He ended the question vaguely – uncertain even whether he should be asking it.

'Why don't you try something else?' I countered. 'Now that you're alone you're free. Perhaps travel writing? Start local and see what happens. Use your insights and investigative abilities. You'd be a lot happier.'

'No, I want to talk about you. About what you've...'

'Go on. Become the real Joe Kayer. Let go of this pretence. If you gave up door-stepping people you'd like yourself more. You wouldn't want the drink.'

He dropped his gaze to the ground and I sensed the acorn of faith germinating within him. The other reporters paused, anxious at this unexpected twist in the usual story they created.

A woman stepped forward, shoving Joe to the side. Her weapons were her beauty as well as her stiletto shoes, deep cleavage and bright red nail polish. Her only defences were her thick layers of makeup and pen and paper. 'Dr Matthews, what did you do to the prostitute you saw? Do you know that she is now clinically depressed?'

Joe wandered off. The other two watched him, wary.

This woman had a strong, immovable faith but not necessarily in God. I looked deeper into her heart and discovered the ache within. 'It's time to move on,' I said to her. 'You've got to stop blaming your father. He did his best but he was only a normal man. He'd always expected your mum to look after you. After all he'd lost her, too.'

'Stop that,' she shouted. 'How dare you? You know nothing about me.' I could see the muscles in her cheeks bunch and her full lips tighten. 'Why won't you answer *my* questions?'

'You know, even if he blamed you for her death, you need to forgive him now. He thought you'd be better off in that home, without him.'

'Stop! Stop! Stop!' She launched herself at me and punched my chest.

I rocked back, breathless.

'You don't have the right to talk about that!' she screamed in my face. 'Answer my questions. What did you do to me... to that woman?'

I could see the angry little girl inside her hiding behind the aggression. I recovered my posture and my compassion. 'When you're a reporter and you ask questions there's always one person missing. You.' I looked at each of the three, so that they could receive my compassion and understanding. 'But you *are* present. You just pretend you're not.'

The two at the back frowned, fidgeting in a Brownian motion that gradually increased the distance between them and me.

I leant forward holding my hands open, palms towards them adopting the universal posture of a preacher. 'Don't forget yourself when you report. You're a part of the process. Don't judge yourselves and don't judge others. That way you could become better at your job. You could expose real stories about the poor and innocent. People who can't tell their tales because they don't have your way with words. Real tragedies that need to be told. You could all do such great good.'

The other two glanced at each other. One looked at Joe wandering off down the road. They disappeared off in opposite directions after some unspoken agreement.

The woman shook her fist in my face. 'You bastard. You had no right,' she said.

She turned and stalked away, proud in defeat.

'I had as much right as you,' I called to her. 'If only you'd accept others more, you might be able to move on. Start a new life with love. The church can teach you how, you know.'

I walked towards the shops hoping to find a café that served a big breakfast.

THE FALL

Proverbs 7:27
Her house is the way to hell, going down to the chambers of death.

I entered from the too-bright, seaside summer's day into the cold and humid gloom of the lobby of the Paradise Hotel. Dr Matthews' Hell would have had much more light so that you could see your torturers and fellow sufferers, but I knew that in reality the next world without His Presence would be a dark, cold, uncaring place full of the regret and despair I was now feeling. The Paradise Hotel's version of Hell smelt of musty carpets and mould.

I waited for my eyes to adjust to the dark lobby after the bright daylight outside. Eventually I could see the faded and peeling blue wallpaper. Sarah was sitting halfway down a staircase, wearing blue jeans and a green sweatshirt, turned sideways so that she could monitor the entrance. I could only assume that she had been silently observing me ever since I had entered.

I smiled at her.

'Hello, Mister,' she said.

'Hello, Sarah, if that is your name,' I answered.

'Sarah's a nice name, really. I don't know why I decided to change it.' She walked up to me and gave me a peck on the cheek.

I wasn't going to get caught again. 'Do you have my...'

She clamped her hand on my mouth. 'Let's go and talk, Mister,' she whispered, conspiratorially as if there was an invisible observer somewhere.

'I'm not a Mister,' I answered loudly. 'I'm a Doctor, you know?'

She turned to walk down the stairs and along a corridor without even looking back. I followed her.

'Yes,' she said, 'but you're a Doctor of Theology. It's not like you can fix people up or anything.' She glanced back at me. 'Anyway, I like to call everyone Mister. It's just my little way.' Her smile warmed my heart but yet again she was hidden from my insights. I couldn't even tell if she had a strong faith or not. I was only certain that she was complex and important.

She led me along a corridor and opened a door. I was panting from the exertion.

She stepped into the room and made a theatrical gesture for me to enter. Just inside I could see a worn armchair next to an old writing desk. In the centre was a double bed, smoothly made up, with a blue duvet and matching, fluffy pillows. The only window was clouded with dirt and what appeared to be a mattress leaning on it from the outside. It matched the continuing sad theme of faded and peeling blue checked wallpaper. A chipped washbasin was set in a cupboard under the window. I could smell a joss stick almost obliterating the faint background odour of mildew.

Sarah sat down on the armchair. 'Come on in, it's not as bad as it looks.'

'No way. I'm not going to let you make a fool of me again.'

She turned to face me and smiled. 'I'm so sorry. Will you ever forgive me?'

'Why don't you give me my wallet and then I can forgive you?'

'In a minute. I've got a special treat for you first.' Her grin was knowing and clever, her lovely big eyes half closed.

I felt a tremor in my stomach. Perhaps she wanted to make up for treating me so badly last time in other ways. I wouldn't do anything wrong, though. I had already sinned enough.

She opened the cupboard, retrieved something and turned to show me a plate with a large round plastic cover. She lifted the cover to reveal biscuits, a knife and what looked to be stilton, brie and cheddar. 'Ta da,' she called out, making a show of offering me the feast. She placed it on the bed. 'Come and sit here with me and we can enjoy this together.' She sat down and pointed at the other side of the plate.

I salivated. 'I'm not sure. I think it might make me sick.'

'Oh nonsense.' She reached down underneath the bed and brought out a bottle of red wine and two glasses.

'No,' I said. 'After you… left, before, you know, I was ill.'

She shook her head and gestured the thought of illness away to the under world. 'You must have eaten too much. Just have a bit. It's delicious.'

Maybe she was right. I had to try. Rebecca might have been lying, just to be nasty to me. 'Alright.'

She poured the wine carefully. 'Sit down gently, now, Mister. You wouldn't want me to spill any.'

I entered the room and gingerly sat, as instructed.

She passed me a glass and I played the party game, trying to keep my drink safely upright in one hand whilst arranging a slice of cheese on a biscuit with the other. Sarah took a biscuit and nibbled at an edge. I handed her the cheese knife and she placed it delicately on the plate.

'Aren't you having any?' I asked.

'You enjoy it. It's my special saying sorry treat just for you.'

I crammed a mouthful of cheese and biscuits into my mouth. I sipped at the harsh wine to wash it down. 'You're very nice, really, aren't you?' I said.

She sniggered. 'Sometimes.'

'Seeing as you're not eating, how about giving me my wallet, now?'

'Okay.' She lifted her sweatshirt to reveal a money belt. She rolled her sweatshirt under her chin, pulling it high enough to reveal a tiny, lacy bra hiding the small mounds of her breasts.

I almost choked on the biscuit.

Her eyes creased into a laughter line as she looked up, still using her chin as an extra hand. She unbuttoned her jeans and used both hands to open her money belt. I could see more lace outlining her knickers.

My stomach was tight, and I could feel my penis filling and becoming very sensitive. I wanted to eat as much cheese as I could but the sight of her bare front was distracting me. Perhaps this time we really could have sex. If she was willing and I didn't pay her, it wouldn't be so much of a sin, would it? Maybe it would be okay?

She withdrew my wallet and passed it to me. She lifted her chin, and as her top fell down, her bra was hidden once more but her jeans remained unbuttoned. She smiled sweetly. 'I am so sorry. I really can't make it up to you enough.'

I forced a huge piece of cheddar down my throat, half eaten – eager to free myself for other activities. I swigged a mouthful of the wine to wash it down and placed the glass safely out of the way.

I opened my wallet. There was no money in it, only a bit of paper. I looked at her, puzzled.

'It's an IOU. I had to use that money for my sister. She's on her own and she's got a baby and she needed help to get some baby food and nappies and it was late last night. I'm so sorry.'

I opened the note. 'Well, I guess...'

'Look I left your credit card. And I'll pay you back as soon as I can. I'll get paid on Tuesday. I'm so sorry.'

'You keep saying that. You keep saying that you're so sorry. Do you mean it?'

'Yes, of course.'

I could see the credit card. 'And you'll pay me next Tuesday?'

'Oh you're being so nice about it. Let me give you a big kiss.' She stood and moved the wine bottle and plate to the washbasin. She leaned forward to kiss me, her jeans still undone. She brushed her lips to my cheek. 'Thank you so much, Mister.'

I urgently pressed my open mouth to her lips but she sealed her mouth shut. She leaned forward forcing me to lie back on the bed, making my stomach stretch uncomfortably. She kissed my ears and throat as she undid my belt, gently touching the growing tautness of my trousers with the palms of her hands. 'Let's get all this off you,' she said.

'Sarah, shouldn't you get undressed, too?'

'Yes of course.' She lifted her sweatshirt off in one deft movement.

I reached for her breasts but she swept my hands aside.

'Let me undo your shirt first.' She seemed able to undo each button one handed with a deft flick. I felt her hand slide across my tumescence as she unzipped my trousers.

She dropped her jeans to the floor revealing tiny knickers that barely covered her essential femininity. 'Stay on your back,' she ordered me. She dragged my trousers off my legs and climbed onto my body.

My stomach was feeling a bit worse. 'But you've still got...' I said.

'Yes!' she shouted at the top of her voice, covering her face with both hands.

The door burst open and yet again I was blinded by camera flashes. Someone shouted questions at me. I lay still covering my face with my hands, waiting in hiding for the intrusion to go away and for peace to return. Eventually the bombardment stopped and Sarah climbed off me.

'What will you do about my bra and knickers?' asked Sarah.

Another voice replied. 'Make them disappear. Would you like to be a double D?'

I sat up. The woman reporter who I had befuddled that morning was standing in front of me, her back to the window. I heard the door behind me close.

Sarah giggled. 'No. A C-cup. And, remember Del, you promised. No one will see my face.'

'Trust me darling, it will look a lot better if you're blacked out.'

'Are you saying I'm ugly?' demanded Sarah.

'No, of course not.' Del pointed at me. 'But it will make him look even sleazier.' She sneered at the window. 'This room is perfect.'

It was like I no longer existed. They were standing on either side of me, barristers presenting my sin to an invisible court. There were tears in my eyes. I couldn't decide which was worse, the physical pain in my stomach or the emotional pain at being tricked again. How could she? Were all women like Del, Sarah and Rebecca?

Del sneered towards me for a quick second. 'Do you want me to stay until you're ready to go? In case he gets nasty.'

'No,' said Sarah. 'You know, I think he's just what he seems. Perhaps we've been a bit hard on him?'

'He deserved this. All that holier than thou. He tells us we're all sinners and now look at him.' Del picked up my clothes and threw them at me. 'Get dressed. You disgust me.'

I sobbed and shook my head. 'What have I done to deserve this?'

'You went too far. I ask the questions not you,' Del snapped.

I twisted my body so that I could watch her go, fearing that she might hit me from behind.

She gave me a final sneer as she left the room, closing the door behind her.

I turned back to Sarah. She was fully dressed again, standing in front of the window staring at me with her head tilted to the side as if slightly curious as to what sort of creature I might be.

'Why did you do it? What did I do to you?' I pleaded.

'For the money, of course, silly.' She was childlike, irresponsible. 'It wasn't much but Del wanted a story and you fell right into. Plop!' She continued that puzzled stare. 'I've got to get by, you know?'

Once again I failed to see into her soul, despite my compassion.

'You *are* odd,' she said. 'Some men would be furious by now, threatening, angry. Others would run. Maybe feeling sorry for themselves. What's wrong with you?'

'Can't you see? I've always cared about you. I forgave you. And you tricked me and now I have to forgive you again.' I stared at the bed, allowing the tears to roll down my cheeks.

'You only wanted me because I looked like a little boy. You're just a paedophile. You deserved to be ripped off.'

'No. I really just wanted to have sex.'

'And you really believed that you could just have sex with anyone who comes along with no consequences or anything?' She waved her hand in the air to emphasise her words.

'I guess so.' I stood up and stared at the floor, still naked.

'Look at you. You're fat and old.'

I looked down at myself. I did seem to be putting on weight.

'What makes you think that anyone would want that?' She pointed at my shamed and hiding manhood.

Why was I given such a horrible body? Why did it have to be inherited from that bastard Dr M?

'And my name isn't Sarah, and it isn't Sandra either.'

'I'm sorry, Sarah or Sandra or whoever you are. I suppose I didn't take care of you like I should.' I picked up my shirt and put it on. A shot of pain went through my stomach and I leaned forward, resting on the bed.

'There you go again,' she said, ignoring my actions. 'You are so strange; so interesting. I've never met a man like you, before. Don't you understand about cause and effect?'

'I can't understand you or anything you do,' I muttered through clenched teeth.

She sat down in the antique chair totally ignoring my obvious pain. 'Perhaps you need a lesson. Listen carefully.' She conveyed an image of a little girl instructing a younger boy. 'For every cause there is an effect. For every effect there is a cause. If the effect is that you want sex, you have got to create the right conditions so that there is a cause.' She waved her hands indicating imaginary sequences of causes and effects.

The pain in my stomach subsided. I stood to put on my underpants and trousers.

'So,' she continued, 'if you want sex, it's either got to be caused by love and wooing which takes forever, or by buying it, which is horrible. Or,' she raised a finger to point at my stomach, 'you've got to be so attractive that women want you for your body.'

'I tried to pay for it. It didn't work either.'

'How can you be this old and not know all this? Have you come from another planet?'

'Sort of.' I stared at the ground.

She laughed. 'Quick! Get Del back. I've got an alien now!'

'I suppose it was cause and effect that made Del and you set me up. I did something to her today and she hates me for it.'

She paused for a second, examining my face carefully. 'Women sure do hate you. It's because of what you keep saying. What did you do to Del?'

'I told her to forgive her father. I guess she wasn't ready for it. That's how I got away to see you.' I paused.

She looked away quickly.

'Wait.' I said. 'I just realised. That was after you rang me. So you two set me up before then. Why did she hate me then?'

She looked down at the ground and turned her back. 'I dunno.' She faced me once more. 'What did you do to her?'

'I have special powers.'

Her eyes lit up with excitement. 'What are they? Show me.'

'I can see into your soul. It might be dangerous.'

'Yes. Even better.' She stared into my face, bouncing on her toes in her eagerness. 'Show me.'

'I can't see your soul properly. But I can show you that I care.' I let my feelings shine out.

'Weird,' she said staring at me. 'You do seem to be really caring about me. It's almost like I can feel something from you. Are you really from another planet?'

I smiled at her. 'No. Heaven. I've been put here. By God. I'm an angel.'

She giggled and then stopped herself when she saw my serious expression. 'Yeah, that's good. But that still doesn't explain why you don't know about cause and effect. Angels know everything and make our lives good and save us and protect us. You aren't doing too well as an angel are you?'

I sat down on the bed to put my shoes and socks on. 'Look. It's like this. There is no time in heaven. No time for cause and effect to occur in.' My stomach was leaden but no longer painful.

'So, if there's no time in heaven, how did God put you here?'

I stopped and stared. She was right. I couldn't answer her.

'Okay.' She stood up. 'Let's say you're an angel, then. What's your name?'

'I don't have a name. I'm only an angel.'

'No. Angels have names, like Michael or Raphael or something like that. One of my friends was into some silly game that had fighting and angels and demons.'

'You're thinking of Archangels. They have names, but I'm not that important.'

'So are you still Dr Matthews?'

'No.'

She was such a strange woman, at first so worldly wise and now suddenly naïve and childlike. She put her hands on her hips. 'Then you still need a name, Mister Angel. What do you want to be called?'

I felt within myself. 'Gabriel. I think that's right.'

She offered her hand. I took it and she lifted my arm, guiding me to stand. She looked behind my back. 'Okay, Gabriel, where do you hide your wings?' She waved her hands above my head. 'Where's your halo?'

'I don't have any.'

'Why not?'

'I don't know. Why should I have them?'

'Well, why did God put you here?' She was bouncing, almost jumping with excitement.

'I don't know that either. I just know I've got a great purpose. And I've been having some dreams. I may have to kill another angel before it brings terrible evil into the world.'

'Really? This is so exciting. I've never met an angel before and now I'm in a fight between two!'

I looked down at my body. 'But I'm still ugly. Wouldn't being with me break the law of cause and effect or would having sex with an angel be more fun?'

She pushed me into the chair and sat on the bed. 'No, I don't mean that. I never have sex with anyone. I don't want to. No, I mean, I've never had an angel as a friend. And since you have not got a clue, it must be my job to teach you all about the world.'

A perfect lotus blossom of rightness burst open within my heart. Yes. She was right.

And so she started my education by pointing out that the credit card she had left for me wasn't mine, that IOUs are never worth anything and that I shouldn't believe anything about sisters with babies unless I saw them myself. It was only after all this instruction that she finally told me to avoid overeating, especially cheese.

FIGHTING TALK

Psalm 144:1
*Blessed be the LORD my strength which teacheth my
hands to war, and my fingers to fight:*

'An army of holy fighters? What like crusaders?'

'No. More like detectives' I answered her. 'Look, Sarah,
it'll work. We need lots of people to help us find this angel
and neutralise it before it kills me.'

'Oh, I understand, like in the Inquisition. Lots of
investigators to get the truth out of everyone,' she frowned
ferociously and turned an imaginary thumb screw, 'no
matter what it takes.'

'No, not murderers and torturers. I couldn't accept that.
No, people who want to fight for what is good and right.
But not with weapons.'

We were in my living room. When Sarah had arrived,
Rebecca was too furious to ask me who she was or why she
was here. She had been icily polite before she disappeared
somewhere, probably the bedroom.

And now my guardian angel was walking around my
living room, holding an imaginary collection box. 'I've got

it. Just like the Salvation Army. There could be easy money in dressing up like them and collecting in pubs.'

We had some snacks, peanuts and crisps that I had bought that morning. 'No,' I said. 'This isn't about money! It's about good and evil. It's about my purpose and enabling me to do it.'

She sat down and giggled. 'You are so serious sometimes. But you still need money to live and make things happen.'

'This will be about love.'

'Right!' She ran her hands from her blue jeans on her hips to the sweatshirt on her chest, pouting and presenting a sexual overture. 'Love. I could wear my sexy red dress and see if any of the boys want me, then we'll have them and you can brainwash them into our cult.'

'No.' I thumped the white cushion of the white sofa.

'Oh, sorry. You don't want boys, then? I forgot. You want girls. I'll wear my jeans and my sensible shoes and my loose top.' She looked down at her body in mock discovery. 'Just like I'm wearing now! I must be gay and didn't know it.'

I stared at her stony faced.

She continued anyway, aggressively strutting up and down, frowning and announcing her lesbian credentials. 'I'll cut my hair even shorter and bring in the girls. But you'll have to pretend to be a girl, too. You could be called Gabrielle! I think you'll look really ugly in a dress. You're too fat. But that should be okay because no one's allowed to talk about people being fat, anymore.'

'Sarah, stop taking the piss. Do you know anything about lesbians at all?'

She sat drawing her knees together, her head slightly bowed, lips pursed and eyes down in an exaggerated pose of contrition. She loved to be the centre of attention. 'I'm so sorry but my name's not Sarah.' She shook her head in a ladylike pose.

This was so exasperating. If she would only sit still and stay on one topic of discussion. 'What is your name, then?'

She was back to her little boy expression, with the wide-eyed smile and wistful look. 'What do you want it to be, Mister?'

'I want to know your real name.'

'Umm, Susan?'

I shook my head. 'No. Not Susan.'

'Katherine. We could have breakfast at Tiffany's.' She adopted a regal pose with her fingers near her mouth as if using a cigarette holder.

'If you're thinking of the movie, I think you'll find the name is Audrey Hepburn.'

Her lip raised in feigned contempt. 'Audrey's an old lady's name. I don't want that one.' She jumped to her feet and leant forward, hands between her legs holding down an imaginary dress and pouting. 'How about Marilyn?'

'I'll never know, now, will I? You could have told me your name and I would have no way of knowing.' I shook my head in despair. 'Why aren't you an actress? You always have to be the centre of attention. And you seem to know all about old movies.'

'Yes, I should be an actress. Shakespearean, of course.' She frowned, stabbed the air and wrung her hands. 'Lady MacBeth.'

'So why aren't you an actress?'

'No, better still, Titania from The Taming of the Shrew.' She scowled at me in contempt. 'I hate all men,' she declared.

This time it was my head that shook in mock despair. 'Titania's the fairy queen in A Midsummer Night's Dream.'

'Yes. A fairy queen. That's it.' Now she was wandering around waving an imaginary wand. She pointed it at me. 'Turn into Brad Pitt.'

'Huh. Now you're talking. Titania turned a man into a donkey. That's what you did to me.'

'All men are donkeys, anyway. They're so easily controlled by sex. Even with my tiny tits I can get them going. Anyway, I want to be called Titania.'

'You can't have tiny tits and be called Titania. It's false advertising. Anyway, I've just remembered something. I don't think it was Titania who turned him into a donkey. I think it was Puck.'

'Puck.' She popped her lips as she said it.

'Actually I think Puck is right. He was a mischievous imp.'

'But I'm a girl. Perhaps.' She smiled at me. Maybe she was still hiding something. 'Anyway, that's a horrible name.' She fell down on the sofa next to me and cuddled up with an imploring expression.

'There's something boyish about you,' I said.

She giggled once more. 'Actually, I don't want to be a girl. There's too much hassle.'

'So, you'd rather be a boy?'

She stood up again, legs wide and pointed at her puffed up chest. 'Possibly. No. Except when I choose, of course. I'd like to choose whether I'm a boy or a girl or neither.'

'What about being a woman?'

She sighed. 'No. Never a woman. Too many complications.' She stared at the plain white wall and, for a few seconds, I felt something. She really was neither man nor woman. Nor boy nor girl. She was unique, magical, always an illusion. There was a soul in there, but it wasn't bound to this reality.

'Puck it is then,' I said.

'What?'

'I'm going to call you Puck. You're a fairy boy, and you're not real.'

'Gabriel and Puck. I guess I can get used to it. But you have to promise never to use it in front of anyone else.'

'Yes, fine, but how do I get my followers?'

I reached the bottom of my crisp bag. Where had they gone? I opened another packet.

She sat down on a chair opposite me and adopted the pose of The Thinker for a few seconds. She became bored of this posture almost immediately, sat back and smiled, her eyes vacant as she applied her mind to the problem. 'Let's see. You'll need money and you'll need people. People should be easy. There's millions of idiots out there. They believe the most incredible stuff. An angel should be so easy. But you want lots of people. All at once. That takes advertising. We'll need a scam to get some money. I know some brilliant scams.'

'No, Puck. Nothing sinful. I'm trying to control myself.' And I really believed it, too. In those days I never noticed how little I cared for those around me, how my only concern was what they could do for me and not who they were or what they wanted.

'But it'll only be taking from the stupid and the greedy. Like, one thing is, you get people to bet on the toss of a coin.' She was excited again, showing an imaginary coin being tossed. 'But you get someone to convince them that the coin's a fake and mostly comes up heads. So, you keep tossing and they start to notice the heads and then they'll bet again and again on heads until they're almost broke.'

'Does that really work?'

'I don't know I've never tried it. I only do easy stuff like robbing old perverts who want to bonk boyish women.' She grinned at me.

'This is no good!'

She pouted.

'It has to be on the telly.' She framed her face with her fingers. 'Are you lost?' Her voice was deep and booming, mocking the reverential tone of a telly evangelist. 'Need to fight a few angels and demons?' A vague American accent came and went at random as she spoke. 'Then join Gabriel and Marjorie as they fight the good fight.'

'Marjorie? Why Marjorie?'

'Isn't that a nice ordinary name? The right name for someone godly?'

'No.'

She frowned, staring at the ground.

'I'm sorry, Sarah,' I said, 'I mean Puck, but I need something that will really work. And we haven't got enough money for an expensive advertising campaign.'

She shrugged and sat down, thoughtful at last. 'Okay,' she said, 'I don't want to be a telly evangelist. People might recognise me.'

'Why would people recognising you be a problem?'

Her eyes became wide and innocent. 'It just would be, okay?' She cocked her head to the side. 'Actually, maybe we don't need TV and we don't need to pay.' She looked at me, thoughtfully. 'You're already in the papers. You can capitalise on that. Maybe get a bigger profile?'

I became concerned. 'Puck, what are you thinking of?'

'No, really. You could use everything that's happened. We could get Del in. Use her instead of her using us.'

'You worry me when you become serious.'

'Is there a big sort of prayer or something that would show everyone how good and holy you are now?'

'It would have to be a big prayer. Or a lot of it.' Her idea had caught my imagination. I smiled at her. 'How about a vigil?'

'What do you mean?'

'A night of prayer. In a church. Asking for God's forgiveness. Showing that I'm a sinner who's repenting.'

She curled her lip, unimpressed. 'It sounds a bit boring. Why would the papers say anything?'

'Because they've been so nasty to me? Don't they owe me?' I opened another bag of crisps. Where did they keep disappearing to?

'Don't be stupid. They don't even care about you.'

'Then why was I in the paper?'

She rolled her eyes to the ceiling. 'Because it's August. It's the silly season and there are no interesting stories. They like the weird stories at this time of year.' She paused and smiled. 'But that gives me an idea. You're an angel right?'

'Yes.' I became worried yet again.

'Well, tell them you're an angel and that you're going to do a miracle.' She was excited again. 'What can you do?'

'What like turning water into wine?'

'Yes. Yes do that.' She bounced on her toes again. 'Create something really high quality, like a burgundy. Anything except that rubbish that I gave you the other day.'

I gave her a dry look. 'I can't do that.'

'Oh, okay, then, a low quality wine. Something cheap. Like from a supermarket.'

'No. I can't turn water into wine.'

She nodded in cynical agreement. 'I thought not. You're not really an angel at all.'

I focussed for a few seconds thinking.

She opened her mouth to speak but I raised my palm to silence her.

'No, let me explain,' I said at last, when I realised that I had run out of peanuts as well as crisps.

She puffed her cheeks. 'Is this going to take a long while?'

'No. Think about a TV, a phone, a radio, anything like that. They're all technical marvels aren't they?'

'Yeah, whatever.'

'If the world wasn't predictable they couldn't be built, could they? They wouldn't do the same thing every time.'

'Guess not. Have you finished?'

I sighed. How could I explain it to her? 'If any old person could do miracles, the world would be impossible and we couldn't make the world our own.'

She patted her open mouth feigning a yawn to show how bored she was.

'If we all did miracles, there'd be no predictability. We couldn't even feed ourselves.' I had run out of snacks. I'd have to buy more next time. 'We'd all have to just hope that miracle workers would look after us, or we'd all have to do miracles and then they wouldn't be miracles any more.'

'What about just you and me then?'

'If I could finish my point,' I said sternly.

She raised the back of her hand to her forehead and looked pained.

'Stop that. All I'm saying is that miracles can only happen very, very occasionally and then only with very special people, otherwise we couldn't have built this world, and I think that God wants us to be able to build things without miracles to see what we can do.'

'Thank you, brother,' she shouted, adopting her vague American accent again. 'Hear De Word of De Lord.'

'Very funny,' I said sulkily.

She frowned. 'I'm sorry. You're talking about cause and effect again, aren't you?'

'Yes. That's it.' I was excited. She *had* understood. 'Cause and effect. Everything's predictable.' I paused and looked at her. 'Except you... And me.' I stared at the floor. There was something important about free will. I shook myself out of my pensive mood. 'So miracles are out.'

'Okay.' She pulled at her lip and looked at me. 'But you can do something,' she said eventually. 'You did it to Del. She kept on going on about it all the time.'

'What's this?'

'Del, from the paper. She was so angry at you. She said you violated her soul. You did it to me, too, but I didn't feel violated.' She thought for a second. 'You know, we could use that. You could read minds.'

'I don't think I can do that. I can just read souls.'

'What's the difference?'

'I don't know.'

'Is that all?'

'I don't know. I think there's something else, too. I can feel it. Like a muscle that could be used but hasn't yet.'

'Really? What sort of muscle? In your face? On your hand?'

'I can't describe it. And it's not really a muscle. I couldn't think of any other way to say it.'

She examined my face once more. 'But you can read souls?'

'Yes.'

'Okay. We have to make a big show of that, then.' She paced, thinking on her feet. 'It's a good time of year. Everyone's on holiday so the papers are really boring and they'll do anything to get a story. They especially like the wacky ones. You do your vigil. Say how you're an angel and you've asked God for powers to help others.'

'It will have to be all night in a church.'

'Yeah, that sounds great. And when you come out of the church, start telling people about their souls. Not journalists, though. They don't have souls.'

'Yes they do.'

'Well only little, twisted ones. No, we have to reach lots of people. And then you can read their souls.'

She was right. I thought it through. 'Yes,' I said finally, rising to my feet. 'Yes! You're right. It's my purpose! To bring people to a new religion! To save their souls. And then the evil will be overcome by the sheer numbers of good people. You're right. I'll have a new religion. I'll sweep aside the rest and start again.'

I ignored Puck's concerned expression.

I leaned closer to her. 'And do you want to know something?'

'No, but you're going to tell me, anyway, aren't you?'

'Dr M was starting to set it up. In opposition to the church. He was so upset about women priests and stuff that he wanted to create his own church. I know how to do it. Let's go have a pizza while we talk about it.'

VIGILANCE

1 Peter 5:8
***Be sober, be vigilant; because your adversary the
devil, as a roaring lion, walketh about, seeking whom
he may devour:***

The thud of the heavy doors echoed through the small
church. At last Del and her cameraman had left. My knees
were hurting from the hard stone floor in front of the altar.
I lowered my arms from their raised position and stood up.
Del didn't believe in me. She even sniggered when I said I
was an angel and then she asked the usual questions about
wings and halos. I was grateful for Puck's advice and didn't
reveal my dreams. As far as they were concerned, I was
an angel, confessing my sins and receiving holy guidance.
This was difficult but it should help to recruit followers to
my church.

It was a warm, late August afternoon outside, but the
high ceiling, stained glass windows and hard stone kept the
church interior in wretched cold. I munched on a packet of
crisps as I paraded up and down the aisle patting my arms
across my body to warm my limbs.

The musty wood and stone smell of the church reminded me of interminable sermons survived through dogged persistence as a child. As an adult I inflicted them on others.

Dr Matthews often preached here and so the vicar had been pleased to support my vigil. I clambered up the steps to the pulpit, and, as I recovered my breath, I looked down on my potential worshippers. I could see them in the pews, people of all colours and creeds turning to me for spiritual guidance. I was filled with pride.

Then I remembered the last sermon I had given, to a church full of fellow malcontents. My murderer had probably been in the congregation. It might have been that weird guy that smiled too much. Or the liberal. Maybe it was someone else who waited outside. He could be outside now, waiting for it to get dark. After all the publicity he was sure to know where I was. Maybe I should lock the door? I felt the chill inside my heart.

No. This was silly. No one knew I was here except Puck, Rebecca, Del and her cameraman. Anyone else would have had to monitor my every movement. It wouldn't be in the papers until after the vigil. No, he didn't even know I was here.

I descended back to the church floor, determined not to panic. I lay down on a bench, but the hard wood was too uncomfortable. I should have been praying, but I couldn't be bothered. I checked my pockets for snacks but I had eaten everything. Instead I found some letters that Rebecca had given to me, demanding that I look at them.

They were irrelevant. I was to be fired, my credit card was cancelled because payments were overdue and I had won a prize, possibly an expensive TV.

I paced some more. This was so boring! I wandered down to the main entrance.

A note was lying on the floor a few feet in.

I stared at it. I could see the name "Dr Matthews" in large block letters. Why hadn't the deliverer opened the door or knocked or called out? Was the murderer watching through the gap at floor height to see what I would do?

I could feel my heart pounding. If my nemesis was out there he must know where I was. He might be playing a cat and mouse game with me. Any minute I would hear him approaching, taunting me before he killed me.

A creak sounded, echoing in the old hall. I turned, but no one was there. I ran up and down the aisle and skirted warily around the communion rail and pulpit. No sign of anyone. Of course, they would have to come through the main door. The side door was locked. I panted heavily as I walked back to the main door.

I lay down on the cold stone and looked out through the crack at the blinding light outside. I couldn't see a thing. I snatched the paper from the floor.

The handwriting was small, scrawled and almost illegible, forcing me to use my glasses.

'Dr Matthews you can help me but if I don't get some help I'm going to OD out tonight I don't want to I want peec what about you are you real or are you like everyone if your here tonight help me you know where you said you could help me come here I can go either way give up and you save my soul or not
??? is God listening ????'

Bethany's signature was carefully written at the bottom of the note, neatly underlined with well formed, round letters in stark contrast to the scribbled handwriting in the rest of the note. I had been an idiot. Imagining murderers when I could have left the door open and let her find me. I could have given her the support she needed immediately. If I wasn't there for her, she might go back to the drugs or even worse kill herself. She needed me and only I could help her. I was needed and it felt good.

My vigil could wait. As long as I was back before the morning, no one would even know I had gone and I would be doing two great acts at the same time. And, of course, my murderer still wouldn't know where I was.

I opened the doors and looked out carefully. No one was around. I half expected there to be a reporter or two waiting to catch me out. The church was quite a way from the centre of town. How would I get down to see her? I had my credit cards. There was probably a cash machine in the local pub a few hundred yards down the road. I could get some money there and catch a taxi downtown.

As I walked I read her note again and again, trying to make sense of it.

The pub was full of drunken men wearing rugby outfits.

Great.

I worked my way through the crowd, dodging elbows as best I could, but several times I had beer and cider spilt over me. Finally, I found the cash machine and withdrew plenty of money. I fought my way back to the bar to get something to eat and also to find out where I could summon a taxi. While I was waiting for a huge man to leave the bar I felt a tap on my right shoulder.

'Shouldn't you be in a vigil, Dr Matthews?'

It was Joe Kayer. I saw him before I was blinded by the flash. He must have been following me.

I had to get away.

I ran.

I pushed wildly to my left and to my right.

Drunken oafs shoved me back and forth, swearing.

I was pushed towards the bar.

I could see a clerical collar.

My head hit something hard.

I fell to the floor, confused.

Something was happening around me. Bodies moved above me.

I was kicked again and again.

I forced myself to my feet. I had to find the way out. Get to Bethany. Save her. A huge hand grabbed my arm.

'Come on,' said a voice.

Had to keep standing. Had to rescue Bethany. Dragged somewhere. Sitting. A door closed and movement. More walking. Another door. More sitting. Bethany.

Gluttony

Proverbs 23:2
And put a knife to thy throat, if thou be a man given to appetite.

Ten, eleven, twelve. She had crammed twelve boiled sweets into her mouth, but to be able to chew she would have to open her mouth and then they would all fall out. She tried to swallow but they were too large. She didn't want to waste food for that would be a sin. What was she to do?

'What are you doing, child?' demanded her father.

She jumped in fear almost choking on a sweet.

Why had he come into her bedroom? She thought she was safe here? She looked up at him. Was she sinning? She wasn't angry, so it wasn't wrath. Envy? Lust? She didn't know what lust was.

'Answer me.' He was angry now. What had she done?

'I'm eating,' she tried to say, but as soon as she opened her mouth, two of the sweets fell out onto the floor. She clamped her teeth shut.

'How many sweets have you eaten?' he demanded.

She paused for a second. She mustn't lie. She subtracted the two that had fallen out and held her hands outstretched to show ten.

'What? I asked you a question, child.'

'Ten,' she muttered around closed teeth, now in absolute terror, for she had obviously sinned but she didn't know what she had done.

'They are still in your mouth aren't they?'

She nodded.

'Gluttony,' he shouted. 'Gluttony. You are eating more food than you need. You disgusting child. You must know by now that this is one of the seven deadly sins. Have you learnt nothing?'

Oh no. A deadly sin. She hoped that her soul was not forever tarnished. She opened her mouth and spat two into her hand.

'Put them back in,' he ordered. 'I will teach you the consequences of gluttony.'

She forced the sweets back into her mouth.

'And the two that dropped out earlier.'

She searched for them. They were covered in carpet hair. She appealed to her father, still unable to speak through her clenched teeth.

'Those as well.'

She forced them in, her stomach turning.

'You will now swallow all of them,' her father stated.

She shook her head. How could she do that without chewing? She signalled.

He seemed to understand. 'Swallow them whole.'

She forced each sweet down her throat. At each swallow her stomach threatened to regurgitate it but her iron will, propped up by fear, overcame the reactions of her body.

By the last sweet her stomach was hurting terribly.

The pain of the beating was worse than her stomach.

Finally the last benediction was announced.

'Psalm 78:18: they tempted God in their heart by asking meat for their lust.'

After that lesson she was always disgusted by gluttony. It was a sin that hurt everyone, not just the sinner. If a person ate more than they needed they damaged their bodies and denied others what they needed. The whole of the western world was sinning. All those people eating far more than they needed while others went hungry. But how could she stop it? How could she save that many souls? There must be a clue somewhere. But, first, she had to make sure that no one could stop her. Not even a sinning, mad lay preacher who thought he was an angel.

CASTING THE FIRST STONE

Lamentations 4:6
For the punishment of the iniquity of the daughter of my people is greater than the punishment of the sin of Sodom, that was overthrown as in a moment, and no hands stayed on her.

The dreadful, beautiful angel draws the observer to it so that he can testify to its work. A woman lies unconscious surrounded by seven hooded figures.

'That's Bethany. What are you going to do to her?'

As always a perfect smile is offered by the terrible angel to the observer.

'No. You can't do this.'

'They say unto him, Master this woman was taken in adultery, in the very act.'

'John 8:4. No! This isn't right. You can't punish her for my sin. I was the adulterous one. She's not even married.'

The angel nods curtly and its tongue touches the woman's head. It rouses the victim who looks around, dazed.

'Am I dead already?' she asks. 'Is this Hell?'

The holy company draw back in shock, holding their ears. They chant, 'Holy, holy, holy,' in a confusion of voices.

The accused woman tries to move, but she is sluggish, so slow that one of the inquisitors can easily push her back onto the floor.

'Do not prostitute thy daughter, to cause her to be a whore; lest the land fall to whoredom, and the land become full of wickedness.'

'Leviticus 19:29. How can you use the Bible like this? It's not right. I'll stop you. I call on God to intervene and save this woman.'

The angel silently laughs and the observer is aware of its contempt for holy intervention.

'Evil and adulterous,' is chanted in that same high sing song voice. 'No one will save you.'

'Is this my judgement?' asks Bethany, apparently resigned to her fate.

The angel and the monks nod in perfect unison.

'That guy. The minister. Could he have saved me? If he was here?'

The angel looks up at the observer and laughs silently at the very thought that anyone could save this wrongdoer, particularly the observer.

'And this is the condemnation, that light is come into the world, and men loved darkness rather than light, because their deeds were evil.'

'John 3:19. But it's not their fault. You are leading them. They're just your tools. A knife can be used for good or evil but it's not evil itself.'

The angel gloats at the observer.

'Wait. I know. Hosea 4:14. I will not punish your daughters when they commit whoredom.'

The angel frowns and looks away.

'Well? What about that Bible quote?'

'Your deeds are evil,' is sung in a monotone. 'You must cease these acts. You are drawing others into sin.'

The prostitute sighs softly, a tear rolls down her cheek. 'Yes. I was going to stop, anyway. Are you going to kill me?'

'Now Moses in the law commanded us, that such should be stoned.'

'John 8:5. What about the rest of the passage? It says "but what sayest thou?".'

The beautiful angel sulks.

I know. This is all an illusion! None of you exist. This is just my imagination. It's my guilt over Bethany. You're just a bad dream. I must have eaten some more cheese.

The monk chants the angel's words, 'now Moses in the law commanded us, that such should be stoned.'

The whore nods. 'I don't suppose I could have something to help me along before you do it? To reduce the pain?'

The monk and the acolytes do not respond.

'I guess not. Will you be strong enough to make it quick?'

In response a monk lifts a large and heavy stone without effort. The terror of her situation finally galvanises a last desperate escape and the guilty one tries to roll away, but her body is weak and slow. A blow strikes her head and she cries out once softly in pain. It sounds much like the calls she made for her clients as she faked the joy of love. Another blow strikes and she lies motionless, dazed but still alive. Blood seeps from the damaged head.

How can she have survived any blows from that stone?

The angel does not care, it is only interested in the scene before it, glowing more strongly, increasing in power as the dying woman's soul becomes detached from her body.

Repeated blows bring more blood and cause more damage until finally there is only uninhabited flesh.

The angel quotes once more.

'The punishment of thine iniquity is accomplished, O daughter of Zion.'

'Lamentations 4:22. You must be an illusion. Please, be an illusion. Why would God let you do this?'

A Bible and cross are placed on the body.

They think they are enacting God's word, don't they? It's your deception.

The angel opens its heart to the observer.

'Asbeel? Your name is Asbeel?'

The scene is further arranged with blood, skin and hair and the angel once again casts the spell of misdirection.

'Let me talk to them. Let me show them a different form of religion. One that is full of love and not punishment.'

The observer is dispelled.

COUNTING THE DANCERS

It is not possible to count the number of angels that can dance on the head of a pin, for counting requires time and space to separate them one from another.

Persecution

Matthew 5:11

Blessed are ye, when men shall revile you, and persecute you, and shall say all manner of evil against you falsely, for my sake.

'Can you hear me?' The voice was faint – a man's.

Something touched my arm.

'See…' It was the same voice.

My head hurt. My chest hurt. I shouted.

I needed…

…to rescue someone.

I was bumped. A shaft of pain sliced through my head.

I could feel sheets. There was an overpowering smell of disinfectant. Someone was speaking. Something was beeping. I opened my eyes and winced as the strong light ignited a pain between my temples. My mouth was dry. I must have been drinking.

There was something I had to do. Save someone.

Bethany.

My dream came back. Was I too late? I tried to sit up but I was overwhelmed by stomach churning agony.

I was in a bed in a hospital ward. A nurse was inspecting each patient. Finally, she looked in my direction and walked over to me.

'How do you feel?' she asked, touching my wrist and looking into my eyes.

'Headache,' I answered. My throat was sore. 'Thirsty.'

'I'll get you a drink.' She poured water from a jug on my bedside table. 'Drink it slowly.'

I was desperately thirsty but I didn't need her advice, as I couldn't drink quickly. She watched me in silence, until I finished the last slow sip. I used my insights to look beyond her middle aged, overweight body and dark, dyed hair to the woman within. Despite her profession she was self-obsessed and resentful of needing to care for others. Her faith was weak.

'The doctor will see you soon.' She disappeared off through a door. I closed my eyes and listened to the noises of the ward, hushed conversations, the occasional beep of a machine, a squeaky wheel on a trolley. And always footsteps coming and going, some fast, some slow.

Sometime later an Indian woman appeared her white coat and stethoscope advertising her status in the hospital. Another nurse followed her. The Indian doctor's faith was deep and strong. The curtain was pulled around the bed, enclosing us, protecting me from the world.

'How are you feeling?' the doctor asked.

'Horrible. But much better than before, thank you.' Was this the wages of sin? Was I being punished for what I did with …?

I couldn't remember her name.

'You had a nasty knock on the head. Do you know who you are?'

I stared at her. This was going to be tricky. I couldn't keep lying and pretending to be Dr Matthews anymore. 'I used to be called Dr Matthews. Dr Gideon Matthews, but I prefer to be called Gabriel.'

'I thought I'd seen you before,' said the nurse.

The doctor and I both stared at her.

'You're in the papers,' she replied.

'What?' I had forgotten about that.

'I'll go get it for you.' She disappeared again leaving me with the doctor.

'Do you know what that's about?' asked the doctor.

I nodded in despair. 'It won't be good. How long have I been out?'

'You arrived here this morning.'

I looked for my watch but my wrist was bare.

'It's 6 in the evening,' she added.

'Enough time for the papers to write something really nasty, I suppose.'

'I wouldn't know about that. Now please, lay still, I need to examine you.'

She did endless tests. I had to watch her finger; she tapped my knees and elbows; she blinded me with a light. 'How are you feeling, now?' she asked eventually.

'I have a headache and my eyes hurt.' It was time I stopped being so selfish. It was time to stop sinning and think of others more and how I could help them.

I opened my heart to her. I could see the detached professionalism that drove her to get everything right, but still protected her heart and her family. What should I say to help her?

'I think you'll be fine,' she said. 'Is there someone at home?'

'Perhaps my wife.'

'Tell the nurses how to contact her and we'll get you home as soon as possible.'

'Thank you doctor.' I touched her arm. 'Take good care of yourself, too.'

Her expression was stern, but I could feel the gratitude within her. She slipped out through the closed curtains.

After a few minutes the curtains were thrown back and more light blinded me.

'You *are* in the paper,' said the nurse. 'It's not very good I'm afraid.'

She dropped it on my lap. I barely glanced at her before I opened the paper.

I stared at the article. It was full of judgements from reporters and an editor who were probably more of a sinner than I was. "PUB VIGIL", "The Pisspot Priest", "Spirit of the Pub" and "Nutcase Angel". I was barely aware of giving Rebecca's details to the nurse as I read it.

'You know that's not right,' she said, nodding towards the paper.

'What?'

'It's wrong. It says you were drunk. We did a blood test to try to figure out what was wrong with you.' She held up my notes on a clipboard to show me.

'I wasn't drunk, was I?'

'No. You were sober. You were concussed. The paper's got it wrong.'

I examined her properly. She was very young, perhaps in her twenties, with brown short hair and brown eyes. She wore no make-up. She smiled easily and lightly. I looked into her soul. She had a good solid faith and cared greatly about people. It dominated every part of her. 'You shouldn't worry about everyone else so much,' I said. 'You need a bit of TLC, too.'

She smiled at me. 'That's very nice of you to say so.' She nodded at the papers. 'But that's not fair.' She called to me over her shoulder as she left for another patient, 'you should make them tell the truth.'

I read some more. There was an article on angels, with pictures. Most of it was rubbish, pictures of God as an old man with a beard, everyone on clouds and halos and wings all round. Ridiculous. They even had a section by another academic whose work Dr M had read, Professor Hakeem. He was an expert on everything to do with angels. The pictures showed one of the medieval hierarchies of angels, explaining the different orders, Angels, Archangels, Virtues, Powers, Principalities, Dominations, Thrones, Cherubim and Seraphim. They declared that if I was an angel I was a nobody, an angel of the lowest order without even a name. Archangels were one above me. All the other angels were still in heaven. It must have been written by Del to be so nasty and so specific to me.

I curled up under my blanket and waited. I talked to several nurses and each time I opened my heart to them. They all needed support to help them in such a difficult job but I couldn't do much other than say a few words.

After many hours I was taken home in an ambulance. A male paramedic accompanied me in silence on the journey home; another person of strong faith. They seemed to be all around me at the hospital, so I had given up telling them to look after themselves.

It was dark as I came out of the ambulance. A flash went off in my eyes. The paramedic shouted at someone to leave me alone as he led me to the front door where Rebecca was standing guard – a one headed Cerberus in a white dress and sensible shoes. She stood aside to allow me to cross the threshold into the safety of the house. Her expression was stern enough to keep the reporters out.

'You go up to your bed,' she ordered, but gently. I thought I detected a hint of compassion in her voice.

I trudged up the stairs, each one an effort, as if Sisyphus' boulder was always above me. I just hoped I wasn't going to start rolling back down again. Another, lesser wave of pain floated through my head as I undressed and climbed into bed.

'Are you feeling better now?'

I winced in the morning light.

'The paramedics said you hadn't been drinking. They were so angry,' said Rebecca.

'Why?'

'About the papers. They said it was unfair. They liked you.' She stared at me, probably searching for something that was likeable.

'My head still hurts.' I pulled the clean smelling sheet close under my neck.

'Why weren't you at your vigil?'

'I'd received a letter from Bethany. That prostitute.'

'What did she want? Did you have any money left?' There was no sign of surprise in her face.

'Don't take it wrong. I've put that behind me. She wanted to give up on the drugs. Go cold turkey or whatever they call it. She wanted spiritual guidance.'

She scrutinised my face for guile. 'Go on.'

'I was trying to get a taxi. To help her, you know.'

'So what happened?'

'Someone pushed me and I fell.'

'How did you get to the hospital?'

'I don't know.' I looked into her eyes. 'Rebecca. I'm trying to be good, but it isn't easy.'

'It used to be.'

'No. I think I paid a high price for being so moral.' I felt nothing but love for her. 'You did, too. I'm sorry.'

'What are you sorry for?' She did not move, focussed entirely on my face, still being so careful of her feelings.

'Everything Dr Matthews did to you. The way he hated you and your body. Could you please forgive me?'

'There's a lot to forgive.'

'I know and I realise it's a lot to ask.'

'You're too late.'

'Really?'

She scowled. 'I'll think about it. I'll make some breakfast. Do you want to eat up here?'

'No. I feel okay. I'll come down.'

She looked back at me as she left the room. I couldn't guess at what she was thinking.

I dressed. My trousers always seemed to be tight these days. I would have to do some exercise and stop eating so much, but everything tasted so good. I eventually found a pair of tracksuit trousers that fitted.

The table was set for breakfast, white bowls, white plates, white bread, white butter, white porridge, with a dash of set honey – opaque and almost white.

The doorbell rang as I ate. I signalled that I was too tired to get up.

Rebecca scowled. 'Reporters. I'll get rid of them.'

She went to the front door. I could hear voices coming nearer. I turned in my chair to see a medium height man and a tall woman in the doorway both dressed in dark suits.

'Doctor Matthews?' said the man.

I nodded. 'But I prefer to be called Gabriel.'

'We're police officers,' he said, asserting his authority. They flashed ID cards at me and muttered some names that I forgot immediately. He spoke with a strong cockney accent.

'We'd like to ask you some questions,' declared the policewoman. I thought I heard a slight Welsh lilt.

Their faith was slow and weak, repressed and understated. I nodded and stood up, intending to go to another room, but they were too impatient.

'Where were you last night?' demanded the man rudely.

'I don't know. At my vigil. In a church.'

Something in his eyes made me wary.

'But I left early,' I added hurriedly. 'To see someone.' Then my dream flashed through my mind. 'It's about Bethany, isn't it. Is she dead?'

'What do you think?'

'Was she... Was she stoned to death?'

'What makes you think that?'

'It was the monk. The angel told him to do it. To kill her. She was a sinner. An adulterer. She was drugged. She couldn't move. He hit her again and again and again until she was dead.' That poor woman. Dead. I could feel the pain as if it was my own.

'Right,' he said. 'Doctor Matthews, I am arresting you for the murder of Bethany Chaff...'

I didn't hear anything more. Bethany was dead and the angel was really out there killing people and hunting for me. And it was so close, now. It must know who I was and where I lived. Nothing else mattered. I had to destroy it before it found me.

As I was guided into the police car all I could see was Rebecca's grim expression.

None So Deaf, None So Blind

Isaiah 56:10

His watchmen are blind; they are all ignorant, they are all dumb dogs, they cannot bark; sleeping, lying down, loving to slumber.

I could not escape the memory of Bethany, emaciated, bloodied and dead.

The interview room was small, featureless. The chair and wooden desk were hard and nondescript. There were no distractions, no comforts and definitely no entertainments, just the smell of cleaning fluid not quite overpowering a slight smell of unwashed bodies and possibly urine. A uniformed policeman stood near the door. His powerful faith was distracting. I laid my head on the table, too tired to do anything else.

The same detectives that arrested me came into the room and sat down opposite me.

'You have the right to a solicitor,' said the woman.

'This is all wrong,' I said, ignoring them. 'I didn't do it. You should be looking for the monk. He's the killer. And his gang.'

How could the angel have found her? Why was she so weak? Did it know my relationship to her? Did it know where I lived? I kept seeing the bloodied stone striking again and again and again and imagining it hitting my head instead of hers.

They fiddled with a tape recorder and announced their names with some combination of the words detective and inspector or something similar. All I heard was that the man was Armstrong and the woman Evans.

'Dr Matthews,' said Armstrong.

I ignored him, pre-occupied with the visions in my head.

'Dr Matthews,' he repeated.

I looked up.

'Do you know why you were arrested?' he asked. He was the bad cop, with his arrogant sneer. He had a pad open and was holding a pen, ready to write.

'You must understand,' I pleaded. 'There's an angel and I have to fight it. I'm a good angel and it must be an evil angel and I've got to beat it before it kills me.'

They stared at each other. The woman shrugged and the man looked back at me.

'Okay,' he said, 'let's start with the night before last, the sixteenth. You said you were at the church. When did you leave?'

'Early. I got a note from Bethany. She asked me to help her get off the drugs. I was in a pub and I got knocked out. I just remember being in hospital yesterday. I must have been there all night.'

'We checked the hospital,' he said. 'You weren't there until the morning. No one could remember you being there before 9am.'

'What?'

'Where is this note now?' demanded Armstrong. He was speaking even more aggressively, demanding my full attention.

I cringed in fear. Was I going to spend the rest of my life in gaol for something I didn't do? Could the angel and monk find me there and kill me before I could find them? 'I don't know. Didn't the hospital know how I got there? Someone must have taken me in.'

The woman spoke, 'they couldn't find any of your records. They seem to have disappeared, just like your note. Can you explain that?' She was more relaxed, less invasive – the good cop.

The policeman in the corner fidgeted. 'Sir, if I may speak,' he said.

'You saw me turn on the tape recorder.' Armstrong seemed to be permanently angry.

'Yes, Sir, but it is important, Sir. I know where this man was.'

'What?' He slammed his pen down.

I flinched at the unexpected violence of such a common day act.

'Sir, I recognise this man. He was here in the cells this morning.' He was bobbing from side to side in barely controlled panic. 'The night before last there was a pub fight. He must have been in a cell all night and then, when he wouldn't wake up someone called a doctor.' He was in a desperate rush, perhaps trying to avoid another reprimand. 'They sent him to hospital.'

Evans intervened. 'Are you sure it was him?'

'Yes, Ma'am.'

'What time did you arrest him?' she said.

I felt hope appear. Her expression was proof that I was innocent. I would escape prison.

'It wasn't me that arrested him. We didn't even know. Somehow, he just ended up in a cell.'

'What does the paper work say?' she asked.

The junior officer's expression showed intense alarm. 'There wasn't any.'

'What?' demanded Armstrong.

'If he had been arrested properly when would it have been?' asked Evans.

'About 9pm, Ma'am.'

'Why wasn't he checked by a doctor when he arrived?' The macho detective was now shouting. His cockney accent became even more pronounced.

'I don't know, Sir.' The poor innocent foot soldier stepped back against the wall in fear. 'There was some sort of a mix up somehow. We don't know what happened. But he was here in the morning and he had to have been in a cell all night. That was the only time the cells were opened.'

'Are you sure?' Armstrong was calming down, now, with only a bitter expression rather than the anger of a few minutes ago.

'Yes,' replied my saviour. He kept glancing at me. He was so young. Perhaps only just out of police school.

'When did you send him to hospital?' asked the woman gently.

'It was at the end of my shift. Perhaps 8am? He went straight there.' He said this as if in his defence. 'In an ambulance.'

She shook her head. 'She was alive at midnight. Several witnesses. Dead at 9am. He was either in custody or in hospital and unconscious all the time. It couldn't have been him.'

Mr Macho looked at me. 'How did you know what happened?' He obviously hadn't finished attacking me yet.

'What?' Everything was changing too fast. Despite the relief that I had an alibi, I was still terrified of this violent man. And a monk and a demon were still out to kill me.

'How did you know that she was hit by a stone?'

'A dream. I get lots of them.' I tried to make myself as small as possible to escape from his anger.

He shook his head. 'We found your Bible and cross there.' He picked up a plastic bag containing both items. 'Your name is in the Bible. That is your cross isn't it?'

I nodded. Blood was smeared on them both, Bethany's blood. I pointed at the holy objects. 'I was robbed. I forgot all about them. It was ages ago. In the spring. I nearly died. I was interviewed by someone. A policewoman. She'll know.'

He held up a report. 'Your DNA was all over the place. Hair, skin, even some blood and semen.'

I looked at my feet in shame. 'I saw her. A few days ago.'

He scowled. 'Your blood was even on the brick.'

'I don't know how that happened. Maybe the angel cast a spell...' Only a great power could have overcome the natural laws of physics. 'What about the monk and all those followers he has?' I asked. I felt sorry for the bobby in the corner if Armstrong was always like this.

His scowl said it all. 'There was no other DNA there.'

Evans shook her head. 'Okay, it's clear that you're innocent.'

'Why did I get arrested?' I asked of the uniformed man.

'You did stink of alcohol, Sir.' He was providing an alibi for someone, probably himself. Either that or someone else had told him what I was like. 'You kept swaying a lot and talking about God and Heaven. You acted just like you were drunk...' He blinked rapidly, still terrified. 'Sir, we didn't... Do you want to press charges?'

A man of faith had provided an alibi at the most important time I needed it. I looked back at the detectives. 'That's it. Can't you see it? This is a holy war. I received holy protection.' I pointed at the constable. 'From him. The murderer got unholy protection. That's why you couldn't find evidence of him.'

Armstrong sighed. 'I don't have time for this. We need to go and look for a real killer.' He pointed at my rescuer. 'You sort him out. We're off.'

As she left the room Evans looked back at me, watching for something. Yet again she shrugged. It was obviously her usual reaction to all of life's difficulties. She left and closed the door behind her.

I nearly collapsed with relief as the most immediate danger passed.

'Look, I shouldn't say this,' said the policeman, 'but they were lying about the DNA. A place like that, there'd be bits of people everywhere. It would be even stranger if only your DNA was there. And it was a bit quick for a test, too.'

'What?'

'To collect all the evidence from the whole room and then put it all through DNA testing? It'd take more than one day. They were up to something. They must have been really sure it was you and so they couldn't be bothered to get the proper evidence. I think that's why he was so angry with me. He didn't believe me and wanted to see what would happen if he mentioned the DNA to you.' He looked down at the floor. 'You aren't going to press charges, are you?' he mumbled.

I smiled and sent all my compassion to him. 'No, of course not. You did a great thing. Something holy. You did God's purpose and saved me from evil.' I felt safer. Even though there was great power threatening me, I had been protected.

He swallowed and blinked furiously. 'Did I? My father always told me to fight the devil.' His eyes were watery.

I nodded.

He stood proudly and smiled back, then led me out the door to freedom that was only delayed by my signature.

'Look at these,' I shouted over the background noise of the office. I threw a handful of newspaper cuttings onto Armstrong's desk. It had taken me three days since I was arrested to collect them all and I was proud of my detective work.

He shook his head. 'We get people like you here all the time. Mystics who can solve everything with just a picture.' He shook his head in cynical disbelief. 'And you're all useless.' He was still Mr Macho.

I was bumped aside by a woman carrying an armful of papers. She was wearing a cheap perfume. It overcame the background stench of coffee and sweat for a few seconds.

'But I'm not a mystic,' I said. 'These are holy dreams. I'm seeing what's happening.' I held up a page. 'Look at this one. The paedophile. You've arrested the wrong person. He was drowned, wasn't he?'

'Yes.'

I could hardly hear his answer because a man at the next desk was shouting at someone on the phone. The office was crowded with all sorts of people, mostly in suits or police uniforms. I had assumed that everyone would be out looking at crime scenes, interviewing people and arresting criminals but instead they were all in this office chatting and writing.

'There, how could I have known that?' I called.

'Because you saw it in there.' Armstrong pointed at my pile of papers.

'Where?' I held up the cuttings for inspection. 'I couldn't find it in any of the papers.'

He shrugged. 'It was announced on the radio. We announced that after we arrested the murderer. And that murderer is awaiting trial with DNA evidence. He had a reason, he had an opportunity. He did not have an alibi.' He stared at me with thin lips and accusing eyes. 'Unlike some people,' he added.

The noisy phone call stopped at last and there was relative calm as the background din reduced to a cacophony.

'But it's this monk and his followers.' I shuffled madly through my clippings, dropping several on to the floor. I ignored the fallen papers, grabbed at one on top of the remaining pile and glanced at it. 'What about Peter Mitchelson? His hand was cut off, wasn't it? That wasn't in the paper was it? I saw the murderer.'

'Okay,' Mr Macho answered aggressively, 'what do you think you know?'

I was elbowed aside by another man who placed a piece of paper on Armstrong's desk. He signed it.

'The monk used duct tape and suffocated him by pinching his nose.'

He stared at me. 'Close, but you're wrong.'

Someone behind me managed to shout 'Fuck you,' so loudly it was understandable despite the noise.

'But you've got to believe me.'

Armstrong stood with his hands on his hips. 'All right, let's pretend you've seen the murderer. What did he look like?'

'I don't know, I couldn't see his face.'

He shook his head. 'Useless.'

I was pushed aside even more rudely by a uniformed policeman walking at a slow pace to answer a ringing phone. 'Did you arrest a member of the clergy?' I asked.

'Yes.'

I smiled. At last I was getting somewhere. 'He was set up. By this angel and the monk. They're trying to kill all the clergy.'

'What, one at a time? This is hopeless. If you have real evidence, something you can prove, someone you can identify, bring it to me, otherwise, stop wasting my time.' He grabbed my elbow and walked me towards the exit.

A group of men and women standing around a table in the corner all laughed at some private joke.

'But I can help. You need me to fight the evil.'

I had no choice but to be led to the door.

'Please I can help you,' I pleaded. 'This is important. They want to kill me. You're my only hope!'

He shook his head. 'Do you know the penalties for wasting police time?' He opened the door and waited.

As I stepped out of the room I sagged. I would have to find someone who could help me. Not this lazy policeman who couldn't be bothered. I needed that army of followers, people who wouldn't need evidence, who could see the angel for themselves. I had to find that monk. I needed more knowledge. I needed to show everyone that I could do miracles.

The door slammed shut behind me.

Miracles Come and Go

Acts 23:8
***For the Sadducees say that there is no resurrection,
neither angel, nor spirit: but the Pharisees confess both.***

Joe Kayer died in front of me.

He fell forward, blue lipped and clutching at his chest.
I caught him and lowered his body gently to the ground.

'Help. Help,' I shouted.

We were on the steps outside the police station.

A policeman appeared, kneeled opposite me and felt
for a pulse. He leaned close, listened at the man's mouth,
rolled him flat on the level ground and started pounding
his chest.

'Call for an ambulance,' he bellowed at a colleague who
ran indoors.

I held Joe's hand, looking at his thin face. He was
wearing a white shirt and a dark grey suit with a thin black
tie. *Dressed and ready for death* I thought wryly.

*I could feel his hand, clammy and cold, jerking with the
violence of the resuscitation.*

Calmness took me.

His soul is ready to cut the silver thread and move on. Pure spiritual love is near.

I call to it.

It pauses.

I call, not with words but with a feeling, a sense of purpose, a request to stay.

The soul yearns to go.

I ask for it to stay, to help, to support, to fulfil my divine purpose.

It pauses, but the soul is in divine harmony, sensing the perfection of pure love. It wants to leave this world, to go to that love.

I ask again; remain with me for a little while, for what is time but an illusion? Just a little time, for we are bound in a holy duty. This extended life will soon end and you can return once more.

And it stays.

I opened my eyes.

Joe was coughing and pushing the first aider away. He looked at me and nodded weakly.

A siren heralded further help.

The resurrected man reached to me and seemed to try to say something.

'Are you alright?' asked the policeman. 'I just saved you. Not this guy.' He was affronted that his heroism had not been rewarded.

Joe nodded at his resuscitator in response to the demand for notice as if to say thanks. But he could also see how important I was.

The policeman echoed the nod, mollified at the late recognition.

The ambulance pulled up and two green uniformed men stepped out from it.

Joe frowned as the paramedics took over, eclipsing everyone else from his world.

I stared unseeing at the world around me in a state of great joy.

I could do miracles.

I could resurrect the dead.

Del was wearing a tight white blouse, red nails, thick makeup and stilettos. Her hair was now a deep and unnatural burgundy. Her heavenly perfume clashed with the disgusting stink of disinfectant. The disinfectant won, but only just.

'Okay *Doctor* Matthews,' she said. She found it amusing to lampoon me. 'Show me your miracle.'

'We have to wait for someone to be dying first. I need to be with them at the time of death. Then I can save them.'

Del shook her head in cynical judgement. 'So what have you arranged?' she challenged.

'What?' I was a bit puzzled. 'We're going to wait for someone to die and then I'll hold their hand.'

'Are you saying that you haven't talked to any of the doctors or the patients or their relatives?' she asked.

'Why should I?'

We were outside the intensive care unit, in front of a pair of huge Perspex sheets, scratched and almost opaque. The doors clattered noisily as a man in casual clothes pushed them aside. He returned my stare as he walked past.

'You don't have a clue do you?' she demanded. 'They'll throw you out as soon as you go in.'

'What? Why?'

'Idiot. Well, I'm not going to go away without a story. I'll sort it.' She undid a button on her white lacy blouse as she swayed through the doors with an exaggerated feminine walk.

I couldn't resist staring at her rounded, blue-skirted bottom in beautiful contrast to her slender waist.

I waited exposed and alone outside the room, watching the steady flow of people coming and going around us. Doctors, nurses and unidentifiable workers were always rushing past, some staring at me, others focussed on some life saving task. Every single person had a purpose and meaning to their life. I wondered if they could see my uncertainty.

I barely recognised Del coming to the Perspex doors from inside the room before she held one side open. A second later a male doctor in white coat and stethoscope opened the other door. Del waved me into the inner sanctum of decisions over life and death. The doctor smiled down her cleavage.

'Doctor Matthews,' she said. She pointed towards the doctor's stethoscope, 'the good doctor here...'

'That's *Mister* Gawain,' he interrupted with a condescending smile. 'I'm a consultant you see.' He touched his stethoscope.

Del frowned for a fraction of a second before she regained her self-control and smiled again. 'Yes, of course,' she agreed. '*Mister* Gawain has very kindly agreed to allow you to bring comfort to the dying for our report.'

'Comfort?' I replied. 'But...'

She interrupted me. 'I've already explained that we will respect the patients' beliefs, so there's no need to explain to him. You provide spiritual comfort to any patient who agrees and, if they want, I can write up their story of how faith has helped them, just like we planned.'

I had to admit, she was clever. She must have thought this up almost instantly.

Del practically dragged me into the room. I expected to hear machines beeping and doctors shouting as they resuscitated people. Instead it was surprisingly hushed compared to the hubbub outside the door.

The disinfectant smell was less intense but I could detect the odours of incontinence and other poorly controlled bodily functions. I stood closer to Del's sweet scent.

A young, blond male nurse in blue medical coveralls with a good, strong faith was talking quietly to an elderly female patient and pointing in our direction. The patient's intense faith was impossible to ignore as she smiled weakly and nodded to us. The nurse muttered in response and then moved on to perform other duties.

Mister Gawain seemed to remember that he had patients to see after a minute of staring at Del's blouse and mumbled something as he walked away.

I took a step towards the believer, but Del held me back.

'You can only talk to the patients that the nurse says,' she whispered to me. 'Stay as long as you want, but if anyone needs resuscitation stay out of the way.' She smiled tightly. 'Once you've saved a life I'll ask the patient how it felt.'

I nodded.

'And for God's sake don't tell anyone anything weird, will you?' she added very quietly, squeezing my arm to make sure I understood.

I scanned the room and felt a strange array of faiths. Mostly they were very weak but growing steadily. Their approaching death was reminding them of more important issues. None were as strong as that one woman who was now beckoning us towards her.

Del shepherded me to her side, staying close on my left, the patient's head to my right. I stood so close to the edge of the bed, that I could feel the iron bar beneath the sheet and smell the body lotion I always associated with old age.

'It's Doctor Matthews, isn't it?' asked the patient.

'Yes,' I replied, surprised.

'The nurse recognised you, too. We've seen you in the paper.'

'Oh,' I said.

'Have you really lost your faith?' she asked. 'Did you really do all those things?'

'My faith is stronger than ever,' I answered. 'Like all of humanity, I have a problem with sin, but I'm working on it with God's help and forgiveness. And I know for a fact that God and Heaven are both waiting for us all and that God is guiding me every day.'

Del bumped against me, probably a warning. I must have been preaching.

The woman reached for my right hand and held it gently. I think she was comforting me as much as I was comforting her. 'My name is Mary,' she said.

'How do you feel about death?' I asked.

Once again Del bumped me.

Mary smiled weakly. 'I look forward to meeting Jesus.' She winced in pain and stared blindly ahead for a few seconds.

'Do you have any fears?' I asked.

'Of course. I know I'll be judged and found to be a sinner, but I trust to God's grace that He will forgive me.'

'If you were to die would you want to come back?' I asked.

Del's sharp fingernails pinched the back of my left arm. I pulled my arm away.

'What do you mean?' asked Mary.

'I mean would you want to continue this life, despite your death?'

'What?' She frowned. 'A sort of resurrection?'

I nodded. 'Or maybe you might have a near death experience.'

'No.' She focussed on my eyes seeking an answer of some sort. 'When it's my time, God will take me. Why would I want to come back?'

'Perhaps for a bigger purpose? To fulfil some task for God?'

Mary frowned. 'I want to go to heaven. I'm in pain. I've done my job.' She stared into my face while I smiled at her. 'There is something odd about you? Are you saying you can bring people back?'

'Gabriel,' hissed Del in warning. Her nails cut a furrow into my arm.

Mary looked puzzled at the use of my new name.

I let go of Mary and used my right hand to hold Del's hand away from my arm in self-protection. 'Perhaps,' I said to Mary. 'I have a purpose. I need followers and supporters. Your faith would be useful to me.'

'How dare you?' said Mary, suddenly furious. 'How dare you?' she repeated. 'Haven't I done my part? Isn't it time to go to Heaven? What makes you think that you have a right? Why don't you save someone else? Someone who isn't in God's grace?'

'But,' I protested, 'what if it was God's will?'

'You don't know God's will. You don't know anything. How dare you think that you could change God's will?' She turned her face away.

I stood stunned. How could she be so angry with me? She had such strong faith.

'Go away,' she said violently snapping her head back to look at me. She winced in pain. 'Go away,' she repeated, this time through clenched teeth.

I backed away from her.

The nurse stepped in front of me. 'Perhaps you need to leave, now,' he said. 'No one else wants to talk to you.'

Everything was going wrong. What had happened to my purpose? 'What's wrong?' I pleaded.

'They're ill,' said the nurse. 'They don't want to be bothered by you. They've seen you in the papers. No one trusts you.'

'But it's all lies. I'm a good man.' I wanted him to believe me.

He put his hand on my arm. 'No, Doctor Matthews,' he said. 'We know about the way you treat women. Your attitude to the church. We don't need you here. Go away.'

We were at the door to the unit. 'Who's we?' I demanded

Del grabbed my arm and forced me out the door. 'I told you not to go all weird,' she snapped at me in a barely controlled whisper.

'But that woman's faith...'

'Just shut up,' she snapped.

'But that nurse,' I whined. 'He knew me. There's a conspiracy going on.'

'I said shut up,' ordered Del. The doors closed behind us and Del grabbed my arm.

I tried to resist as she pushed me down the corridor but, even though she was a small woman, I was helpless. 'But I have my purpose,' I said.

She stopped and held my shirt in her hand. 'Could you have really healed those people?'

'What?' She was suddenly so aggressive.

'You said to that woman that you would resurrect her and heal her. Can you do that?'

'I don't know.' I looked away from her intense stare. 'I did it once. I saved Joe. Joe Kayer.'

She grabbed my chin and forced me to look at her. 'And how many times have you done that?' she demanded.

Her lips were compressed so tightly I could barely see her lipstick.

'Once.' I looked at the ground. Something about her question made me feel uncertain.

'Is that all? Just Joe? And how do you know that you really did it?'

'He looked at me as if he had been saved.'

Del kept hold of my chin and made me look right into her eyes. 'There's one more thing you can try and that's it. No healing, no nothing.'

Her intense beauty overwhelmed me. What man could resist her? Beyond the make up and clothes was a beautiful woman who grabbed your attention. I had to win her over.

'Okay,' I said decisively. 'No more messing about. We wait in Casualty. If the opportunity comes up in the next couple of hours, I'll resurrect someone. If not, we move on.'

Del smiled and my heart exploded in delight. I resolved to be more of a man for her.

'Come on then,' I said. This time I was in charge as I gently took her arm.

We had been sitting and waiting for four hours. Del had managed to find dozens of discreet little tasks for herself, mostly grooming her appearance or taking notes on the appearance of those around her, but I was bored.

'Come on,' I said. 'It's not going to happen, is it?'

'Nope,' she agreed. 'I don't have any story. It's a good thing that my editor fancies me or I'd have a real problem,' she said.

I stood up. If only I could get her to dress less like a tart and more like a real woman. Not so much face make up, less flesh showing and more sensible shoes. Perhaps then fewer men would keep staring at her. Perhaps then she would be more interested in me.

'Let's go home,' I suggested walking towards the door. She stood and followed.

I paused. 'Del?'

'Yes?'

'Could you give me some advice? On my appearance?' Perhaps she could come to like me, too.

She inspected me. I waited for her judgement.

After only seconds she gestured to my stomach. 'Lose weight, get some decent clothes, have a shave and look after yourself.'

I led her through the doors into the street.

'Do you think I'm attractive?' I asked her.

'Oh God no. Just for once, can't a man just leave me alone?' she asked of the world.

'It's that obvious is it?'

'Yep. It happens to me all the time. Men just want to fuck me.'

Her crude language surprised me. 'But look at the way you dress. All that thick make up. Do you really need it?'

'I know,' she muttered. 'It's my own fault.'

A woman collapsed to the pavement a few yards in front of us. I ran to her and held her arm. I didn't know what to do.

'You stay here and do your stuff,' said Del. 'I'll go get a nurse.'

I felt the calm of the spirit take over.

The soul clings to its body. It does not know of the presence of the pure love all around it.

Stay. God has a task for you. You can help.

But the soul cannot hear. It remains clinging to its body but the silver thread has already broken. The soul separates from the body.

Look around you. There is pure love here.

The soul yearns for love but cannot experience it. It does not know how to return to its body

Stay. I can help you find it.

The soul disappears.

The arm I held jerked as a man pounded her chest.

A trolley appeared with a doctor who examined her, but I already knew that she was dead.

Del stared at the body, white faced and rigid. The doctor stopped the resuscitator.

'Come on,' I said to Del. 'It didn't work.' I couldn't remain in the midst of this failure.

I took her arm and gently led her away, breaking the hypnotic control of the scene of death.

She walked with me for a few feet and then stumbled up against me, sobbing against my side. I put my arms around her in comfort.

'She's gone,' said Del, barely comprehensible through her sobs.

'Yes. And I couldn't bring her back. I'm a failure again.'

She looked up at me. 'No.' She had stopped crying but she continued to cling to my body.

I opened myself to her fully and felt the sadness within. I also realised that she was talking about her mother. We walked into a park opposite the hospital, my arm protectively around her shoulders. I was calm and strong to support her. I felt that we could almost be a couple. I would be so proud to have this beautiful woman as my companion and partner.

We sat on a bench.

'Was that how your mum died?' I asked.

She shrugged, sobbed and hugged me once again. 'Please,' she said.

I didn't know what to do. Perhaps she wanted more than comfort? Yet again I opened myself to her and felt the need within, but there was no place for romance, she needed fatherly support. My lust was frustrated, but my purpose here was more important, and so I held her as if she was a tiny child, stroking her hand and muttering the comfort words like "there there" and "it's okay". These are the words that no one actually listens to, for their effect is in the saying and not what is said.

As I waited for her to recover her composure I scanned the everyday activities in the park. A woman and child were feeding the ducks. Another woman pushed an enormous pram that must have contained a baby secreted within its components. A couple rested on another bench eating sandwiches. None of these people seemed to be concerned with death or the meaning of their lives.

Eventually Del dried her eyes and put her feelings away in her purse with her handkerchief. 'Don't ever mention this to anyone,' she snapped at me. She was angry once again and I could see why. All those years of having to protect herself for there was no one else to protect her, using her beauty and constant offers of love to hide the desperately unloved woman within.

'It's okay. This was just between us.'

She stood. 'And you were useless. Why couldn't you save her?'

I sagged. I had failed them both and I had lost my opportunity for more than friendship. 'I don't know,' I said. 'Her soul was lost. Maybe she didn't have enough faith? Maybe she needed more physical healing?'

'You stupid bastard.' She leaned towards me, face close to mine. 'I wanted you to do it. To bring someone back. To stop the ending of life.' Her anger was burning and hateful.

I was confused. My insights had been wrong. Why was she angry with me?

'Ring me again when you've got a real story, Loser,' she said. She walked off, leaving me confused and lonely.

Was I supposed to save people from death? Perhaps, only God or Jesus could resurrect, and I couldn't do anything. Had I even saved Joe?

Know Thine Enemy

Matthew 7:22

Many will say to me in that day, 'Lord, Lord, have we not prophesied in thy name? and in thy name have cast out devils? and in thy name done many wonderful works?'

Puck looked into the demon's face. The facetted red eyes glowered down at her, talons raised, ready to torture her.

'That demon's job is to torment the unbeliever for eternity.' Professor Hakeem spoke in a rich baritone with an Oxbridge accent.

Puck's expression fell into a frown as she touched the jewels in the statues' eyes. 'Why?' she asked.

'That's what demons do, they torment. It's usually a punishment because your side has been beaten. Your only hope is that God will provide punishment for your ungodly attackers.' He shrugged. 'Or maybe they do it because they're just plain nasty. What did you say your name was, my dear?'

'Samantha,' replied Puck without a pause.

'A lovely name,' he said. He looked at me and his smile transformed into a scowl. 'So why have you come to see me here at the University, Dr Matthews?'

I was staring in awe around his room. Thousands of books surrounded us in ramparts of knowledge on all the walls. The ancient books dominated and occluded any evidence of modernity in the large, purpose-built office. Even the picture window was partly obscured by the stacks of learned tomes on the windowsill. Small pictures and woodcuts of angels and demons were squeezed onto shelves displacing volumes of lesser depth into the dark recesses. The terrible bronze demon was companioned by a tiny, carved, ebony imp next to it and constrained by a twelve inch, ivory angel looking down from the shelf above. Pictures of demons and angels were scattered throughout the room. An enormous ancient book, which could only be measured in cubits and had to be carried by more than one person, was open on the massive desk at a coloured picture of God casting Lucifer into Hell.

'Dr Matthews,' prompted Professor Hakeem.

'Yes, sorry.' I concentrated on his fulsome, white beard so that I would not be distracted. 'Please, I call myself Gabriel.' His faith was the strongest I had ever seen.

He frowned even more. 'Why have you come to me?' If not for his enormous beard and powerful faith, the professor would have been very ordinary. He was slim, of medium height and wearing a plain white shirt and dark trousers.

'How can I say this?' I stumbled.

'He thinks he's an angel,' said Puck. 'And we need your advice.'

Professor Hakeem stared at me in obvious amazement. 'An angel?' He inspected my face and head. 'I see.' He walked behind me and gently slid a hand down my shoulder blades. 'A very ancient angel or you would have a halo and wings. Why the name Gabriel? Are you an archangel? Any tendencies to want to be a telephonist?'

I wrinkled my nose. 'A telephonist?'

He smiled. 'Gabriel is the patron saint of communication workers.'

'No. I'm just an angel. I just like that name.'

'Ah. An ordinary angel. No name.' He shook his head at me and grimaced. 'Have you come all this way just to mock me?'

I sighed. 'Look, Professor, I really need to know about this. I'm not Dr Matthews. He was murdered and then I appeared in his body. I need to know all about angels and you're the expert. This is a battle between Good and Evil.'

Professor Hakeem turned on Puck, 'I really believe in angels, you know.' He picked up a picture and waved it in her face. 'That's Raphael.' He pointed at a wood cut. 'And that's the real Gabriel.' He turned back to me. 'And you're not like him. Not at all. Not even a bit.'

'Is that why he doesn't have wings?' asked Puck.

'That's not so important,' said the expert, waving his hand to dismiss such irrelevant details. 'Angels didn't have them originally.'

Puck grinned at me. 'So you can be an angel and still be a randy old man desperate to get into my pants,' she declared.

Professor Hakeem's eyebrows rose. 'Really?' he asked me.

'I'm not perfect.'

Puck snorted. 'That's for sure,' she said.

He smiled. 'Perhaps you two had better sit down.' He gestured towards some very ordinary looking chairs at a small round table.

I stared at a small pile of books on the nearest chair. The Professor frowned once more and waved his hand as if it didn't matter where I put them. I placed the stack on the floor and sat.

The scholar's lower lip slipped forward to trap his moustache in his mouth as he examined my face. 'So, Dr Matthews, you are obviously not immediately recognisable as an angel as you're not of extraordinary beauty. You don't have a body of beryl or a face like lightning, nor eyes that are lamps of fire. And I expect that your feet are not like polished brass.'

He winked at Puck and gestured under the table towards me. She giggled and ducked under to inspect my feet for angelic properties. Professor Hakeem waited sternly with eyebrows raised as she returned from her investigations. Her lips pursed in exaggerated sternness as she shook her head to signify a lack of a heavenly pedicure.

'Not to worry,' he continued, 'let's see what else might make you an angel. Can you fly?' His expression was carefully neutral.

'No, of course not.' I felt like I was sitting an angel exam. 'I'm in a human body. I'm still governed by the laws of physics. And as you said before I don't have wings.'

'And as I said, that's okay. Wings aren't that important. They're just an artist's way of showing that an angel is an elemental creature of the air. I don't suppose you can become invisible?'

'I'm not a psychopath, either.'

Puck interrupted, 'are you sure?'

The professor sighed this time. 'Sorry, but you must agree, this is odd. And it's more likely that you would be schizophrenic than psychopathic,' he added as he stared at me.

'Well, I'm not mad,' I muttered.

My examiner leaned sideways towards Puck, keeping his eyes focussed on me. 'Have you seen him do any sacrificial fire?' he said to her in a stage whisper.

'You mean like lighting a cigarette without matches?' she asked, continuing the mock seriousness.

'I was thinking a bit bigger.' He leaned toward me with that investigative attitude once more. 'Have you now or have you ever consumed sacrifices by fire or created fire by supernatural means?'

'Like I said, I'm in a human body. Just like everyone else.'

'How do feel about smiting? Do you want to wipe out the armies of the ungodly?'

Puck laughed and banged the desk.

'Professor!' I almost shouted at him in frustration.

He smiled at last. 'Okay, okay. I was just having some fun.' He sat back and shook his head. 'Look, it doesn't sound like you're an angel at all,' he said. 'You're corporeal but you don't have the bright spirits and beauty of a creature direct from heaven.'

'What's corpor whatever?' asked Puck.

'Corporeal. In a body,' responded the demonologist. 'Don't you know the arguments?'

She shook her head.

He continued. 'How many angels can dance on the head of a pin? If they're corporeal...'

She frowned.

'...if they have bodies,' he explained, 'then only so many, perhaps one or a thousand or a million can fit on the head of a pin, but if...'

I couldn't let this go on. I had to interrupt. 'But if they have no bodies because they are souls, then none can dance because only a body has legs to dance with!'

He smiled at me. 'Why yes, Doctor, you're right!'

'Please call me Gabriel.'

'Well, seeing as we're being so friendly, you can call me Solomon, my dear,' he said to Puck, winking once more.

She smiled at him.

'And what's more,' I added, 'souls have no time or space. That's why bodies are needed. All these other things are illusions.'

'Possibly,' he agreed.

'What about the New Testament?' I said. 'Perhaps I'm an angel in the sense of the word "Angelos"?'

'What do you mean?' asked Puck.

'Angel is actually a Greek word for messenger,' I answered. 'Anyone can be an angel and still be a messenger.'

'Yes,' the professor explained to Puck, 'as St Augustine wrote, "angelus est nomen officii". Angel is the name of the office. You don't even need a name.'

'So I can be an angel without all that other rubbish. I can be constrained by physics, have a normal body and still have a holy purpose.'

'True,' he agreed, 'but they do have a message. Can you reveal your message?'

'No, I don't know what it is.'

'He's got magical powers,' volunteered Puck.

The professor raised his eyebrows to me.

'Look, I only have spiritual powers. Powers that link me to souls.'

'Describe them!' he demanded, loudly.

'I can see into what drives people. Their emotions.'

'It sounds like you're very sensitive to people. But nothing supernatural?' he asked.

'Couldn't it be that I'm here because God doesn't want to change the laws of physics?'

'What do you mean?' His sat back into his chair and fiddled with his beard. It was a well-practised and unconscious act.

'Puck has explained to me that there is a cause for every effect.'

'Yes, it's the most important...' chimed in Puck.

'Let me go on.' I interrupted. 'But, you can have an effect with no cause if it comes from a person. A person has free will and a moral choice. If God makes something happen, it's a miracle, there is no physical cause for an effect. So to affect the world without subverting physics God must work through souls which can initiate effects.'

Solomon meditated on my words, sucking at his moustache once more.

After a few minutes Puck stood up and walked around the room looking at every statue and book, deliberately making a lot of noise. She obviously didn't like the lack of attention.

'Interesting,' he said at last. 'You think you're an angel and you're an agent of God. But, this is only what you say. Do you have anything substantial to prove it?'

'I really do have powers,' I said, defensively. 'It's not just that I can feel people's souls. I brought someone back from the dead.'

He sat up, quickly. 'How?'

'I don't know. I could feel his soul and I called it back to serve God.'

He smiled. 'That doesn't sound like an angel. It sounds more like a delusion. Do you also think that you're Jesus? Do you want to start your own religion?'

Puck giggled. 'He couldn't raise anyone else from the dead but he's already trying to get followers.' She walked back to her chair and sat.

I looked at the ground, embarrassed. 'I'm not Jesus. I can't do miracles or anything. I'm an angel and I've come here for a purpose and it involves saving people. The religion would be to make that happen. To protect me.'

Solomon wiped his damp moustache with a hand. 'Protect you?'

'From the *baad* angel,' murmured Puck, dramatically drawling the word "bad" with an exaggerated American accent.

'What?' He scowled.

'Yes. I keep getting dreams. I think I'm in the middle of a holy war.'

He tutted and shook his head in disbelief.

'Please, you must understand,' I pleaded. This man was my only hope. 'Another angel appears in my dreams. It makes a monk kill and murder people. It quotes the Bible. I think this killer is real and he's targeting clerics.'

'Why haven't I heard of this serial killer?' asked Solomon.

'Because the angel is protecting it from the police. It keeps on casting spells to confuse the crime scene. They keep arresting religious people for the crimes of the monk.'

The professor shook his head. 'An angel? Casting spells? You just said that you can't change the laws of physics and yet this other angel can?'

I stared dumbfounded. 'You're right.'

Once again his head shook in refutation. 'What are these dreams, then? What does this angel look like?'

'A beautiful man.'

'I see. Perhaps an angel from the Hebrew tradition.'

'He has no genitalia, and a very long tongue. And he instructs a monk and he only quotes from the Bible.'

'Which Bible?'

'Christian. I know every quote.'

'New or Old Testament?'

'Both.'

He shook his head. 'This all sounds very odd. I can see nothing angelic in you and this other angel seems to be more the product of a good imagination.' He glanced at me, assessing my sanity. 'Or schizophrenia,' he added after a second. 'It sounds like an illusion. What makes you think it is an angel?'

'I just know it. It wants to kill me. I think it tried to kill me before, when the monk stabbed Dr Matthews and stole his cross and Bible. They used them to frame me for a murder. But it didn't work. I was knocked out by a cleric and ended up in prison and then hospital.'

Puck tapped on the desk. 'Please, Mister, he's telling the truth. He was arrested and all.'

'I see. A holy war between two angels. Hence all these references to clerics. Are you sure? Don't forget, angels aren't always nice.'

'Yes, they are,' shouted Puck.

'Not always, my dear,' he defended. 'Sometimes you can't tell who angels are and they're not necessarily being nice to you. They might be doing you a favour by being nasty. The message is not always a good one. Look at the Angel of Death. It's the ultimate in nasty angels.'

'What about guardian angels, then?' said Puck, clearly upset. 'We all have one of them.'

'Maybe, but the biblical evidence is weak. Only a few special people or places may have guardian angels. But there are many more references in the Bible to angels with swords.'

I held up a hand to stop Puck from arguing further. 'All this is irrelevant. This angel is dangerous and I am absolutely certain that I'm here to counter it. I think the word Asbeel is important.'

'Asbeel?' Solomon stared at me carefully. He walked to a shelf retrieved a book and opened it. After a few seconds he said, 'Asbeel is a Fallen Angel. A demon. An agent of the devil.' He flicked through the pages. 'In Enoch I. "He imparted to the holy sons of God evil counsel and led them astray through the daughters of men."' He sat down again still holding the book open. 'That was in one of the Apocrypha. You said he quoted from the New Testament.'

'Yes. What's the problem? What am I up against? Is he powerful?'

He snorted at me. 'You tell me, you know all about it.'

'I don't know,' I moaned

The professor sucked at his moustache again. 'Many people believe that God always maintains a balance between Good and Evil. At least until the final days, anyway. And then the devil will be allowed to control the earth.'

'Yes,' I called out. 'You're right. A balance. I must be the balance against this demon's evil. I am enabling people to have a choice.' I stood up. 'So they won't be dominated by God's holy goodness or this demon's evil.'

Puck stood up, too. 'Yes. We're the good guys.'

Solomon stared at us both. 'Unless, of course, this is the time of the Apocalypse and then it would mean that this other angel truly is more powerful than you.'

I could feel panic rising within me 'But I must overcome this demon. There must be a way.'

Again a wipe of the damp moustache. 'Perhaps there is. He works through women. But it's not that simple.'

'What?' I asked, calming down.

'It's just that many Christians don't believe he exists. Although I suppose it depends on your point of view.'

'Is there a way to counter it?'

'I don't know. Perhaps an exorcism,' the professor said, shaking his head. 'This is complicated. There are many views of demons and the devil. Some people say that they don't exist. They are just metaphors. I prefer the medieval approach with its real physical demons, but I have no evidence. It's easier to believe that they are evil souls which may inhabit bodies. Much as you claim to do.' He frowned at me.

'What?'

'Are you sure that you're not this angel that kills? After all you seem to be acting quite demonically.' He leaned towards Puck. 'Trying to get into your pants, I believe you said?'

She nodded, passing the judgement on my behaviour. 'And other things,' she whispered.

He pointed an accusing finger at me. 'Are you sure you're not Asbeel?' he demanded.

'But I was in prison when the last dream occurred!' He couldn't be right could he?

'You could have travelled as a soul to this monk. You could be instructing him through your spiritual body. Prove to me that you're not Asbeel. Now.'

This was no good. I needed to know more. 'No! You know I can't. He really is different to me. He is a demon and he's making someone else kill clerics. I am on the side of Good. I've come to you haven't I? As Jesus said, *Mark 3:25 "and if a house be divided against itself, that house cannot stand"*. He was talking about demons, then.'

'If you say so,' Solomon agreed, his head shaking, denying his words.

If an expert and believer of angels didn't believe me then who would? 'We need to find out about Asbeel,' I pleaded. 'How did it get here? Has it been summoned? Is there a way to dispel it?'

He tapped the table and stared at me. 'It could be inhabiting a woman.'

'Perhaps there's a woman instructing this monk?' I asked. 'I only know about the demon and the murders from my dreams. We need to find answers. To destroy it.'

Solomon shook his head once more. 'Look, I know that you're from the old school of the Bible, Dr Matthews. Like me, you believe in angels and demons but a lot of people will think you're mad, you know?'

Puck giggled. 'I already know it, mister,' she said, leaning over to him and holding his arm. 'But he's a lot of fun. Things really do happen around him.'

'Be quiet,' I snapped at her. 'What are you getting at?'

He leaned forward towards me. 'I said it earlier. You know what they say. That angels and demons are just metaphors.' He tapped my head. 'Internal processes. Dreams, illusions, products of schizophrenic minds. Medieval and non-existent.' He gestured towards Puck. 'Ways to scare the uneducated, unthinking and credulous.' He pointed at himself and then at me. 'Not for the likes of you and me.'

Puck poked her tongue out at him.

'Honestly,' he said, 'I don't know what I can do for you at the moment. You have to find this demon or its monk.' He paused. 'And you have to prove that it's not you.'

'You've got to help us professor,' I shouted. 'We're in a holy war. You and me and Puck. And we've got to win it or lots more people will die.'

'I'm sorry,' he answered, quietly. 'I can't help you. You're on your own.'

CHEMISTRY

Ecclesiates 10:13
The beginning of the words of his mouth is foolishness: and the end of his talk is mischievous madness.

'Am I mad?'

The psychiatrist compressed his lips. 'Madness is such a pejorative term, Doctor Matthews.'

We were in a grey office with a desk, three chairs and a single sad bookshelf. Even the computer on the desk was grey and smelt slightly of cleaning fluid. The doctor had no faith at all. He was wearing a blue pin striped suit and bright red bow tie. The wooden clogs provided another clue to his eccentricity. How could he diagnose me as mad when he was so weird himself?

I frowned at him. 'Please call me Gabriel.'

'Ah, now this is an important part of your treatment. You must stop calling yourself Gabriel.'

'Why? Anyone can change their name.'

He shook his head. 'If it's for a good reason, perhaps, but I think it's a part of this false persona you have created.'

I leaned forward to stress my point. 'It's not false. I am now Gabriel. I am no longer Doctor Gideon Matthews.'

He leaned back and smiled tautly. 'I'm not going to hurt you. You're okay,' he said. I think he was trying to be reassuring. 'You don't think I'm a demon, do you?'

'No. That's only in my dreams.'

His grin remained strained.

'I'm not dangerous,' I said settling back into my seat. The chair was utilitarian, hard backed and uncomfortable with slats placed in the perfect position to dig into my back muscles.

He relaxed slightly. 'That's good,' he said.

Perversely, I felt I was under attack even though he was clearly fearful of me. 'But you've got to admit that these dreams are prophetic and I really was set up for this murder.'

He adopted a patronising smile. 'Gideon, people in your condition feel that it is all sensible and rational.'

'But I was able to know about these murders before I read about them.'

He leaned back again, his hand slipping under his desk. 'How do you know? It is only your memory. Memory is a tricky thing, you know. It reconstructs itself. Perhaps you only remember it that way now after you have all the facts. Or possibly you heard it but didn't notice it on the radio. A glance is enough for the unconscious mind, you know.'

I stared at the floor. Could he be right? 'But what about when I was in prison?'

He visibly relaxed and put his hand back on the desk. I realised then that he must have had a panic button underneath the desk. 'A coincidence at most,' he assured me. 'There are no demons. There is no conspiracy. The world is as you see it. There is no Holy War going on.' He looked at me. 'I believe that you have a faith. That is very good, but perhaps you shouldn't let it affect your way of life so much.'

How could he say that? Don't let my faith affect my way of life? This man was outrageous. My faith was my way of life. 'But I really am a different person. I have a new soul.'

His fingers drew a circle on the desk as if he was overcoming an impulse to slide his hand back under his desk again. 'We have no evidence of this. I can see you here now and I can see all the evidence.' He held up some papers. I guessed they were my notes. 'Whoever you think you are, the only continuity I and everyone else have between who you were and who you are now is your body. I'm afraid that for all useful purposes you are still Dr Matthews. You just think you're someone else. Identity is a complex thing, but I can assure you, it goes with the body.' His speech was too polished, too well prepared. He must have given it a thousand times, probably at abstract academic conferences throughout the world without any practical use.

'Why do I think I'm an angel?'

He smiled. 'You have a chemical imbalance in your brain.'

'What?' I shouted, leaning forward and placing my knuckles on the cold desk.

His hand slipped back below the desk. 'Calm down, calm down. It's all right.'

I settled back in my chair. Perhaps he was right. 'Ok, then. So why have I changed?'

'It's probably the trauma you experienced. Maybe your brain was damaged. Something may have released an inner tendency towards schizophrenia. The brain is complicated, you know. Who can know why?'

I shook my head. I had a holy task to perform. I knew my faith was right and that it was the most important aspect of my being, more important than anything physical. I could feel what I had done and felt and experienced. I knew the demon was really there. I had called Joe back from death. He'd even said so.

I realised then that this lazy doctor only knew my name because it was written on a piece of paper. He wasn't interested in me, only in chemicals and reactions. I wasn't even a person to him, just another patient, with no meaningful identity other than what was written down on his notes. He couldn't be bothered to investigate anything that was even the slightest bit difficult. Were all psychiatrists like this?

He retrieved a prescription pad from his desk drawer and started to write on it. 'Now then,' he said. 'This is an excellent medication that can really help your condition. It may have some side effects. You may feel a bit tired or detached but it will help you to see reality as it is. You'll feel much better once you're on these and you'll be able to get back to your normal life, although it may take a while to get another job.'

He tore the sheet from the pad and passed it to me without even looking up to see how I reacted. The drugs had been supplied and that was it. Over. The easiest option had been taken.

'Thank you, Dr Matthews. I need to see my next patient.' He stared at his computer.

I walked out the door scrunching his inadequate chemical solution into my pocket, worrying that perhaps he was right and there were no angels.

SLOTH

Proverbs 15:19
The way of the slothful man is as an hedge of thorns: but the way of the righteous is made plain.

At the time she didn't know it, but her father was dying and that was why he had ignored her sin. She was terrified that her immortal soul was in peril. She was wrathful and it was his duty to provide a path to salvation by punishing her.

But he would not do it.

She had never really understood the danger that sloth posed until then. But now she realised that because of his laziness she was in danger of going to Hell for eternity and he didn't care!

What was she to do? How was she to be punished?

She remembered the pain of muscle cramp after heavy exercise and decided that this would be a good way to punish her body, but it wasn't enough just to work out until a muscle hurt. She would need more pain than that. She started with a stretch that pushed her sinews until they were taut and hot. She ran, carrying the heaviest weight she could until she was exhausted and convinced she could run no more. And then she ran again with her body screaming in pain. Eventually, she stopped and her body shook in pain and exhaustion. It was so bad that she could barely think, even to say a benediction.

This did not have the immediacy, urgency and clean finish of a beating but it would have to do. If her father continued to be slothful she could exercise regularly. It also provided extra physical benefits that might be of use one day. She found a Bible passage to suit her sin easily enough. There was always something about punishment to be found in the Old Testament.

Ecclesiastes 8:11. Because sentence against an evil work is not executed speedily, therefore the heart of the sons of men is fully set in them to do evil.

It wasn't the best quote but it would be enough for now. Having shrived herself of sin she returned to stare at her father. He was sitting in an armchair, slumped when he should have been bolt upright. Before she had disappeared her mother had always explained that men were weaker than women. Now she could see the proof. He was lazy. A woman would not give in until her duty had been performed.

Her father had died a few short months later. He had refused all medical help praying to God for a miracle. It never came. Over the years, as she had grown in understanding she discovered why God never intervened. Like so many men her father had committed a deadly sin and thus there was no help for him, not even from God.

But that was long ago and right now there was yet another man who was interfering with God's plans to place women at the top of the church. She had only recently learnt of the true gospels, removed from the Bible by men in the first few centuries. The true gospels showed the importance of women in the Bible and in Jesus' time.

Yet again, a man was encouraging others to sin and it was her duty to stop him by whatever means she could. Just as she had stopped the lapsed priest and the paedophile. Souls were at stake and so the petty pains of one or two bodies were irrelevant.

She had performed her holy duty as instructed and killed this wretched man who was interfering with God's purpose but somehow he had survived and become someone new, someone lustful and slothful and who knows what else? He was jeopardising his soul and those of others around him. Because she had failed in her duty he was now her responsibility and so she must save his soul or do away with him before even more people listened to him and doomed themselves to an eternity of suffering.

Arranging the right circumstances would be effortless.

WHERE ANGELS FEAR TO TREAD

Psalm 86:14
O God, the proud are risen against me, and the assemblies of violent men have sought after my soul; and have not set thee before them.

The demon appeared.

My legs almost collapsed underneath me. My heart pounded in fear. I may have wet myself.

It was a few yards in front of me, standing in the moonlight outside the house I was going to visit. It smiled at me and my stomach convulsed in fear.

The note was a trap. There was no rich benefactor. It may not even have been a note from Puck.

The angel beckons to the observer to come closer.

'No. No.'

The monk and many followers are gathered in a semi circle, on their knees and ready to execute the angel's holy judgement. The angel speaks.

'Take heed, brethren, lest there be in any of you an evil heart of unbelief, in departing from the living God.'

'*Hebrews 3:12. I am not an unbeliever. I have not departed from God. You have.*'

The chant echoes, 'evil heart of unbelief'.

'*Stay away from me.*'

The monk and followers rise and stand beside the terrible angel.

'**To execute vengeance upon the heathen, and punishments upon the people;**'

'*Psalm 149:7. What punishment?*'

The angel announces another judgement.

'**Wherefore doth a living man complain, a man for the punishment of his sins?**'

'*Lamentations 3:39. Me? You don't have the right to punish me. God has given me a Holy Purpose.*'

'**And Gideon said unto him, Oh my Lord, if the LORD be with us, why then is all this befallen us? and where be all his miracles which our fathers told us of, saying, Did not the LORD bring us up from Egypt? but now the LORD hath forsaken us, and delivered us into the hands of the Midianites.**'

'*Judges 6:13. I refuse to believe you. God has not forsaken me. Why are you attacking me?*'

'**And they shall bear the punishment of their iniquity: the punishment of the prophet shall be even as the punishment of him that seeketh unto him.**'

'*Ezekiel 14:10. So I'm being punished for seeking you out? To save myself.*'

The angel smiles.

'**The people answered and said, Thou hast a devil: who goeth about to kill thee?**'

'*John 7:20. I'm not the demon. You are.*'

'**Of how much sorer punishment, suppose ye, shall he be thought worthy, who hath trodden under foot the Son of God, and hath counted the blood of the covenant,**' *wherewith he was sanctified, an unholy thing, and hath done despite unto the Spirit of grace?'*

'Hebrews 10:29.'

'No. You are the demon,' I shouted. 'I call on God to return you to Hell where you came from.'

I could see the moonlit street once again.

The monk pointed at me with strangely glistening hands. 'He's the paedo,' he shouted in a high pitched, almost feminine voice.

The acolytes stepped forward, brandishing sticks and iron bars.

I turned and fled.

I could hear feet pounding behind me. My heart was thudding and my legs were burning. I could hear them running behind and around me. Any minute now, I would feel the first blow. How long would I be able to survive? How much pain would I feel before I lost consciousness?

I glanced over my shoulder. They were almost on me. The fear drove me to push myself harder despite the agony in my legs.

Within a few more steps I was puffing furiously and starting to slow. I was an old man, unfit. I stopped and wheezed while the pain in my side passed. I expected once again to feel the dull thud of a knife entering my back.

I looked back over my shoulder and two men in cowls were standing behind me. I could just make out their cold, thin smiles under their hoods.

I looked forward to see a trio of monks standing a few feet in front of me and to my left. How had they managed to appear right in front of me so quickly?

There was an alley to my right. I had no choice but to run down it. I stumbled for a few feet into the dark shadows and then saw in front of me another two assailants.

I had been herded into this dark alley. That was why they hadn't hit me before. They were pushing me into a place where they wouldn't be seen. I was helpless.

They closed in muttering. 'Fucking paedo.' 'Bastard.' 'Child killer.' I could smell beer and sweat. I could almost feel the blows already. I wanted to live. I didn't want to die. I had to do God's bidding. Who would stop the demon? No one else could find it.

I turned around and around and around saying, 'no, no, no,' to each of them.

I dropped to my knees to await the first blow of the unjust judgement.

As I waited to die I realised paradoxically, that there was so little faith in these creatures that even the demon was unable to receive worship from them and so it had disappeared.

I prayed for a miracle to occur once again.

Urgent Actions

The ego has a constant urgent need to act, always fearful, belligerent or seeking pleasures with at most short-term consideration of the consequences. It is only the quiet, easily ignored presence of the soul that can modify this selfish desperation with long term plans and proper morality.

ANOTHER ANGEL

Luke 22:43

And there appeared an angel unto him from heaven, strengthening him.

A flash of white pain.

A blow to the back of my head.

I fell forward onto my hands jarring my body from elbows to teeth.

More pain in my ribs as a foot connected with my side.

There was a pause.

I raised my head a few agonised inches.

There was a space between two of my attackers. A foot kicked me in the head, but lightly and at an angle. I waited for the follow up.

None came.

There was movement above me. My attackers were ignoring me.

I rolled to the side and looked up.

A Goliath stood amongst them.

He hit the nearest hooded man with his elbow. His quarry collapsed.

Another tormentor hit out at my rescuer with a crow bar. Almost lazily, the giant slipped forward, took the weapon and threw his assailant aside. Somehow he always seemed to be ahead of them. Moving slowly but always where he wanted to be.

Two more were struck down, almost in one blow. The remaining three turned and ran.

One of the acolytes on the ground stumbled to his feet and limped away looking back over his shoulder in terror.

Yes!

Jubilation!

God had sent my rescuer!

So my purpose *was* right and good. We could defeat the demon. Surely this Holy Crusader was more than a physical match for a demon. He and I would track it down and destroy it. We would vanquish our enemies.

The pains in my body were dissipating already washed away by the joy of victory.

My rescuer effortlessly lifted a hooded man from the ground by his jacket and carried him to me. 'Are you okay?' he asked of me. His faith was powerful.

'Yes. Yes.' I could have kissed him in my joy.

The captured monk squirmed, trying to escape the powerful grip. 'Let me go. You can't hold me. It's against the law,' he shouted.

My rescuer grunted in derision. 'Why were you attacking this man?' he demanded.

Our prisoner tried to turn his face away, almost tearing his clothes in terror of his captor. He was a teenager, slim and scruffy with a bleeding nose and a nasty scrape across his face. His hooded sweatshirt and baseball cap simulated the monastic vestments that tricked me into thinking he was a holy man. 'He's a fucking paedo,' he accused, pointing at me.

'No, I'm not,' I answered.

'Liar.' He shouted into my face. 'You're Donald Pleasance.' Self righteous anger had overcome his terror for a second.

'No, look,' I said. I took out my wallet and showed him my credit card and driver's licence. 'My name is Matthews. Who told you I was a paedophile?'

The big man remained silent throughout all this, regularly surveying the surrounding area.

'I dunno,' said the boy, clearly confused and trying to make sense of what had happened. 'We just were sort of told. Jimmy told us where to wait for you.'

'Who's Jimmy?'

'Me mate.' He looked around in fear and puzzlement. He stank of sweat and fear.

I had to find out what he knew. 'Do you know anything about a monk?'

'What?'

'A man wearing a hood. Not like yours, though. Like in the past.'

He was puzzled.

'You know like in the movies. Someone who quoted from the Bible. Or chanted?'

He nodded. 'Yeah. Jimmy talked to her. She was weird, man. Jimmy didn't know her or anything. She sort of was there and said something.'

A woman? Asbeel worked through women. 'What did she look like?'

'I dunno.'

'How tall was she?'

'A bit short. Not very.'

'What colour was her hair? Was she fat or skinny? Did you see her face?'

He fell back in fear, unable to cope with my percussive questioning. 'I didn't see nothing. She was wearing a coat, like a hoodie but bigger. Like you said. Like from the movies. You know. Obi-Wan Kenobi. And she said weird stuff.'

'How did you know she was a woman?'

'Her voice?' He seemed unsure of everything.

'Did you notice anything?'

'Nuh. Let me go. You can't keep me. You're breaking the law. I didn't see nothing.'

'Where's Jimmy? I can ask him.'

The boy squirmed in terror once more. 'Nuh. He don't know either. She just sort of said and we knew what to do. She said you're a paedo.'

I opened my heart to him. I could see his pain and frustration. The message "you're worthless" was carved so deep into his soul that it had even dampened his faith. I could also see that he was telling the truth. The demon and the monk were too clever. They had cast a spell of confusion over the whole gang. They were helpless dupes, ready with fists and weapons but not with their brains. And definitely not ready to listen with their souls.

'You thought you were doing something right didn't you?' I offered.

He hung his head.

I tried to reach him again. 'You were just protecting the kids in the street, weren't you?'

He still would not respond, though I could see in his heart that he wanted to.

'Listen,' I said, 'you need to think for yourself. You let other people think for you. You were tricked.'

'Yeah, right,' he said in a carefully flat and unresponsive voice, but I could see the flicker of hope deep within him.

'Why don't you try something different?' I said. 'Something that'll teach you what's right and what's wrong. The Church maybe.'

He looked at the ground. To anyone else he was ignoring me, but I could see the tiniest spark of faith glow within his soul.

My Goliath shook him. 'Are you listening, you little turd?'

The spark of faith vanished and he snarled at the ground in a well-practised response to patriarchal aggression.

I gently grasped the huge hand holding the boy. 'Let him go. He needs a chance to find God. A demon was controlling him.'

They both stared at me wide eyed. The boy was confused and the man was worried.

'It cast a spell,' I continued. 'We won't find out anything this way. It's too clever to reveal itself. This boy could become someone good if he can just avoid the demons.'

They both continued to stare at me silently, but I felt the hard muscles in the massive hand relax.

'Are you sure?' rumbled my protector at last.

'Yes. I'm sure. He won't know anything. I can tell. Trust me. He's been tricked by The Great Deceiver, the Devil Himself.'

He let go and the boy staggered to his feet, walked backward for a few steps and then turned and ran. I could hear others running from the shadows to join him.

'Thank you,' I said. 'You saved my life.'

The big man nodded once.

'I'm Gabriel.' I forced myself to my feet, ignoring the spike of pain in my side and the spots before my eyes. 'How did you know where to find me?'

'I didn't. I was in the bus shelter and you ran past.' We walked out of the alley and into the penumbra of a streetlight. Or at least I stumbled out and my saviour strode. He had to stop every few feet and wait for me. He was wearing combat trousers and a plain, green sweatshirt. He was tall, maybe seven foot, and very broad shouldered.

The world tended to spin around me and my head hurt again. 'Well, thank you,' I said. 'You did a holy act. What is your name?'

His expression was stern. My insights told me that he was a mighty scowler, angry at the world for not being as it should be. No one crossed this man twice.

'Sam. What did you mean with all that stuff about demons and the devil?' he asked.

I smiled at him and showed my compassion. 'It's true. There's a demon about and it's casting spells and influencing people. It's tried to get to me three times. First Dr Matthews was stabbed from behind, so he died and I appeared and then it set me up to be accused of someone's murder and now it's tried more direct means.' I nodded towards the direction where the thugs had disappeared.

He grunted yet again. His expression showed puzzlement. 'You appeared?'

'I'm an angel. Sent by God.'

He nodded. 'Yeah.' He didn't seem to be surprised anymore. 'I know. I've had a dream, too. It was about you. I need to protect you.'

'Yes!' I shouted.

He looked around to see if anyone had heard us.

I touched his shoulder in what I believed were love and thanks. 'Let's go talk to a couple of my friends. I'm starting to understand now.'

Trust

Luke 11:17
But he, knowing their thoughts, said unto them, Every kingdom divided against itself is brought to desolation; and a house divided against a house falleth.

'It wasn't me,' shouted Puck. 'I don't know anything.'

She was still opaque to my insights. Was she telling the truth? Had she written that note or not? Was she the monk? Once again, somehow, the paper evidence had disappeared.

'Well someone is trying to kill me,' I said.

'I thought it was a demon,' said Del.

'Yes, so did I, but I think the demon isn't corporeal. It has to work through someone. A woman.' I pointed at Puck. 'Like her.'

Puck was in her usual uniform, jeans and sweatshirt. 'I told you it wasn't me,' she shouted back. 'I don't have any reason to hurt you. I like you. How do you know it's not your wife?'

'I don't. It's just that I don't know anything about you, do I? I wait for you and perhaps you'll turn up. Where do you live? How do you survive?'

'That's my business, okay? No one needs to know.' Still not even a clue as to who the real Puck was.

'And what about my religion?' I demanded of Puck. 'Have you found me any followers? Have you found a way for us to get the money we need?'

'Whose religion is it?' demanded Del.

I was distracted by Del's skimpy T-shirt top. It highlighted her figure wonderfully, exaggerating the taut roundness of her breasts. Her jeans exaggerated her thin waist and rounded bottom.

'It's my religion,' I answered her.

'Then why does Sarah have to do all the work?' countered Del.

'Because it's me the demon's trying to kill. I have to hide while she gets an army of followers and then we can get enough money to hunt it down and neutralise it.'

Del held Sam's arm. Her slender fingers could not even reach all the way across one bicep. 'But now you've got Sam to protect you. Shouldn't you be out spreading the good word yourself?'

Sam puffed himself up in foolish pride.

I didn't like the way that Sam and Del had become so close almost instantly. I wanted to impress Del, but she only seemed to have eyes for this shallow hulk of a man. 'Okay. But what do we do about my religion?' I demanded.

'I thought you said Dr Matthews had organised it,' said Puck.

'Well, yes,' I answered, 'but I don't like the people that were helping him.'

'And that's why we need money,' said Del. 'Lots of money.'

'We were going to do something on the telly,' said Puck.

'I'm not happy about that,' I said.

Del held up a leaflet. 'I think we should see how these people get their money.'

So, as usual, Del had been planning something. What was she up to?

Puck reached for the leaflet but Sam grabbed it first and stared at it. I didn't expect him to be able to read it all. With that much muscle how could he have a brain as well?

'Well, tell us all about it,' demanded Puck.

'It's a spiritualist group,' explained Del. 'They can fill a big hall. I've looked at them before. They're con artists but we can learn from them.'

Puck jumped up and clapped her hands. 'Really? Is it a scam? I love scams.'

'Let's go and find out,' said Del.

Spirits

Ephesians 6:12
For we wrestle not against flesh and blood, but against principalities, against powers, against the rulers of the darkness of this world, against spiritual wickedness in high places.

'I have mystic powers,' announced Puck as she entered the room.

'What's that on your head?' I demanded.

'It's my pyramid of power,' she answered. 'It concentrates the magic rays that give me my insights.'

'It looks like it's made of aluminium foil,' commented Del, smiling.

'It was, but I've magically transformed it,' Puck answered.

'Let me see it,' I said.

'Never,' said Puck in a regal pose. 'For then you might learn my secrets and it is only the initiated that can use these powers.'

'It's just a wire frame pyramid made of twisted foil,' rumbled Sam. I was surprised that he was even able to use words like pyramid.

'Go on, tell us how it will make us lots of money,' demanded Del with a grin.

'It's not about the money. It's about my powers,' said Puck. She was even more supercilious now.

'Okay then, let's see your powers,' I said.

'Right,' said Puck. 'First, let me concentrate.' She rolled her eyes into her head in a marvellous send up of spiritualists. 'Now, I'm getting something. Is the word angel, meaningful to anyone here?'

'That's cheating,' yelled Del. 'You know it is. Tell us something we don't know.'

Puck looked away, disdain emanating from every part of her body. She was such a wonderful comic actress. 'You who have little belief will never understand me, but I will show you a fraction of my powers whilst I wear the pyramid.'

In a serious humour failure Sam shook his head slowly.

Puck closed her eyes and her face creased in mock concentration. 'I'm getting a name. It's a name close to someone here.' She opened one eye to see if anyone was reacting yet. 'If you don't help me it will be your fault, you know, not mine. You've got to answer if you recognise something that's relevant to you.'

'Come on,' said Del. 'Get on with it. Show us something really clever.'

'Okay,' said Puck, closing her eyes again. 'I'm getting a message from the other side.' She moaned gently. 'It's a name with a *vowel* in it,' she announced as if it was a great achievement.

I laughed.

Del smiled. 'Come on,' she muttered.

Puck shook her head gently as if to cast out the nay sayers and foolish. 'Very well. Does the letter S mean anything?'

Del and I shook our heads.

'It's becoming clearer. S, S, J, J,' she peeked at us from the corner of her eye. 'J, Jo, John. No, Joan. The name Joan means something to someone here.'

'You're a complete sham,' said Del.

'No,' Puck said. 'It means something to you, doesn't it, Sam?'

That was the first time that I noticed that Sam wasn't just scowling. He was glaring at Puck.

'Joan has hurt you, hasn't she?' said Puck. 'My powers are working now. She was very close, wasn't she?'

'Stop it,' said Sam, low and mean.

'No, it's starting to work. I can see it now. She cheated on you didn't she? You loved her but you couldn't trust her.'

'Shut up,' he repeated.

'Sarah,' said Del to Puck, 'I think…'

But Puck wasn't listening. 'Did you catch her with her lover?' said Puck. 'Did you want to hurt them both? But you couldn't could you? You could have broken both their bodies with your hands. Killed them with a flick of your fingers. Like that.' She clicked her fingers. 'But instead you walked away.'

Suddenly Sam was standing an inch away from Puck, his huge body looming over her, his hand raised open palmed.

Puck's eyes widened in fear.

I sat terrified and impotent. I wanted to save her but how could I? He would destroy me if I even stood up.

Del was just able to reach Sam's arm. 'Come on, now. She's just a silly girl.' Her tone was gentle and persuading. 'A huge man like you doesn't need to treat her like this. She's just a bit stupid.'

Puck nodded slowly. Her whole body was shaking.

'It's okay,' comforted Del. 'Forget her. You've got me, now.' Del gently leaned her whole body against him.

This wasn't fair. I wanted Del to treat me like that, not him. Still it was working. He looked down at her.

'I bet I'm a much better catch than this other bitch who never deserved you anyway,' said Del.

He lowered his arm and Puck took a step back.

'Come on,' said Del. 'Let's go outside and get some fresh air.'

He nodded.

Del led him gently to the door. At the last moment she glared back at Puck and shook her head.

Puck waited until the door closed behind them. 'It was only meant to be a joke,' she said. 'I didn't think it would work so well.' She started to cry. 'I don't have special powers.'

I took Puck in my arms to comfort her. 'I know.'

'I only said it because I could see him recognise the name.'

'Yes. It just shows how easy it is to fake powers. It wasn't even luck. Everyone has a problem with love,' I said bitterly wishing that I was hugging Del and not Puck.

'Should we use this to make lots of money?' she asked.

'I'm not sure,' I said. 'It could be a bit dangerous. We need a lot of money.'

'It was so easy,' said Puck.

'Yes, I know. Let's see what else turns up in the next day or so.'

CONTACT

1 Corinthians 14:1
Follow after charity, and desire spiritual gifts, but rather that ye may prophesy.

'I've left you, your demons and your friends until last, Gabriel,' the spiritualist declared to the audience of thirty people in the hall before him.

I stared in stunned amazement. 'How do you know my new name?'

'You first,' the spiritualist said pointing straight at Sam. 'You've not much time left. Enjoy what time you have. Forget the past. Think of now. Your death is near.'

Sam glared.

The spiritualist was a very ordinary man, with a strong Welsh accent, casual trousers and a shirt. You expected someone with his ethereal abilities to be dressed up in stars and magic symbols, but this man had real ability and didn't need any pretence to trap the credulous. He had been pointing at people and immediately saying the right words or names. Things he couldn't have known or would have had to spend many days researching. I couldn't see any evidence of the usual vague starting point in the hope that someone in the audience would respond. He pointed at Del. 'You have so much pain already. It will get worse before it gets better.'

Del shrugged her shoulders.

'You must stop the lies,' he said to her.

She frowned.

He continued. 'It's time to put your past behind you and become true and straight. Death will surround you but you will escape it.'

Del stared at him, clearly puzzled and confused.

Why was he so vague with her? Not a mention of a name or anything.

He met Puck's eyes. 'You have many names,' he said. 'You need to reveal everything to Gabriel. Until you do, many lives are at risk.'

Puck shook her open hands at him to silence him and then looked at me in alarm.

'You will find out that you are at the centre of all these deaths,' the spiritualist said to Puck.

She shook her head. A tear formed in her eye.

'But it's not really your fault,' he added in comfort.

He looked straight at me. 'You're running out of time, Gabriel,' he said. 'You need to get on with it.'

'What?' I said.

'You will die again before your purpose is fulfilled.'

I trembled in fear. 'No. Not again. I'm protected. By God.'

He shook his head. 'No, that protection must end. The time is near. Don't fail, for the consequences for the world will be too great.'

'No.' I looked around the room for the demon. Was it here? Was it the demon telling him what to say?

'You have brought the only demons present in this room,' he said.

Had I mentioned the demon out loud? I was certain I hadn't said a thing. Everyone was staring at me.

'I'm afraid death follows you everywhere, Gabriel. As you knew right from the start. Prepare to die thrice times.'

He looked at all of us with compassionate sadness. 'I'm so sorry. Death surrounds you all. There is much sadness yet to come.'

He walked back to the centre of the stage. 'That is all. I hope I have been of comfort to some of you.' He stared directly at me. 'And where I could not bring comfort, at least perhaps I have provided direction. Accept your fate and you will all be happier even if only for a short time.' He walked off the stage.

We sat stunned.

God Forsaken Places

1 Timothy 6:10

For the love of money is the root of all evil; which while some coveted after, they have erred from the faith, and pierced themselves with many sorrows.

'We could use you as bait,' rumbled Sam.

'What?' I said.

He smiled. 'As Sun Tzu wrote, "Hold out baits to entice the enemy." If we want to catch an enemy that's good at hiding, draw it out. Make yourself really visible and let it chase after you.'

'Yes,' said Puck. 'Trap it, smack.' She clapped her hands together simulating a demon trap.

We were in my house again, holding yet another council of war. Last night's visit to the spiritualist had left me terrified. We didn't want anything to do with spiritual powers any more, not even for money.

'But what if it catches me instead?' I asked. 'You heard what he said. I'm going to die.' I knew I was whining, but I couldn't help myself. I was so scared. I didn't care about them or their needs. They weren't real people, just puppets and players to support me. They were no more to me than my personal army sent to protect and care for me.

Del grasped Sam's arm with both hands and leaned her body against it. 'You'll have big strong Sam to protect you.'

This was no good. I wanted to say that I didn't need his protection so that Del would admire me instead of him. I had to show her I could be just as brave as Sam. 'Okay, but where? Where would the demon be?'

'It would have to be on its territory,' said Sam.

'Yes, good idea,' agreed Del. 'Where would a demon be?'

'It wouldn't be in a church,' said Puck, 'because that's the opposite of it. That's where God is, so it must be somewhere really unholy.'

'In a shopping centre,' I said. 'That's about as far as you can get from a holy place. In a shopping centre God has been replaced by consumerism.' And I should be safe in front of all those people.

Del was appalled. 'No. That's just a tired old cliché,' she said. 'Shopping centres are wonderful places.'

'But there are lots of people there,' said Puck.

'And lots of money,' added Del.

'Okay, that's it.' I said. 'I'll go to the shopping mall, this evening and preach. Perhaps we can take up a collection?'

How long did I have? Would this be the end of my life?

GREED

Isaiah 56:11
Yea, they are greedy dogs which can never have enough, and they are shepherds that cannot understand; they all look to their own way, every one for his gain, from his quarter.

It was such a pretty dress. Her mother had helped her to choose it. It was so lovely with little flowers on it. She tried it on to see how she looked.

'Where did you get that dress?'

She turned and crouched down in a single smooth movement, ready for anything. She must have been paying too much attention to the dress otherwise she would have heard him. Sometimes he moved so quietly.

'Mama,' she answered. It couldn't be a sin if Mama bought it. Could it?

'You have enough dresses. You didn't need another.'

'But I'm going to a party.'

'Never. Think of the evil.'

So it was to be another beating. 'What is my sin?'

'Greed, child, greed. You have taken more than you need. It is the path to your downfall.'

'But Mama…'

'I will talk to her,' he answered.

After the beating, her legs still smarting, she lay on her bed and listened to them arguing. Mama didn't think it was a sin. How could that be? Who was right, Mama or Papa?

A scream. It was Mama. So she was being punished, too. She must have sinned.

A door slammed.

She never saw Mama again after that day. It was the day that she learned of the consequences of sin, for it can drive away even those you love. Papa never mentioned her again, but *she* remembered Mama, treasuring every little memory and hidden memento.

She was appalled by the greed of that dreadful ex minister who actually thought he was an angel.

She felt even more guilt at her previous failure. He and his demons would condemn so many others to Hell. She wanted him to turn aside from sloth and instead he had turned to greed. His fears had driven him to demand money, as if that could save him from death and the ensuing holy judgement.

She had prayed for guidance and it had come so easily. Her plan was effortlessly arranged, his guardian would be distracted at the right moment and then she would be able to send *him* on to be judged by God.

What a pathetic creature he was, man or angel. He was doing all this to protect himself from a demon that did not exist.

Stony Ground

Mark 4:5-6

And some fell on stony ground, where it had not much earth; and immediately it sprang up, because it had no depth of earth.

But when the sun was up, it was scorched; and because it had no root, it withered away.

'Angels and demons walk among us!' I called to the passing crowd. 'We are surrounded by demons. Real demons. Disguised as people.'

Del, Puck and Sam were on each side of me. They formed my protective phalanx as well as acting as my emissaries for those that were able to hear me and respond.

I paused for breath, reviewing the passers-by to judge the reaction. It was almost as if I had become invisible. Men were staring at Del, but no one was looking at me.

I continued on. 'I have seen depraved and deplorable acts, sexual exhibitions.'

A grey haired, middle-aged woman in a flowery blue dress and sensible shoes paused and stared.

'These are the acts of demons!' I shouted.

She waited.

I was getting to her. 'I have seen demons in our very midst.'

She nodded thoughtfully.

'I tell you, some demons have even taken over the Church,' I said to her.

She moved closer, eyes wide and interested.

'Are you ready for the good fight?'

'What do you mean?' she asked.

A few more people, men and women, mostly elderly were gathering around, to see what was happening.

'As Revelations has predicted,' I shouted at them all, 'The Apocalypse may be upon us and God has allowed the Devil dominion over the earth.'

A couple of teenagers dressed all in black paused.

'The Devil tricks and confuses us all. It is only by constant attention that we see through the deception and avoid the steel trap of lust.'

The teenagers sneered and walked away.

'Are you interested in learning more about Angels?' I asked the audience.

An elderly man shook his head and dragged his female partner away. A few more people herd-like followed them.

'Give up on your worldly goods,' I said. 'Forget about shopping. Come and help me fight the demons.'

The face of the woman in the blue dress transformed instantly into a frown and she turned away.

A last couple turned and wandered away.

'This isn't working,' I said to Del.

'You've only been here for two minutes,' she replied. 'You can't expect it to be that easy.'

I scowled at her. 'It's not fair. Dr Matthews had lots of listeners. Now that I have a real message, no one wants to know.'

She scoffed in my face. 'A real message? You don't know what it is other than to protect yourself. You don't even have a reason, just some vague purpose.'

'What I should do?'

'Useless,' she judged. 'Wait here,' she barked at me. She grabbed Puck's arm, 'come on, let's do some shopping.'

'Goody,' cheered Puck.

They disappeared off into the crowd.

'Is this what you expected?' I asked Sam.

'It takes time. Don't be so impatient,' he answered, his eyes focussed on where Del had disappeared.

'But what if it doesn't work?' I moaned at him.

'Then we need to do more thinking,' he replied.

'Like what? How I could be killed? How long should we wait?'

He said nothing, his sunglasses hiding any possibility that I might relate to him man to man.

I stared at the surrounding shops and people. There was colour in everything. The shop displays showed some nice clothes and gadgets and I could smell the cookies baking. I noticed a dash of white on the other side of a huge potted palm. It was interesting for some reason. I moved so that I could see it more clearly. It was Rebecca seated on a bench in her usual white dress. She jumped up and almost ran into a department store. She must have been spying on me.

I went back to stand by my muscle bound protector. He didn't even nod in my direction. Perhaps he was looking for Del. This was getting worse. Any minute now the demon would appear.

A hand touched my shoulder.

I leapt forward and turned.

'No!' I shouted.

'Calm down,' said Del, laughing, 'it's only me.'

I looked around to see if anyone had seen me. Sam was grinning and Puck was clapping her hands and jumping up and down in glee.

'You jumped straight up then,' shouted Puck for everyone to hear.

'God, you're dreadful,' said Del, shaking her head.

'You scared me,' I needed to defend my honour but all I could feel was my hot face showing supreme embarrassment. 'This body nearly died, remember.'

Del tipped her head to the side. 'Yes, I suppose you have had it a bit rough. I'm sorry.' She held my arm and drew me to her so she could kiss my cheek.

I could feel the softness of her breast compressed against my arm and my body became light and strong. What a woman.

She handed me a silver statuette with semi circular bands coming out from either side. It was an angel, about four inches high with wings wide, holding a sword, point down.

'What?' I was confused.

'I know, it's crap but it will do.'

'What is it?'

She sighed. 'I've got one, too. I bought one for Puck as well.'

'What are these?' I asked, pointing at the bands extending from the sides.

'It's a tiara. Look,' Del put hers on her head, carefully positioning it so that the angel stood in front.

'Aren't they great?' demanded Puck. I hadn't noticed it on her until then, but now I couldn't see how I could possibly have missed it. The tiaras made Del and Puck look stupid.

'I don't...' I said.

Del interrupted me. 'I'm trying to help you here. This is the way that you can be noticed.' She held up a clipboard. 'Sarah and I will go around asking people about angels and that sort of thing. Like it's a questionnaire. And then we'll send them to you. They can find you because you'll be wearing one of these.'

'We're fighting for equal rights for angels to exist,' grinned Puck. I could almost see a spiritual energy glowing from her eyes. 'Did you know that the church is going to ban angels because they're not Politically Correct?' she demanded of me.

'That's not true,' I said. I looked at Del for guidance. 'Is it?'

Del shushed me. 'No, of course not. I just made it up, but most people don't know that and it will be an ice breaker and we can start a conversation.'

'Where did you get them from?' I couldn't guess who would sell such rubbish.

'From the new age shop,' answered Del.

'What, three of them? Why would anyone want to buy these?'

Del scowled at me.

'I suppose they're right for us, though,' I added hastily.

Del and I watched Puck as she looked at her reflection in a shop window. 'I think they're a child's toy, really,' said Del. 'It was odd, though,' she added. 'It wasn't in the shop. A man said they were for me. He wouldn't take any money. He said something about God's will. What do you think he meant?'

I stared at her. 'Another angel?' I looked at it again. I could see some writing underneath but it was too small for me to read. 'What does that say?'

Del held it to the light and squinted. 'The Archangel Gabriel smites the demon,' she read.

We stared at each other. It was a sign from God.

'So what,' grumbled Sam.

I had forgotten all about him. There was no way that the big lunk would understand the meaning of a mysterious stranger with angel icons.

'What about him?' I asked Del. 'Shouldn't he have one, too?' His face went white and his hands formed tight fists. I hoped that he wouldn't twitch one of those massive fists into my face.

Del grinned at him. 'I don't think so,' she said to me in a side whisper. 'Anyway, you need to be visible, not him. He needs to be your protector.'

As if someone that big could hide. Still she was right. Anyone asking him for religious advice wouldn't get very far.

'Okay,' I agreed. 'I'll wear it. Perhaps it will work.' I rammed it on my head and Del fussed at it. I thoroughly enjoyed her close physical presence.

Somehow Sam managed to scowl even more deeply than he had before. I guess I was becoming more sensitive to his moods.

Del and Puck disappeared into the crowd once more and I looked up at Sam. 'How do I look?' I asked.

He grunted. 'I'll watch you from over there,' he muttered as he walked off to stand in front of the door.

After a few minutes another middle-aged woman with deep grey hair and a lined face came up to me. 'Can you contact my dead sister for me?'

'No,' I said. 'She's dead. There is no time where she is. She can't have conversations.'

'How dare you?' shouted the woman. 'She's in heaven.'

'Yes,' I defended, 'but she hasn't got a body anymore. She can't talk.'

'What about through you? Aren't you a spiritualist?'

I shook my head.

'Useless bugger,' muttered the woman as she walked away from me.

My first convert lost because she couldn't tell the difference between the spiritual and physical worlds.

No one else talked to me for an hour and the crowds gradually dissipated. Sam had disappeared. A security guard approached me.

'Do you want to talk about angels?' I asked him.

'No,' he replied. 'I've come to ask you to leave.'

'What?'

'We've received a complaint that you're carrying on some sort of religious thing here. It's not allowed.'

'Why not?' I asked.

'We don't want to offend anyone.'

'Who will be offended?' I demanded. This was ridiculous.

'A Muslim person.'

'No. The Muslim people respect angels and other people's religion. They like it that Christians are religious.'

'Someone said she was offended, so we're asking you to leave.'

'This is absurd. Why can't this person tell me that they are offended?'

'I'm sorry, Sir, but we don't allow any religion here.'

'So, you, a white middle class man are deciding who would be offended and who would not. What right do you have to speak for others, you patronising bastard?'

He frowned at me. 'Look, mate, if you don't leave now, via that exit,' he pointed at the nearest door, 'I'll call the police and have you thrown out. Now go.'

I felt a bump behind me and looked around to see another guard. He was equally threatening. I looked around for Sam but he was still absent.

It was time to give up. There was no faith here anyway, not from either of these guards nor from the crowds of people desperate to grab some trinket to distract them from realising that their existence was always under threat and ultimately worthless.

I proudly walked through the exit with the guards escorting me closely. I left the soulless shopping centre behind me. I hoped that Sam would find me soon,

I was in an enclosed alley, lit only from the waning evening light and the reflections from the shop windows. Miraculously, there was no else around. This must have been a rear entrance.

The demon was standing at the entrance to the alley.

My heart thudded painfully.

I looked around in desperation seeking a way out.

How did it know where I was? How could it have found me so quickly? Where was Sam?

I ran back to the entrance to the shopping centre, but the door was locked. I could see the guards walking away. I banged on the window, desperate for my life but they kept on walking, unheeding and uncaring now that the threat that I represented to their world was safely ejected.

I looked back to the end of the alley. The monk was standing in front of me dressed in brown robes. Except that she was a nun of course. I stumbled backwards further into the alley, past huge rubbish bins and litter. She withdrew a knife from her robes. The demon glowed more brightly and its tongue lashed out towards me.

CAPTURED

A person cannot exercise full free will as long as they are held captive by the inner demons of irrational beliefs, mind numbing fear and over protective arrogance.

THE BATTLE

Jeremiah 50:22
A sound of battle is in the land, and of great destruction.

Where was Sam? Everyone had deserted me, and now I was caught by this dangerous woman.

The demon glows even more brightly. It speaks to both observer and punisher.

'For false Christs and false prophets shall rise, and shall shew signs and wonders, to seduce, if it were possible, even the elect.'

'Mark 13:22. This is irrelevant. You're talking rubbish. I'm not a false Christ and I'm not a false prophet.'

The monk shakes her head. 'No,' she chants. 'You are the enemy. You are staying my hand from my holy purpose.'

She raises her holy sword. It glows with a righteous light.

The accused scrambles backwards in fear. 'But I'm the one with a holy purpose,' he defends. 'Not you. You are stopping me.'

'And these shall go away into everlasting punishment: but the righteous into life eternal,' *announces the* **demon.**

'Matthew 25:46. Wait I know. How about 1 Timothy 4:1? "Now the Spirit speaketh expressly, that in the latter times some shall depart from the faith, giving heed to seducing spirits, and doctrines of devils." It is not I that has left the faith, but you. You are violating a commandment. "Thou shalt not kill." You are the seducing spirit and next to you is the devil with its doctrines.'

The execution pauses. 'Satan is the great deceiver. God has instructed me. I am his agent.'

Gabriel desperately pleads. 'If you are bringing death aren't you bringing evil? Are you the Devil's agent?'

'The Devil only acts with God's approval,' chants the monk.

'So you are doing the Devil's work.'

'No! I am holy. I am righteous. I shall smite the ungodly!'

The sword point rests upon the chest of the condemned man.

The judged man calls out in fear. 'I am an angel. I have a purpose. Your angel is a demon.'

From his brow a glow appears. It is a light from the sword held by the true angel Gabriel on the observer's tiara. The holy light blazes up and forms into holy armour. Asbeel darkens in colour and shrinks in size.

'Look,' calls Gabriel. 'Your demon has been defeated.'

The monk turns and sees the demon's impotency. She looks around, confused and desperate.

'Its instructions are wrong,' calls Gabriel. 'You can't trust it.'

'You wear a demon,' declares the monk.

'No. It is an angel.'

The monk looks up to Heaven, lifts the holy sword and, with the light blazing from it, strikes at Gabriel's chest.

The slow strike with eyes heavenwards gives him time to twist to the side and the sword misses. He reaches up to take the handle of the sword.

The light of Gabriel dispels the demon.

I held the handle of the knife against her surprisingly powerful grip, forcing it into the ground. I still couldn't see her face. Who was she?

She snatched back the knife, spun gracefully on one toe and ran from the alley.

Seconds later Sam appeared.

'Did you see her?' I called.

'What?' he said.

'The monk or nun or whatever. You must have seen her run out of the alley.'

'No. No one,' he shouted in response. He ran around the small alley, looking into the bins, kicking up the litter.

'She got away again,' I said. 'But I was able to defeat her demon.' I smiled at him. I showed him the tiara. 'It was this, it saved me.'

He finished surveying the alley. 'You're okay, then.'

I held the precious ornament close, auditing every feature. 'Yeah, what happened to you?'

'I had to go to the toilet. Why are you out here?'

'I was thrown out by some guards. They said I was offending people.'

'Why just then? Just as the shop was closing.'

'They said they had received a complaint... From a woman.'

Sam nodded. 'I'm not surprised. She's got amazingly good timing. How did she know that I would go to the loo then and for so long? Let's go.'

I put the tiara carefully into my pocket.

A House Divided

Mark 3:25
And if a house be divided against itself, that house cannot stand.

'It's your wife,' declared Sam. 'She's the one trying to kill you.'

'What?' I asked. We were waiting for the bus outside the shopping centre. 'How? Why her? Why didn't I recognise her?'

'Did you actually see her face?'

'No. She was hidden behind the cowl. And I suppose she was about the right size.'

'There you are,' announced Sam. 'She knew where you were. This killer knows all about you. Right from the start. Even before you met us. She knows where you'll be and when.'

'What about Sarah?' I asked. 'She's got a similar build and she's much younger so she could have been able to fight me much better.'

He nodded. 'Maybe. Sarah gave me a sandwich and then I had to go to the toilet.' He stared at me for a second. 'No offence,' he said, 'but I think it doesn't matter how good they are at fighting. You're pretty hopeless. Even your wife could have beaten you.'

My stomach rumbled. 'I didn't get a sandwich,' I muttered, hurt and angry.

'It could be either, but at the moment I'd bet on your wife.'

'She does hate me. Something to do with babies and sex.'

'Yeah,' he grunted. 'You know women have a problem with sex?'

'What?'

'They get bored with men. As soon as they get used to you, they never want it again. Except to have babies.' He was obviously remembering some past issues with bitterness.

'Are you sure? I thought that women were always lustful.'

He stared at me in puzzlement. 'What? Where did you get that rubbish? It's men who are always after sex. Porn, pros, mistresses. Men need sex. Women don't.'

'Are you sure?'

'Yes. All women. They're all like that.' He was so certain and very angry.

'I guess you know more than me. I don't know anything. Doctor Matthews never understood it. Is that why I got caught with that pro, Bethany?'

He nodded. 'Yeah. Maybe someone set up Bethany, too. That was no coincidence. Wives hate prostitutes. It's like they don't want to have sex and they don't want the man to have it either.' His pursed lips and angry stare showed the strength of his bitterness.

'Is this about Joan, too?' I said, realising at last that perhaps he wasn't such a good judge of character. Just a very bitter man.

He frowned. 'What about that sandwich? Do you think Sarah doped it to force me to go to the toilet?"

He obviously didn't want to talk about Joan. 'But why would Sarah want to kill me?'

'Maybe she's crazy. In a nasty way.'

'She doesn't seem to be crazy.'

He shook his head, his eyes focussed vaguely in the far distance. 'No. The really mad ones don't. They don't feel guilt or anything. That's why you can't catch them with a lie detector. They really think that they are right and they don't feel fear or guilt. They do whatever they want. They can't be controlled through fear.'

'So it's fear that controls us? That stops us from killing each other? Take away the fear and you have a killer?'

'Or sometimes it's that fear that makes you a killer,' he said. He was frowning to himself.

'And are you a killer? Did you kill Joan?' I asked him.

He paused and continued to look into the distance. 'Sarah got it wrong. Her name was Jean.' He stood and punched the bus shelter. He walked away, fists held tight. After a few seconds he paused. 'Forget it,' he finally said.

This was another part of his life that he didn't want to discuss. Which came first, the anger and bitterness or the difficulties in his life? I would probably never know. For, as the spiritualist had foretold, we did not have not much life left between us.

'Why not Del?' I asked. 'It could have been her.'

'No.' His tone was flat. Certain. 'It wasn't her.'

I wasn't so sure. I couldn't remember anything about this woman who had tried to stab me just a few short hours ago. She could be anyone. I couldn't even remember how tall she was or whether she was stocky or slim. What had happened to me? Was it the demon? Had it cast a spell on me? 'My wife was at the shopping mall,' I suggested to keep the conversation going.

He snapped around to look at me and nodded once. 'Let's rule them out one at a time. We need to find out which one it is, your wife or Sarah. Your wife first. After that find out about Sarah and where she got that sandwich from.'

'Okay, what do you have in mind?'

He told me his plan. I only needed to add a few more steps to make it suit my purpose as well.

Rebecca's face was white, her hands were shaking. I looked around in case there was a knife nearby. Perhaps I shouldn't have told her in the kitchen where there were so many potential weapons.

'When is it due?' she demanded. A tear had appeared in the corner of her eye.

'I've only just found out,' I answered. 'I guess in nine months.'

She shook her head at me. 'It can't be nine months. She wouldn't know yet.'

'Well, I don't know,' I improvised. I hadn't expected that question. 'It was a while back. Before I saw that prostitute.'

'Are you lying?' she said staring at my face. She didn't seem to be angry any more, but she was still pale.

I wished I was a much better liar, but Sam had convinced me that there was no other path. 'No. I just don't know about women.'

Rebecca shook her head slowly. Her eyes remained focussed on my face, attempting to burn away my falseness.

'I'm afraid she wants to keep it. It will cost us a lot.' This should bring Rebecca to the peak of rage. I remembered

Sam's words in my head "if your enemy is easily angered, irritate him".

Rebecca stopped looking into my face and stared at the ground, silent at last.

'I'm going to go and see her later on. At 2pm,' I added. 'I'm meeting her at the church. Sort of in celebration of where Doctor Matthews finally died.'

Rebecca stood stunned. Perhaps the church celebration was a bit too far, but we had to make sure that we would be isolated and that she had plenty of time to get there. I hoped that she would be so angry that she wouldn't realise what an odd place it would be to meet Del. I also hoped that she wouldn't detect all my lies.

As I entered the church, I reviewed in my mind the last memories of Doctor Matthews, the people in the pews, his leaden belief in the wrongness of the church and his contempt for all women, especially Rebecca.

A woman was kneeling at the altar rail, her head covered by a scarf.

My heart thudded once, enough to shake my whole my body.

It was Rebecca. This was it. She was the one. Sam was already hiding somewhere, even though I could not see him. Still, she was only one small woman. As long as the demon wasn't around, I should be able to defend myself from her. She wouldn't catch me off guard like she did at the shopping mall.

She turned to face me and pulled back her scarf.

'I didn't expect to see you here,' I lied.

'I felt I owed it to you.'

'Are you going to admit to it then?'

She looked into my eyes her mouth open, surprise in every part of her body. 'How did you know?'

I slipped into the pew a few rows behind her, standing with plenty of barriers in case she drew a weapon. 'I guess it was obvious. You were the only person who could know wherever I was.'

Her brow furrowed. 'I guess so. You're more observant than I thought. There must have been more, though,' she said.

I sat and felt the cold hardness of the wood through my tracksuit trousers. 'Yes. Your anger of course. It would lead you to justify anything, even this.'

She nodded. 'Justification, yes. You *are* far more sensitive than I thought. Perhaps you really are someone new. How much do you know?'

'No details, of course. I didn't realise that you knew so much about the Bible, though.'

She shook her head. 'I don't understand.'

'All those Bible quotes.'

Again she shook her head in puzzlement.

I looked out for the demon. 'Where is he?'

'Here,' a voice called from the back of the church.

Once again my pulse raced. Where was Sam? Why wasn't he here now? I was about to confront the demon. I needed him.

The minister for the church, Peter Abeer, walked in wearing jeans and a checked shirt. So the demon did have a human form. It was a minister, someone I had trusted. Someone I knew so much about. The father of all lies.

And I still couldn't see Sam.

'If you're looking for a very large man,' the minister said, 'I'm afraid he left about half an hour ago.'

'What?'

'You have nothing to fear from us,' he added.

Rebecca looked around at him. 'What's going on, Peter?' she asked.

He walked up the centre aisle. As he came to my pew I stood and edged away, ready to run, but I needed to know where Sam was so I could run to him. Peter continued to the front. Rebecca stood as he came to her. He put his arm around her shoulders showing a practised intimacy.

Rebecca leaned against his body. 'I'm so sorry, Gid – sorry Gabriel, but it wasn't only me was it?'

I was being tricked by confusing statements. The devil is the master of disguises and tricks. Peter had lied. Sam couldn't really have left already, could he? 'What's going on?' I demanded.

'Things are a bit different to what both you think,' said the minister-demon that was Peter.

'You can't trick me,' I declared. I sidled closer towards the end of the pew away from the aisle. The demon in ministerial form released Rebecca and walked in parallel, tracking me.

I had made a mistake. It was hard to sidle between the pews, my progress was hampered by the narrow gap. My enemy, unconstrained would be able to anticipate any retreat and block it off. 'You can't defeat me,' I shouted. 'I have holy protection from you.' I thrust the angel tiara to my brow.

'Gideon... ' he started.

'No,' I shouted back. 'I am Gabriel. I will not die as that man! I am the angel Gabriel. I mean, an angel.' I realised at last that being an angel was pivotal to my life.

He smiled. 'Gabriel,' he said nodding in acknowledgement, 'you have nothing to fear. There are no tricks.' He had moved to the end of the pew only a few yards away. He held his arms open, mocking the benediction posture that I had given so often before.

I retreated one clumsy step at a time.

This evil creature could only kill my body. I tried to focus on my soul. At least it would be safe. Even if I died, God would bring me back. I still had to do His will. But my body did not understand. I felt the fear shake it once more. What of Rebecca? She might even now be sneaking up behind me. I was trapped. I started to cry.

'I'll not listen to your lies,' I shouted. 'Sam, where are you?' I ran to the end of the aisle and looked up and down everywhere as I searched for him. Rebecca was still at the front of the church. I still had a way out via the back door.

'It is your lies, Gid – Gabriel that I will start with,' said the Deceiver. 'You didn't get Del pregnant did you?'

'What?' called Rebecca.

'It was a ruse, my dear,' he answered. 'He thinks you're a murderer. He thinks you tried to kill him.'

She shook her head slightly in confused denial.

Something was wrong here. Once again the demon knew everything. Even about this trap. But why didn't Rebecca know?

'Gabriel,' she said. 'You poor man.'

'He doesn't really know about us,' said Peter.

She didn't seem to acknowledge Peter's strange words. She dabbed a hand to her eye. 'I know it's wrong,' she said, 'but I was hoping that the two sins would cancel out.' She clasped her hands as if begging for something from me. 'For all your sins, Gabriel, it is I who have done so much more.'

'What do you mean?' This was so wrong. Any minute now one of them would attack me. 'I don't understand,' I whined at them.

'Rebecca is pregnant,' said the minister, 'and I'm afraid it's my child.' He looked at her with such love in his eyes. 'Ours,' he added.

'But,' I said. I tried to understand. 'The demon?'

Peter returned to the front of the church leaving me an escape route. 'Think about it,' he said. 'Would a demon be able to come into a holy place?'

'No,' I muttered but I wasn't sure.

'Exactly,' he continued. 'And, according to the story from that Goliath of yours, you were always drawn out from here before you were attacked.'

I thought back through every battle with the demon. He was right.

'And as for Rebecca and myself,' he said, 'I'm afraid that we were together when you were preaching, and that is our greatest sin. I am sorry Gabriel.' He hung his head in shame.

I was safe. And Rebecca had what she wanted. 'What wonderful news,' I called out. The words echoed in the church.

'But, we have sinned against you,' said Rebecca. Her face was creased in puzzlement.

'Only in ways that I wanted to sin, too.' I was so proud of myself.

Her face radiated confusion. Peter looked at me quizzically.

'Don't you see? You and Doctor Matthews were hopeless together. It was a terrible marriage. Can you imagine what it would be like to have that bastard as a father? No, you two should be together. Get married!' Something inside me cried out in anger. I had been cuckolded. My wife had been snatched from me. She was mine, not his. But I would not let it take me over. I controlled it.

Hope appeared in Rebecca's face, but Peter frowned.

'We can't do that. Not without you getting divorced,' he said.

'Okay, then, we'll get divorced,' I said to Rebecca. This made such good sense, but still a part of me was angry.

'But that's a sin,' she answered.

'And I can't marry a divorced woman,' added Peter.

'And isn't it a sin to live without love? To hate and shout and to make each other's life so unbearable.' My words came out too fast. 'Aren't we all sinners anyway? This is a lesser sin to a life of pain and unhappiness.' Yes this was true. I didn't need to be angry. I didn't want to be angry. I felt my hand form a fist. I stared at it and forced it to unclench. I would not envy them for loving each other.

'But the church won't allow it,' said Peter. 'It will reduce the importance of marriage.'

'You're a bit late on that one aren't you?' I snapped back. The anger had said that. 'I tell you, never trust the churchman or a politician when they say it sends the wrong signals. They're trying to change the inevitable and consigning a lot of people to unhappiness.'

'We can't marry,' he said. His manner was flat and uncompromising.

At that point my holy insight came to me. 'Then wait a while,' I answered. 'For I will be dead in a few weeks time, my purpose fulfilled and you can then marry properly.' My heart became bitter and heavy for I would never have the life with Rebecca that he would. 'If you want, pretend that the child is mine. Rebecca, you can live at my place and see Peter whenever you want.' My body shouted at me that this was wrong, I should have had Rebecca's love and this baby should be mine, but I held it in check.

The happy couple stood and stared, dumbfounded.

'Oh, of course,' I added. 'You're worried about money. I know, I'll sell my car.'

'What?' said Rebecca. She stumbled to the nearest pew and leaned heavily on its back.

'Yes. It's in a pound somewhere. It got confiscated,' I explained to Peter. 'I need to get some money to get it out and then I can sell it and give you the money. Would it cover our debts?' And now I was on the moral high ground. They were the sinners and I was the forgiving victim.

Rebecca nodded her head, mouth agape as she stared at me. 'But you love that car. It's the only thing that you ever really let yourself enjoy. You've only had it for a few months.'

'It's only a car,' I answered. And this part was true, for what could I do with a car if I had no living body? All those years of envying other people for their cars and now it was worthless. My sinning was subsiding at the thought of my death.

'But you saved for years to buy it' she said. 'You wouldn't take a loan. You drove around in that old banger for years, embarrassed in front of others, cursing it. You were so happy because you had a top of the range Mercedes like everyone else.'

'So? I'm a different man, now.'

Peter nodded. 'Are you sure?'

'Positive,' I said. 'Treat it as my dowry to help you bring that child into the world in love and happiness.'

'In that case,' replied Peter, 'I could lend you the money to pay for your fines, then we can sell it and you can repay me and your debts.'

I felt so proud of myself.

Tears appeared in Rebecca's eyes. 'You'd do that for me?'

'Of course,' I answered. 'It's only fair. I'm not interested in material possessions. I have something important to do.' *And then I'll die.* 'Hurry, though,' I added. 'I have to implement the next part of my plan.'

Seeking the Truth

Deuteronomy 13:14

Then thou shalt enquire, and make search, and ask diligently; and behold, if it be truth, and the thing certain, that such abomination is wrought among you;

'Are you sure this is Puck's house?' I asked Sam as he opened the gate to a tiny, overgrown garden leading to a small, decaying Victorian terraced house.

'What?' he said. 'It's Sarah's house? Who's Puck?'

A surge of guilt washed through my body. That was supposed to be a secret. 'It's my name for her. Don't tell her I told it to you.'

'Whatever. Sarah's not her real name anyway.'

'What?'

'It's not her real name.' His tone was matter of fact. 'It's Miriam.'

'How do you know that?'

'Del told me. She also told me where she lives.' He knocked on the door.

'Should we do that?' I asked. 'What if someone answers?'

'If someone is at home I'd rather know now,' he snapped at me.

'Who?'

He stared at the door. 'Her housemate.'

The door remained unanswered.

'Housemate?'

'Yeah, she's a student. She shares this house with another woman.'

'How do you know so much about her?'

'Like I said, Del told me.'

'How does she know?' I was so scared. This could go so wrong. I could be caught by the police and be put back into gaol again.

'She's a bloody reporter,' he said abruptly.

We glared at each other while we were waiting for a reply to our knock.

'You don't have a clue, do you?' he said finally. 'I can't see why you're such a threat to this demon. You don't even know the most essential tenets of warfare.'

'What tenets?'

'The Art of War: "If you know the enemy and know yourself, you need not fear the result of a hundred battles." You're not a threat to it. The enemy knows all about you. You know nothing about it. You hardly even know about yourself. By all rights you should be dead now. If the enemy even exists, of course.'

I could feel my anger rising. I tried to think of an answer to this unfair accusation.

He looked away, glancing up and down the street. 'Look at the house to the right, focus on the window,' he muttered to me.

'Okay.' I stared at the window just a few yards away.

Out of the corner of my eye, I saw him moving.

'Did you see any movement?' he demanded.

'Yes. You.'

'No. In the bloody window.'

'Oh. No.' I wished I understood what was going on. I felt helpless and exposed, dependent on a powerful man that I hardly knew.

'You can stop staring now.' He reached to the door handle and fiddled with it his body obscuring my view. It opened.

'What did you just do?'

'A little trick. Now let's find out what we can about Sarah or Puck or Miriam or whoever she is.'

'You're not supposed to use that name.'

'Shut up. We need to find her room.'

He entered first and I followed. He held me by the arm in a painful grip. 'Stand there. Touch nothing,' he said as he closed the door behind me. He was fiddling with something

'What?' I could see almost nothing in the half-light of the hallway. I could smell a mixture of perfume and cleaning fluid.

He placed some plastic objects in my hands. 'Put these on,' he instructed me. His hands felt odd and glistened slightly.

I peered at them closely trying to figure out what they were.

'They're gloves and a hair cover,' Sam said. His eyes appeared to be able to see more easily than mine. From the sound of his voice he was becoming even more exasperated with me.

He tucked his hair into a plastic hat. I could see now that he was wearing plastic gloves and that was why his hands glistened. He had come fully prepared as if he knew exactly what to do for breaking and entering.

'So we don't leave too easy a trail. Just in case,' he added.

I carefully tucked my hair into my hat and pulled the gloves on. If anyone came to the door it would be obvious that we were up to no good. This felt so wrong.

My guide in crime walked along the corridor and opened the first door. 'We don't need to look any further,' he muttered, standing and staring.

'How can you be so sure?' I asked.

He remained silent in the doorway.

I looked in around his great bulk and immediately understood even in the semi-dark of the curtained room. On the opposite wall there was a large picture of my head and shoulders. Above it was an equally large picture of a demon. There were numerous smaller pictures on every wall, too small to see properly in the weak light.

'Del was right,' said Sam. 'She must be the one.'

He led me into the room. 'So you do have a real enemy,' he grunted, perhaps regretfully.

I could smell the mustiness of windows closed against the fresh air and curtains closed against the daylight.

I walked around the room, slowly. Puck had gone to a lot of trouble. All of Del's newspaper articles that made fun of me were on the wall behind the door with references to women circled. There were pictures of Doctor Matthews giving lectures and preaching on the wall opposite the door. The wall to the left of the door consisted entirely of pictures of demons with neat notes under each. The largest demon was drawn from a Hollywood fantasy, red muscular body and huge horns. It was labelled Asbeel.

The rest of the place was a mess compared to the catalogued neatness of the walls. There were books and notes everywhere, mostly on weird theology and new age rubbish. Several were on witchcraft including a laughable, glossy book "Encyclopaedia of Spells." Sam sat at a desk against the wall opposite the door, half hidden by a pile of paper and notes. He lifted some documents to uncover a keyboard and mouse, turned on her computer and fiddled with it.

I looked over his shoulder. I couldn't see what he did, but he soon had pictures of demons and angels appearing.

'This is the last thing she was looking at,' he said at last.

He had stopped at an article on the Apocalypse, with the typical fantasy view of the four riders staring out at a destroyed city with barren land all around and a glowering red sky.

'Do you think she's trying to create the Apocalypse?' I asked.

'I don't know. Maybe she's at war with you.' He looked up at me quizzically. 'Unless she thinks that you're the Rider for War.' He laughed.

I ignored his derision. 'I'll have to have a word with her, then,' I answered. 'I may not know much about war, but, I do know all about the Bible, and that's not right. There are four riders, but they aren't like everyone thinks they are.'

'Whatever,' he replied. 'Let's focus on what we're here for. See if you can find a diary or something.

'You won't,' said a voice from behind us.

We both turned in alarm.

It was Del.

'What the …' I started.

'How did you move so quietly?' asked Sam.

'You weren't listening,' she replied. 'Anyway, what are you going to do about that door?' She nodded her head in the direction of the main door. 'You forced the lock.'

'Yeah,' he said. 'Nothing. Most people never notice it for years, happily locking and unlocking it. Never testing after they locked it. Nothing will be missing, so they'll assume they never noticed it.'

'Has this worked before?' asked Del, coming over to us. She gave me a peck on the cheek while smiling haughtily at Sam. 'Hello, Gabriel,' she said.

Sam's smile disappeared. 'She's the one,' he said. 'Do you think she has a diary?' he demanded.

'Don't be silly,' she said. 'It's only in movies that you get a nice convenient diary to prove and explain everything. But I agree she is the one.'

She inspected a picture on the wall above the computer, resting her body against mine. 'Look at this one,' she said. She grabbed my arm.

I forced myself to focus on the picture rather than Del's perfumed presence. I leaned forward to see it clearly. It was of a lecture theatre with a few dozen students and Dr Matthews talking. 'I gave a talk at the University,' I explained.

'Before you were stabbed?' asked Del.

'Yes.' I inspected the picture this time, rather than just focussing on Dr Matthews. I pointed at a picture of a girl with brightly coloured hair. 'That's Sarah, isn't it? Or is her name Miriam?' The superficial differences in her hair and clothes had deceived me in my first quick scan, but now that I had examined the picture carefully, I recognised her.

And I had a new path to follow in my version of Sam's plan.

Del stood away from the wall. 'I think it's rather obvious isn't it?' She smiled first at Sam and then at me. She gestured to the walls and shrugged.

I sighed. There was no escaping the next step. 'Come on Sam. Just like you said. You do your part and I'll do mine.'

I could also add my own variation now that I had seen that picture.

He nodded darkly. 'It should work,' he said.

Del laughed. 'I'll have a great story either way.'

So she knew Sam's plan, too. I hated it when she used me like this. It was just as well that I had seen that picture of Puck.

THE EXORCISM

Mark 16:17
And these signs shall follow them that believe; In my name shall they cast out devils; they shall speak with new tongues;

'Nice curry,' said Puck. 'You reheated it really well,' she added cynically.

It was nice to think that the accused could have a good meal.

Sam grunted. 'It was too strong for me,' he growled.

'You've eaten it all, though,' I said.

'I was hungry,' he mumbled back.

'Why didn't you get Rebecca to cook us something,' asked Puck. 'I thought she liked you now.'

Sam and I exchanged a guilty glance. 'She's at the hospital for an overnight check up,' I lied. Thankfully, she had agreed to leave us alone for the whole night. I didn't want to think about where she really was and what she was doing. It would just make me envious again.

The doorbell rang. I checked my watch. He was right on time.

I nodded to Sam as I went to the door. He followed and stood behind me as I opened it to a short, thin, black man in black clothes and clerical collar.

He wasn't anything like the man I expected. 'Are you Mr Paulette?' I said.

'No,' he replied. 'I am Doctor Choob. Surely you are expecting me?' His African accent was so strong I could barely understand his words.'

'What?' I said.

'It's okay,' said Sam. 'I got him instead. Mr Paulette wasn't right for this job.'

'Who is this man?' I demanded.

'It's okay,' repeated Sam more forcefully. 'I know what I'm doing. You do your part and he'll do his.'

Sam returned to the kitchen leaving me with the cleric at the entrance to the house. This change would upset my plans.

'I believe that Ndoki has visited you many times in dreams,' said the cleric.

'A demon,' I replied, getting very worried. This was not right. 'I don't know anything about this Ndoki.'

We heard a rapidly stifled scream from the kitchen. I ran in to make sure everything was okay. Sam was holding Puck effortlessly from behind, one hand on her mouth and one arm around her elbows. She was struggling terribly but his strength was too great for her. He forced her to sit in a chair, holding her from behind.

'I'm sorry, Sarah,' I said to her. 'It has to be this way. It won't take long. Trust me.'

Tears rolled down her cheeks. She stopped struggling.

The exorcist entered the room behind me.

'Do your stuff,' snapped Sam.

He nodded in reply, and walked up to Puck. He leaned forward and sniffed at her face, then at her chest his nose almost touching her and then finally just a few inches away from her crotch despite her sitting position.

'What are you doing?' I demanded.

'I have detected the stench of Ndoki on her,' he answered. 'She is possessed. The demon must be driven from her.' He stood and withdrew a Bible from his pocket. 'Do you admit that you have the devil inside you?' he demanded of her.

She shook her head.

'She must be able to speak,' I ordered.

Sam scowled. The black man shrugged.

Sam removed his hand from her mouth and adjusted his hold. She tried to wriggle free but Sam's hands moved incredibly quickly to hold her arms to the chair.

Tears rolled down her cheek. 'Why are you doing this?' she appealed to me.

'I'm really sorry,' I said to her. 'It's for the best.'

'I am here to expel this demon,' shouted Doctor Choob. He threw the Bible into Puck's lap. 'I will drive this devil from you.' He slapped her across the face.

'No,' I shouted. 'This is not how you do an exorcism! You cannot beat this creature from her.'

Sam shook his head.

'I know what I am doing,' shouted the cleric.

'No, you don't,' I shouted back. 'A demon is from the non-physical realm. You can't use the physical to control it. You must use the scriptures and faith.'

He raised his hand to strike her once more. I grabbed his arm and held it back. He threw me to the ground effortlessly.

'Sam, are you going to allow this?' I demanded struggling to my feet.

He shook his head, clearly confused.

'We need to tie her up,' bellowed the exorcist. He pointed at me. 'And you, too. We cannot allow you to stop us.'

'Sam, why did you get this man?' His answer was the key to all my plans.

'Because I said so,' said a voice from behind me,

I was the only one who was not surprised to find that Del had let herself in. Right on cue.

'Sam,' I said once again. I had to get his attention despite his confusion. 'Why him?'

Choob grabbed my arm and held it. 'You are the demon,' he shouted at me.

Puck squirmed once and escaped from Sam's grip. She leapt to the cleric and surprising him totally, kneed him once neatly in the groin. 'That's for that slap,' she crowed. She then punched me in the stomach. 'And that's for not trusting me.'

It hurt. I knew that my plan was risky. This was my punishment for being forced to lie to Puck. I deserved this pain.

Sam collapsed to the floor, groaning.

'What's happening?' demanded Del.

'You!' I shouted at the cleric to make sure he heard me. 'You are going. Now. Puck, make sure he leaves.'

Puck glowered at me, clearly not yet finished. The cleric scowled but when Puck approached him he withdrew out to the corridor. She followed him.

I checked Sam to make sure he was helpless. My body was weak with relief. If he wasn't under control then I was in mortal danger.

'What's happening?' repeated Del.

'You'd better sit down while I explain.' I pointed at the kitchen chair and went to the sink. 'Would you like a drink?'

'What?' she said. 'Why can't you explain?' She sat.

I picked up the apron I had ready and threw it around her, tying her quickly to the chair. I grabbed both her arms from the front and held them down, my face close to her breasts.

Puck walked in. 'Have you gone completely mad?' she demanded.

'He has,' screamed Del. 'He's mad. Let me go.'

'No,' I answered. 'I'm right. It's you and Sam isn't it? You're the monk or nun or whatever and he's the demon.'

'You have gone mad, haven't you?' said Puck, eyes wide in wonder and fear.

'Don't be so stupid,' shouted Del.

'There's some string at the side of the sink,' I said to Puck. 'Tie Sam up now. He won't be sick for long.'

'Let me go,' growled Del through clenched teeth. She didn't seem to be struggling as much as I expected.

'What have you done to him?' asked Puck.

'I've just given him a stomach ache. It'll pass in a few minutes. You've got to tie him up. Now.'

'Gabriel, stop this,' shouted Del right into my ear.

Every time I turned my head to look around my ear brushed against Del's breast.

'How can you be sure?' asked Puck.

'It all fits. Del knew all about me all the time. She knew where I was. She set the punks on to me and then made sure that Sam saved me. She's been toying with me. Who else knew all about where I would be? She was always there. Who else could have kept stealing all the evidence?'

'Don't listen to him,' shouted Del. 'He's mad. He hates women. He always has. He's not an angel. He's just a man who can't cope with his own lust.'

Puck picked up the string and hesitantly approached Sam. He groaned once and she retreated.

238

'Hurry up, he's recovering,' I shouted at her.

'Yes, hurry up little Puck,' said Del. 'Do the mad man's dirty work.'

Puck frowned at me. 'How did she know to call me Puck?' she demanded angrily.

'Sam told me,' said Del.

'You were going to have me beaten up by that bastard,' said Puck.

'No. I wanted someone else. Someone gentler. Del admitted that she chose that brutal bastard. She's trying to get at us both.'

Puck nodded, but still glared at me angrily.

'Listen to me, Sarah' called Del. 'I was trying to see how far Gabriel would go. I thought I would have more time before he started becoming brutal. I'm sorry Sarah, but he thinks it's you. I didn't realise how crazy he is.'

'No,' I said appealing to Puck. 'I knew it wasn't you as soon as I saw a picture of you and Sam told me your real name. Miriam. You're a student at the University. I've lectured to you. You have faith. I checked with a colleague. He said I could trust you. That's why I used you to trap them. I'm sorry Puck.'

'You weren't supposed to use that name in front of other people,' shouted Puck.

Why was she angry over that?

Sam groaned and rolled to his knees. 'You bastard,' he spat at me.

'You're too late,' I said to Puck. 'He's going to kill me.'

'No I'm not,' he said. 'But I should. My guts are killing me. Let Del go.'

I stood away from Del. I had no choice.

'Don't you touch me,' I shouted at them all. 'God will protect me. He'll stop you both.' I held my Bible and cross in front of me to protect myself against the demon's evil. I tried to drag my tiara of Gabriel from my pocket but it was caught.

'Doctor Matthews,' said Del quietly. 'You're not well.'

'What?' I said.

'You're not well,' she repeated.

'I'm not Doctor Matthews. I'm not that bastard. I'm Gabriel.' I backed up towards the door. 'I'm an angel.'

'Don't you see?' she said. 'You're still Doctor Matthews. Everything else is just your imagination. There are no angels or demons.'

'But what about everything that's happened? All those coincidences? My ability to read people's souls?'

'All in your imagination,' she answered. 'Perhaps you were a bit sensitive, but you weren't right about me, you know? My dad was a bastard, but mum's still alive. We left him.'

'But all of you. You're all part of my purpose.' She could not be right.

'We're just people that have all come together,' Del said. She sounded so caring. 'Why should you be so special? You have no more purpose than any of us.'

Puck reached out to me, showing real sympathy. I could feel her faith at last and it was enormously powerful.

'But the demon is real. Look.' I pulled up my shirt to show the scar. 'I've been attacked by it.'

'You were attacked by a person. All this has come since then. Don't you see? You keep accusing people of being demons but no one else has seen the demon or even this nun or monk or whoever she is. It's just in your mind.'

'Sam,' I appealed. 'Didn't you say that you'd been guided to protect me? Didn't you see the demon outside the shopping centre?'

'No,' he said and groaned.

'Okay, Sam, you may not be a demon, but do you remember that sandwich that Puck gave you? It was poisoned wasn't it?' I appealed to Puck next. 'At the shopping centre. Del gave it to you, didn't she?'

Puck nodded.

'It was poisoned,' said Del. 'It was in the cheese.'

'See. She admits it at last,' I shouted.

'Haven't you heard?' said Del. 'There's a load of cheese contaminated by salmonella. There's a big scandal about it. It wasn't my fault. Thousands of people are getting sick.'

Puck wandered out of the room, an oddly thoughtful expression on her face. She was the only person who I could persuade and she had now left me alone with these two maniacs.

'Very well,' I said. 'It's not you, Del. But what about these tiaras you gave us.' I finally dragged it out of my pocket. 'Didn't someone mysterious give them to you? That must have been a part of my religious purpose.'

'No. I bought them,' she said. 'I bought some Alice Bands and those awful cheap statuettes and glued them together. I made them into tiaras.'

'Why would you lie?'

'I wanted to see how stupid you would look. You've always been such a bastard about women. I wanted to see you ridiculed.' She frowned and looked at the ground. 'I'm not very proud of it, now. You couldn't help yourself.'

'Why would you do that?' I begged.

'You were supposed to appear in the papers. I had a complete exposé on you. Pictures. How crazy you are. How much you hate women.'

'But,' I said. I turned to each of them.

'It's okay,' she said. 'It didn't get printed because of this salmonella scare. It was a better story.' She turned to Sam. 'We'd better take him to get some help.'

'No!' I shouted. I was ready for this. I knew they would lie. I opened the door, dived outside and locked it from outside before Sam could catch me. I ran out into the moonless night. The demon would follow me. I prayed desperately for holy protection.

The Death of Gabriel

2 Samuel 22:6

The sorrows of hell compassed me about; the snares of death prevented me.

I could only run for a few yards before I lost my breath. I could hear Sam banging against the door and bellowing. I had to run and hide.

I half jogged and walked to the church where it all started. It was closed. There was no sign of anyone. Of course, the minister, Peter, was out with Rebecca. I had encouraged it. There was no sanctuary here.

By now Sam would have broken the door down and he would be following me. I might not be able to get away another time. I had to hide. I ran to the lane next to the church and stumbled a few feet down it when I heard a noise behind me.

My heart paused between beats.

My breath stopped.

I knew what it was.

It was behind me.

I smelt its sulphurous breath. I could feel the heat of its body.

I turned to look into the eyes of the beautiful demon which had come to take my soul to Hell for all that I had done wrong. I didn't need God's judgement to know what I deserved. This demon's lesser judgement was enough. I had hurt people, both as Gideon Matthews and as Gabriel.

The demon reaches out an arm and holds Gabriel.

I tried to turn from its grip. I shouted at it.

The demon laughs.

I could hear its laughter. 'No!' I shouted at it. 'You can't take me. You don't have the right! Leave me alone.'

My heart thudded rapidly. I could hear my breath rasping. I could feel the heat of its touch. I couldn't remember a single Bible quote even though I knew it was my only hope.

The demon smiles and opens its mouth. Its tongue comes out and wraps around Gabriel, pinning his arms and drawing him in.

I fought. I hit and thrashed and punched and kicked and screamed and twisted and shook.

The mouth opens wide. Wider. So wide that it can consume an entire man.

I was terrified as my head entered into its mouth. The sulphurous stench snatched my breath away.

The head is forced into the mouth followed by the shoulders, the torso, the arms, the legs, the feet. Finally, even the soul of Gabriel is consumed.

I gave in. I stopped. I couldn't fight any more. I had to die now. I had done so many things wrong. It was my punishment.

And now I was going to Hell.

It consumes Gabriel the filthy mucous surrounds him and burns his skin and his soul as he passes through its body. Eventually, Gabriel is defecated onto the ground covered in excrement and filth.

Gabriel is dead.

The demon laughs and dances on his body. It is victorious and Gabriel is driven into the ground.

It was all over. I didn't move.

Love engulfed me.

Pure spiritual love surrounded me.

I lay bathed in a greater joy than I had ever felt before. I could experience this love for all time without getting bored or restless. I knew without a doubt that I was in God's presence.

I did not need time or space anymore. They were distractions. Illusions. Only this love of God existed. I had no need for logic.

I was in heaven once more.

ENVY

Proverbs 27:4
   Wrath is cruel, and anger is outrageous; but who is able to stand before envy?

'Those other girls have mothers,' she said as Papa escorted her from the school. 'Why don't I?'

She was angry for he would not let her talk to the other girls after school, but she was very careful not to show even the smallest sign of it.

His arm shook as he held her arm so tightly that she could feel the blood flow stop. She recognised the signs. She had sinned. He was going to punish her and so save her from her eternal damnation. But which sin was it? He couldn't see her anger. What could he see?

As they walked, she felt elation and fear. Over the years she had come to appreciate the importance of pain. She reviewed each of the seven deadly sins all the way home. By a process of elimination she decided it had to be envy. She was envious of girls who had mothers when she had none.

She looked into his tight-lipped face as they entered the hallway. He was angry. No he was wrathful. He was showing a deadly sin! And she had caused it. So she was sending her father to Hell, now. This was worse than a beating. She was the cause of another person's downfall. Someone she loved. What was she to do? She couldn't punish him.

The beating was terrible. It left bruises on her arms and legs. Thankfully it was winter and she could hide them under many layers of clothes. She had learnt to hide everything ever since that woman had threatened to take Papa away. No one seemed to understand the importance of a soul, not even the authorities.

She would never talk about Mama in front of Papa again.

That terrible man had escaped her every trap. And it was her own uncertainty that stopped her. There could only be one reason for that. It was God's will. God wanted him to survive. But why? He was disgusting – one minute hating women, preventing them from serving God and the next a lustful sinner. He must have committed every single one of the seven deadly sins in the last few months. And he was about to gain power. He was going to spread his sin and send many, many people to eternal damnation.

She saw it then. Of course. That was why he still survived. He did have a purpose and that was to die but not yet. She had been looking too small. Just one or two men. It was the time of the Apocalypse. This was God's will and why he had been saved so that he could be the means to bring on Christ's realm when evil would be expelled and the new world would begin.

But first there would be a lot of suffering and one third of the world's population would die.

THE HORSEMEN

Revelations 6:2
And I saw, and behold a white horse; and he that sat on him had a bow; and a crown was given unto him; and he went forth conquering, and to conquer.

In the void the Observer has no purpose for there is nothing to see. A soft seed of light within the enveloping love appears and grows into a beautiful sexless angel. Not a demon and not Asbeel, a new angel.

Are you the angel Gabriel?

The angel does not respond, as if indicating that such questions are irrelevant. It turns and the Observer, Gabriel who was Gideon, follows its gaze to see...

The demon Asbeel is sitting on a white horse, holding a bow and wearing a crown, standing on a hill overseeing a huge army with deadly weapons prepared and ready to destroy.

The vision moves rapidly to the sea. This time Asbeel and the white horse are on the deck of a massive warship armed and dangerous.

And now the vision is in the air amongst shock waves of planes that disappear before Gabriel has registered the impact of their arrival. Once again, the white rider is present, hovering in the air.

The angel now leads Gabriel to the massive bedroom of an important man, a world leader. Horse and demon are present yet again. Gabriel feels he must speak. He appeals to the angel who nods once.

Demon Asbeel, I don't believe that you really are the first horseman.

Asbeel looks at Gabriel and snarls silently.

I scare you, now, don't I? This angel has power over you and now so do I.

The angel casts a spell of light and love over the demon. It darkens and weakens.

Gabriel is confused. What are you up to? What are you doing?

The angel speaks.

'Let no man deceive you by any means: for that day shall not come, except there come a falling away first, and that man of sin be revealed, the son of perdition.'

'2 Thessalonians 2:3. So I have been deceived. We are equal now, Asbeel. And I feel no fear.'

Asbeel screams silently in rage.

The angel's spell allows Gabriel to enter the Sleeper's dream. The Sleeper stands at the front of the massed armies of Land, Sea and Air facing the threat of evil that comes from all sides. Asbeel and the white horse stand in front. The demon instructs the Sleeper, demonstrating how to make the world a safer and more religious place through war and conquest. The Sleeper understands.

Revelations 6:4

And there went out another horse that was red: and power was given to him that sat thereon to take peace

*from the earth, and that they should kill one another:
and there was given unto him a great sword.*

Gabriel is once again with the Angel, but this time in
the East. Asbeel is now on a red horse, holding a sword aloft.
The blood from the sword drips down onto the demon's arm
where it spreads rapidly to turn its whole body red.

Once again the angel's spell weakens the enemy and
reveals the truth. Before them there is a rough bed. It's
occupant is dirty and thin and holding a huge gun in his
sleep.

Gabriel enters his dream. The occupant of the bed is a
leader of violent and fearful men. Asbeel is advising them to
defend themselves against the coming onslaught of mighty
technology with the blood of martyrs. War and bloodshed
will continue for many years and spread to every part of the
world. Isolation and innocence are no longer protection
from this world encompassing evil.

Revelations 6:5-6
*And I beheld, and lo a black horse; and he that sat
on him had a pair of balances in his hand.*

*And I heard a voice in the midst of the four beasts
say, A measure of wheat for a penny, and three measures
of barley for a penny; and see thou hurt not the oil and
the wine.*

In another abrupt change, Gabriel is led to great barren
fields of crops, dry and black, overseen by a black horseman
holding balance scales. Poor people are begging for food
whilst far away the rich are fat even though they discard vast
quantities of wine and oil.

This time the disguised nun appears, the woman
of Gabriel's nightmares. She is in a huge food factory,

contaminating a vast vat of cheese with the contents of a small vial. She is creating a balance between rich and poor by making the wealthy hungry despite having food.

Revelations 6:8

And I looked, and behold a pale horse: and his name that sat on him was Death, and Hell followed with him. And power was given unto them over the fourth part of the earth, to kill with sword, and with hunger, and with death, and with the beasts of the earth.

The context switches once more and the demon is now on a horse with a pale green tinge to it. Again it snarls at the beautiful angel.

The nun, Asbeel's hooded servant is working at a laboratory bench, creating a lethal plague to affect the last quarter of the earth's inhabitants.

The angel gestures to Gabriel.

It is time to act.

THE PURPOSE OF AN ANGEL

In their short time in this world, bound as they are by physical reality, humans have choices and options to create or destroy but at the end of their time, the choices have been made, the consequences have occurred and no changes can be made to the past.

The Peace of Death

John 14:27

Peace I leave with you, my peace I give unto you: not as the world giveth, give I unto you. Let not your heart be troubled, neither let it be afraid.

'Gabriel.'

I ignored the voice. I was at peace.

'Gabriel.'

The voice was soft but insistent.

'Gabriel.'

I felt someone touch my arm.

'Gabriel.'

I opened my eyes.

It was Joe Kayer.

I was on the ground. In the early dawn light I could see a bush above me.

'Come on, Gabriel,' he said gently and with warmth. 'Time to get up.' He smiled. 'We've got work to do. We've got a purpose.'

I could still feel the comfort of heavenly love.

'Gabriel,' he repeated yet again.

I sat up.

'Come on,' he said, softly. He offered his arm in encouragement.

I reached up to him.

He held my hand.

I searched for signs of any supernatural beings. There were none. I hoped that I was now past all that sort of thing. I didn't want to be insane anymore.

I rolled to the side and kneeled.

After a pause I stood.

'I guess it was me that saved you this time,' he said.

I smiled. 'Yes. Thank you.' I was in the lane near the church. I stared at the ground. There was no sign of demonic excrement. No sign of blood. Even the bushes seemed unruffled and ordinary. No evidence of the violence of last night.

I no longer felt the fear of the last few months. I had been eaten by a demon. What could happen that was worse than that? I also seemed to have lost the obsessions of my body, for the moment at least. I was calmer and in control.

'You brought me back from the dead, you know,' he said. 'On the steps of the police station.' He grasped my arm so that he could share his comfort with me.

'What?'

'When I was dying I felt something spiritual when you held my hand. Perhaps that's why I stayed when you called to me.'

'So I'm not mad, then.'

'Maybe. Who knows? Maybe I'm mad. I know what I felt, though.'

'They said I'm not an angel,' I said.

'I know.' He smiled and gave me a hug. 'They don't understand. They don't know what an angel is. Anyone can be an angel. You just have to show God's love to another person and you're an angel.'

I laughed gently. 'How do you know so much?'

'I've talked to lots of people since you brought me back. I've been thinking a lot.'

'Does anyone believe me when I talk about Heaven? About what it's like.'

'Yes. Some. But there are a lot of people that won't believe it until they experience it, too.'

'Yes.'

'What have you felt?' he asked.

'God's love.'

'Yes.' He held my arm and looked into my face. 'Did it feel real?'

'Very.'

'Other people will say that it was a trick of your mind; like my near death experience of Heaven. And there are some sceptics who reject all explanations unless they too can have the same experience and measure it using instruments.' His caring smile almost overwhelmed me.

'So it's real? I'm not just deluded?' Hope appeared in my heart.

'You mean Heaven?' he said.

I nodded.

'Either trust your experience now or doubt everything.'

He was right. All I could do was accept what I had felt. After all, I believed what my eyes saw and my ears heard every day. My experiences of last night were more unusual, that's all.

He still held my arm. He leaned forward so that all I could see was his face. 'And your purpose? Do you feel it still?'

I shook my head. I had attached too much of my survival, my body's needs and my ego to having a purpose. I was no different from anyone else. I had to create my purpose for myself. It would probably be far more ordinary than starting yet another religion.

But I had another problem. 'Am I Gabriel or Gideon?' I asked.

'They're only earthly names. You are whoever you are.'

'So am I the same person as Gideon?'

'Well, there is the continuity of your body.'

'And that requires time,' I said, starting to understand. 'And it means that I am Gideon.'

He frowned. 'Maybe. But perhaps you also changed into Gabriel. You can be one person at one time and another later. Names are only labels, despite what we think and feel. You seem to be much calmer now, so that might make you someone else other than Gideon. Someone other than Gabriel, too.'

'I want to be someone else. Why should it matter?'

'Your ego, perhaps?'

I nodded. This made sense, too. 'Yes.' I felt a need to preach. 'Do you understand? In Heaven there is no time and space. Only eternal love.'

Joe watched me carefully as if listening to every word.

It was my turn to explain. 'Without time and space and within God's love there can be no way of following that continuity that we talk about now. Every sentence must have a verb and every verb is based in time and God created time and space.' I laughed at my own inconsistency. 'I just said that God created time and space, but the verb "created" requires time so I've made another mistake.'

I was talking to myself now. Joe was just an innocent bystander, silent, waiting patiently for me to finish.

'I can't explain it in words,' I said. 'It's worse than that. My brain uses time to think, reason requires an "if" and a "then" and a "therefore" all of which require time.'

He took my arm and led me somewhere. I didn't care where.

I rambled on. 'When it comes to Heaven and God and everything beyond this physical world we can't use our brains, only our hearts and our souls. There's nothing physical. Nothing to think about logically. Only love to experience.'

We were still walking.

'I know,' he replied. 'I felt it, too. Even though I can't see it or explain it or anything.'

'Yes!' I said. 'There is something more to us and to this universe. It's not just illusions of our bodies or our minds. We *are* souls within God's love. It is only while we are here that this physical world distracts us while our egos demand that we must survive in an ever-changing world. A soul and an ego are different.'

Joe nodded indulgently. 'Perhaps.' He must have seen that I was crestfallen at his lack of understanding. 'Yes,' he added quickly.

Why did I need this constant re-assurance? 'It sounds a bit egotistical,' I added. 'I must make sure that I put others first if I want to avoid all that sinning again. I wouldn't want to commit the sin of pride, now.' This time I hugged Joe. 'Watch out for me, won't you?'

He smiled at me. 'If I can. Let's go find the others.'

I finally remembered my dream. 'I've got to stop the Apocalypse. The end of the world. We've got to do something.' I grabbed his hand and pulled him along. 'Hurry it might be too late. Where are Sam and Del and Sarah?'

'They're waiting for you at your house,' he said, stumbling as I dragged him forward.

'Are they still mad at me?'

'No. They're very worried. They were looking for you. We were going to ring the police this morning.' He saw the panic in my face. 'It's okay. I've already rung them on my mobile. Eventually, I guessed that you'd be here, where it all started. I've looked here before but I couldn't find you in the dark hiding under that hedge.'

We were walking so fast that I was puffing.

We marched on in silence. Despite being breathless, I was at peace. I could feel love all around me even if I was in a hurry.

Dreams

Genesis 37:6

And he said unto them, Hear, I pray you, this dream which I have dreamed:

Joe and I finally arrived at my house, foot sore and exhausted.

Sam and Del were in the hallway as I opened the door.

'Thank God you're all right,' said Del. A tear appeared on her cheek and she ran to hug me. 'I thought you might be dead.'

I smiled at her. 'I was. The demon killed me.'

Her eyes widened in alarm.

Sam pushed past her, hands reaching to me, ready to stop me before I could hurt Del.

'It's okay,' I said holding up my arms to fend him off. 'I know it's not real.'

He lowered his arms but I could see that he still didn't trust me.

'The demon was inside my mind all along,' I said. 'I think it was my way of holding all the horrible things about me that I didn't want to acknowledge. The things Doctor

Matthews believed about women and suffering. The sinful and selfish things I did to everyone, especially Bethany.' I looked into their faces in turn. 'And you three. I was arrogant and manipulative and uncaring. I used my insights to control you rather than heal. And despite all this you've put your lives on the line for me. I'm sorry.' I wanted to say more, at the very least apologise for ignoring their needs, only seeing them as my servants, but I didn't. I had to hope that they had forgiven me already for there was nothing I could say to change the past.

Del peered closely at my face. Perhaps trying to assess me for signs of violence.

Sam scowled and shrugged as always. He continued to watch me closely.

'Let's go inside,' suggested Joe.

Sam stood to the side in the narrow corridor so that first Joe and then I had to push past him to follow Del into the living room.

As I entered the room, Puck ran up and hugged me. I was surprised at the power of her fierce grip.

'I was so scared,' she said in her smallest little girl voice. She stood back and inspected me. 'You look a mess. Did you sleep in a hedge or something?'

'Yes.'

She did a classic double take.

'And I have a dream to tell you,' I added.

I collapsed onto the sofa. Del and Sam shared the other end of the sofa, Sam on the arm. Del rested her hand on Sam's leg. I was aware of a twinge of jealousy at this tiny sign of closeness but I was now aware of my body and its needs so, armed with my newfound calm love for everyone, I easily controlled the inappropriate feeling. Joe sat in my favourite armchair. Puck sat by my side on the arm rest, only letting go of my arm for a second when she had a sneezing fit. I could not understand how she could be so worried about me after the way that I had treated her.

I laughed. 'I thought I should have the cold, not you. After all, I slept in the hedge.'

She shrugged.

They were waiting expectantly. It was time to explain. 'What do you know of The Apocalypse?' I asked the group.

'Four horsemen, isn't it?' said Del.

'And more,' I said. 'Seven seals, the end of the world, Jesus appears, God's kingdom returns but only after the most appalling things have happened.'

'War, famine, pestilence and death. Nearly everyone dies,' said Puck. She stared blindly at a wall. 'A quarter of the population for each horse?' She was hesitant.

'Think about what the Bible actually says, though,' I suggested, 'not just the Hollywood fantasies.'

'I don't know it that well,' she replied.

It was time for me to lecture again. 'There are many explanations, but the best interpretation is of conquest, war, famine – that's shown by a high price for food – and plague. The last horse rider has a greenish tinge.'

'Green?' said Puck. 'I thought it was pale. The riders are white, red, black and pale.'

'I thought you didn't know it that well,' I said.

Puck poked her tongue out at me. I had patronised her again.

'Anyway,' I continued, 'the original Greek version translates as sickly green, not pale. That's why it's translated into plague.'

She nodded and shrugged at the same time.

'What's that got to do with us?' asked Del.

'The most important part,' I said, 'is that no one will know that the end of the world is coming for, as the Bible

263

says, it "comes like a thief in the night". When no one expects it. But I have had a dream. I have been told that this nun is trying to make it happen.'

'What the end of the world?' asked Del.

'Yes. According to my dream three of the major events are already happening to the world. There's the aggression and power of the USA - that's conquest. The second part is the response of the terrorists and the war on terror. The third part was about the injustices of poverty and starvation in Africa. That just leaves the plague.'

'And people calling out for justice,' said Puck. 'That's the thing about the Apocalypse. It's mostly about the bad guys who are hurting the good guys getting beaten up by the angels, especially the Angel of Death.' She stared at me, aghast. 'You're not the Angel of Death are you?'

'No,' I said, shaking my head and smiling. 'And I'm not the demon,' I added before she could ask. 'I don't think I have to stop the Apocalypse. I think I only have to stop this woman.'

'What makes you think that?' asked Del.

'The dream was much more local. This woman dressed as a monk was in it and she was poisoning a big vat of cheese. As if she was trying to create hunger here.'

'You mean like all the cheese with salmonella,' said Del.

We all stared at her.

'What?' I said.

'It was in the news,' she replied. 'Remember we talked about it. There's been this big fuss. Someone added Salmonella to a big pot of cheese and it's affected lots of people. But not that many. Only ten or so. It's not like it was famine.'

Puck squeezed my arm, very hard. 'Which food company was it?'

'Manna Cheeses,' said Del.

'Cheese is important to you, isn't it Gabriel,' said Puck.

I nodded. 'I like it but I can't have it.'

She stared at me intensely. 'Is there any more of this dream?' she asked me in a strangely quiet voice.

'This woman was bringing on the Apocalypse' I said. 'She was creating a plague. Somehow she believed it was only going to affect one quarter of the world's population.'

'I know who she is,' said Puck. 'She's my housemate, Bella. She's a biochemist at Manna Cheeses.' She held my arm. 'I'm sorry I doubted you Gabriel.'

'How can you be so sure?' I asked.

'You'll never forgive me.'

'Why? What have you done?'

'I talked to her all the time. I told her all about you. From the start. I told her what a bastard you were.' A tear formed in her eye. 'You gave a lecture about women in the church.' She shook her head in unconscious denial. 'We both hated you for the way you used the Bible and everything. We planned for me to set you up. When I met you at the hotel. She rang me to say you were there. I thought it was just a bit of fun.'

'How did she know?' I said. 'Why would she do that?'

Puck bowed her head to so I couldn't look into her eye. 'She's a real strong feminist. She hates men and she's also very religious. She gets really worked up about things.'

'Sounds like a psychopath to me,' said Del.

'She must have been following you,' said Sam. 'She must have seen you at the hotel.'

Puck's expression declared her guilt. 'But I never thought that she was dangerous. I thought it was a laugh, when I had you standing around in your underpants. I took your wallet to prove that it was you that had chatted me up. She set up the next bit. She got me to ring Del to photograph you. To get you in the paper. I even told her about the shopping centre.'

Sam stood up and walked closer to Puck. 'So, you're telling me that you were playing games with Gabriel's life by talking to this insane woman about everything he was doing?'

Tears were rolling down her cheeks. She withdrew partially behind me, seeking protection from his anger.

'Why didn't you tell us before?' Sam bellowed.

'She's not to blame,' I said calmly. 'I used you all, and Dr Matthews was a terrible man. He deserved it just as much as I did.'

'Yes, but it explains a lot,' said Del.

Without warning Sam grabbed Puck's arm. 'Which is your room?' he shouted at her.

'What?' she screamed, holding me so tight with her other hand that I could feel the blood stop flowing.

'Let her go, Sam, you're scaring her,' said Del.

He released her but he stayed where he was.

I held her arm gently and leaned forward so that she could look into my eyes. 'In your house. Which is your room?'

'At the back of the house,' she said. She looked at each of us in confusion.

'Is Bella's room at the front?' I asked.

Puck nodded. 'Yes, how did you know?'

'What about the plague?' Sam barked at me.

'What?'

'In your dream. How was the plague spread?'

'I don't know,' I said. 'She was at a laboratory bench.'

'And she's a biochemist,' asked Sam. 'So she'd know what to do.'

Puck sobbed once. 'What have I done?'

'It's not your fault,' I said comforting her with my hand on her arm. 'It's because of my purpose. As long as she was attacking me, she wasn't killing people.'

'Except with the cheese,' said Joe. 'Salmonella kills too. Now she's having a go at everyone.'

'We have to go to the police,' said Del.

'They won't believe us,' I replied. 'They already think I'm mad. We only have my dreams.'

'But she's killing people,' said Del. 'Like Joe said, salmonella kills.'

I thought about it. 'We could tell them that she did the salmonella, but what else is she planning?'

'To kill a quarter of the world's population through plague,' muttered Sam, shaking his head.

'Oh God, no,' said Puck, squeezing her whole body against me. 'She's gone to a conference somewhere. She said something to me about being sorry, but God might protect me if I deserved it.'

'What do you mean?' I asked.

'She was really apologetic,' said Puck, almost babbling in her anxiety to say it all. 'She said something like it had to be done now before she was stopped. She got really upset and started to get into a real hurry. She said her room had been burgled but nothing was missing and we couldn't see anything, except that the lock was broken.' She buried her head in my shoulder and sobbed. 'I didn't even think about it.'

Sam stamped his feet in frustrated activity. 'We've got to do something. Now.'

'I'll ring the police.' said Del.'

'No,' answered Sam. 'If we tell them about the Salmonella they'll take all the evidence and go through it so slowly that it'll be too late.'

'Then it's our job to stop her,' said Joe.

'Let's go,' said Sam.

'Where?' asked Puck.

He stood by the open door. 'Your house, of course.'

THE SORCERESS

Exodus 22:18
Thou shalt not suffer a witch to live.

Puck used her key to open the front door. Sam pushed her aside and strode into the corridor to Bella's room.

'It'll be locked,' called Puck.

He opened the door without effort.

'That's odd,' said Puck.

We followed Sam into the room. I felt guilty about our lies, but Puck didn't seem to notice. At least this time we had been allowed in legally.

'What are we looking for?' asked Del.

'A diary,' suggested Puck. 'She takes it with her everywhere.'

'Then she'll still have it with her, won't she?' said Del sarcastically.

'Oh,' said Puck in a little voice.

'Why does everyone expect to find a convenient diary?' muttered Del yet again. 'This isn't the movies where it's all laid out and easy to see.'

'Does she have a lab book?' asked Joe.

'What's that?' said Puck.

'I know,' said Del. 'Every time I've ever interviewed a scientist or anyone like that they always have a lab book. They write everything in it.'

Joe nodded in agreement and started to sort through the piles of books.

'Won't she have that with her, too?' said Del.

'Maybe we can find an old one?' suggested Sam.

'You lot look for a lab book. I've got another idea,' said Joe. He went to her computer.

We searched the room. No explanations or instructions were required. Each of us established a territory and started looking. Sam picked up a chair and looked underneath it, so we all followed his lead and turned over the nearest item of furniture. Puck crawled under her bed but soon came out sneezing. Del and Sam sneezed in response.

I could see the dust floating in the air. I sneezed, too.

'Anything?' I asked.

'Nup,' said Joe.

Del shook her head.

'She is so neat,' said Puck. 'She even lines her drawers with cardboard.'

Sam strode to her in two steps, snatched the drawer from her and upended it. Puck retreated in fear at this sudden aggressive act.

The big man pulled out the cardboard and a hard cover notebook fell out.

Puck was jubilant, punching a fist into the air as she jumped. 'Yes,' she shouted.

He flicked open the pages and read as fast as he could. We all stared, waiting for the verdict.

'Well,' said Del, 'what's she going to do? How's she going to do it?'

Sam shook his head. 'I dunno. It's all rubbish.'

'Let me see it,' demanded Del.

Puck was nearest, so she grabbed it before Del reached her.

'Don't tear it,' I warned.

Del looked over Puck's shoulder.

'I can understand some of this,' said Puck. 'Some of it's in Greek. It's full of biblical quotes and diagrams, too. Demons and angels. Maybe they're instructing her.' She flicked back and forward through the pages. 'I don't understand the biochemistry, though. Anyone know what "adenovirus" means?'

No one answered.

'Here's something,' said Del. 'Look it says "Chinese lactose intolerant" there. It's got a web site. Show it to Joe.'

Puck showed and Joe typed.

'Something here about 'flu,' added Puck.

'An adenovirus is a vector for inserting genes,' said Joe. He pointed at the computer screen.

Sam and I waited.

'I think I know what she's planning,' called Joe after some more typing.

'What?' I asked. I was just a passenger. They were doing all the work.

'It's only a guess,' Joe added, 'but I think it's all got to do with cheese. Remember she poisoned the cheese with Salmonella. That web site explained that the Chinese have a genetic intolerance for lactose and that's why they can't eat cheese. I also looked at the last document that she opened and guess what I found?'

'What?' demanded Del.

'There's a conference being held in Devon tomorrow. It's on marketing cheese in China. It's trying to find ways to overcome the intolerance problems. I'll print it off,' said Joe.

'So?' said Puck.

'Don't you see?' said Sam.

'No. What?' I asked. This was too confusing.

Sam walked to the door as if ready to leave. 'She's creating a virus that attacks anyone with a genetic tendency for lactose intolerance, so it will affect the Chinese. That's a quarter of the world's population.'

'So, is this what triggers The Apocalypse?' I said. 'A conference?'

'It would be more apocalyptic if there were world leaders there,' said Del, as always with an eye on the news story.

'That's the thing about bio warfare,' said the military man. 'You don't want the enemy to find out about it until it's too late. Important people have security people everywhere and it would probably be exposed too early. Ideally you want a few innocent people to travel a long way and infect a lot of people before it's discovered.'

'Ah, I understand,' said Del. 'I'll bet there's only a handful of people going to this conference. Maybe half a dozen from all parts of the world. Bella can do whatever she wants.'

'It really is time for the police,' said Del.

'No,' said Sam.

'What?' she answered. 'You can't be serious? We can't handle this.'

'No, there're some other people I know,' he replied. 'Experts on plague and stuff. They're kind of a part of the emergency services. I'll contact them. I'll give them the book. They'll know what to do.'

'How do you know about all this?' asked Del.

He grinned back. 'I used to be a soldier. In the SAS. I had a special briefing once.'

Joe laughed.

'What's the matter,' I asked.

'The conference. It was already on the printer. She had already printed it. I never thought to look there until now.'

Something was wrong. The explanation wasn't right and yet I felt a strong tug from my purpose. This was important and it was urgent. It was time to act but still something was wrong.

'Joe, could you drive us all down to Devon?' I asked. 'To this conference?'

'All of us?' said Puck. 'Won't that be dangerous?'

Del smiled. 'Think of the story.'

'I was going anyway,' said Joe. 'I can't miss this. You'll all have to put up with my camera equipment. Sam?'

'Yeah,' he replied. He took the lab book from Puck. 'I'll need that. We need to make a detour to London first.' He picked up his mobile phone.

'Make it quick,' I shouted. 'We need to go now. It may be too late already.'

ARMAGEDDON

Revelations 16:16
And he gathered them together into a place called in the Hebrew tongue Armageddon.

The road wound into a small valley surrounded by trees. At the end of a narrow, isolated lane there was a two-story, boxy building. The overdue sun was rising over a hill behind us. We stopped in a small parking space next to the house.

'It looks like it was built in World War Two,' said Sam.

'It looks like it was bombed then, too,' echoed Del.

The rotting window frames were one of several signs of severe dilapidation.

As each of us climbed from Joe's car we stretched our limbs. It had been a long all night drive from London and Joe wasn't exaggerating when he said we would have to put up with his camera equipment. Even though it was a large multipurpose vehicle we had travelled with tripods on our shoulders and boxes on our laps.

There was no sign of human presence, not even any farm animals, just wild birds and insects.

'Where *is* everyone?' I asked. 'Where's the conference? Where're the people you contacted, Sam?'

'Dunno,' Sam replied. He stared at his mobile phone.

'Maybe the police have come and gone and taken everyone away?' suggested Del.

'Have a look at this place,' said Joe. 'There's no conference here. There never was.'

'Yeah,' said Sam. 'Are you sure it's the right house?'

Joe waved a sheet of paper. 'On the conference leaflet it says Megiddo Hill,' he said. 'What do you think?'

I stared at Joe. 'Megiddo Hill? There's something important about that name. It reminds me of something,' I said.

Sam inspected the map, shrugged and looked at the surroundings. 'I'll ring my contact,' said Sam.

I felt very uncomfortable. 'There's something wrong,' I said. 'If God really wanted to stop The Apocalypse there should be police and authorities here already.' Unless God wants it to happen, I added silently to myself.

We waited in silence while Sam walked back up the hill to get a better signal. He started talking in the phone. He paced back and forth and I heard a shouted expletive. I had never seen him so angry.

The name Megiddo kept annoying me. It was ancient and biblical. It was coming to me, now. The Old Testament, a place of battles. A Hebrew place straight from the most ancient parts of the Bible. Battles. Of course. Armageddon.

'Joe, how did you get that map to here?' I asked, knowing the answer but needing confirmation.

'It was on Bella's computer,' he replied. 'It was the last document she had looked at. And it was on the printer,' he added after a few seconds.

'So we were supposed to find it. It's a trap, isn't it?' I said.

Joe nodded, unsurprised. 'I guess I realised that as soon as I saw this place.' He shook his head in despair. 'We were so gung ho.'

Sam came into shouting range. 'They're not coming,' he called. He rammed his mobile phone into his back pocket.

'Why?' demanded Del.

'Apparently, there's no danger. She doesn't know enough to create a plague. Her notes are mostly rubbish. She'd need a huge lab to do anything dangerous and it definitely wouldn't be a virus that affected cheese haters. The worst she might give us is the 'flu, but anyone could. My friend was laughing at me,' he shouted angrily. 'He thought I was taking the piss with that notebook. He thought I was hoaxing him and when I said that I believed it...' He shrugged roughly. 'I still want to look around,' he added.

He couldn't accept that he had been made to look such a fool.

We walked towards the building. Joe carried his video camera, recording our story.

'I did think it sounded a bit odd,' said Del. 'You know, changing all the Chinese.'

'It happens easily,' said Joe. 'We all get excited and we rush around without thinking. She created that conference leaflet just for us and left it on her printer. I'll bet this place isn't even called Megiddo Hill.'

So we've entered a trap at Armageddon, I thought to myself. *This is where it's all resolved.*

Sam shrugged. 'At least someone else knows where we are.'

'What do you mean?' asked Puck.

'He means that we don't know what Bella and her followers are capable of,' said Del. 'She may have lured us here to kill us all and not just Gabriel. She's obviously living in a fantasy world.'

Puck laughed. 'Really?' she said sarcastically.

'Or maybe she just hates Gabriel this much,' said Joe.

'Don't we all,' said Del. 'After all, look at the way he treats us.'

Joe and Puck laughed and I looked at the ground in shame.

Sam grunted and the laughter stopped. He stared at the house, eyes narrow as he looked around. 'Let's see what we can find out, first,' he said.

'We'll be okay, won't we?' said Del. She was hesitant for once.

My death was very close, now. I could feel it. Hours or minutes, I wasn't sure. I had to walk into Bella's trap and die at her hands. I decided not to say anything. It would only frighten the others even more and I should be able to save them if not myself.

'We'll be all right. God has sent us to stop the Apocalypse,' said Joe, half joking.

'It sounds so pretentious,' said Del. She adopted a deep voice imitating a news announcer – or a movie preview. 'The only ones that can stop the end of civilisation as we know it are these few people.'

'Yes,' shouted Puck, too loudly. 'We're the ones to stop the end of the world.' She raised her hand to her forehead in that theatrical gesture of hers. 'We're such heroes,' she muttered bitterly to herself in contrast to her theatrical gesture. She walked out of sight around the side of the building.

I breathed out a sigh. 'That's what makes me think this is so wrong. Heroes are about big egos. That's not God's way. I'd be happy just to see Bella and talk to her.'

'Come on everyone,' called Puck from around the corner.

We all followed the sound of her voice. At the back of the house there was a path leading from a door to steps that descended into the impenetrable dark of a forest. A mixture of colourful plants and long grass grew free and wild between the house and the trees.

Puck was impatiently pointing to the open door.

I stood midway between the forest and the house. I felt exposed and observed but I didn't want to get any closer to the house.

Puck stepped inside. 'It's disgusting in here. All damp and smelly. What should we do?'

Sam and Joe inspected the entranceway. Del wandered towards them. I could feel something threatening in the forest. I turned to face it.

It was the demon.

It was huge with claws, tusks and red skin – like in Hollywood movies.

My death was imminent.

'Look...' I started to say.

Crack!

A pot plant near my right leg exploded.

'Down,' shouted Sam.

I stared at the demon. It pointed at me and drew a line across its throat.

Crack!

A pot to my left shattered.

'Get inside,' ordered Sam. 'Gabriel!'

The demon bared its enormous teeth.

I was dragged toward the house.

Crack!

A plant near the doorway was destroyed.

'Keep down,' shouted Sam.

Joe dragged me inside and slammed the door.

'Did anyone see the gunman?' asked Sam.

'I saw the demon,' I said. 'In the forest.'

We were in the hallway. It stank of damp and mildew. Sam was next to an open doorway on the left. I could feel water trickling down my face. I wiped it out of my eyes.

'Can you show me where?' said Sam. 'From in there?' He gestured to the room.

I nodded and stepped forward.

'Keep down as we go in,' he instructed. 'Look once and tell me exactly where the demon is.'

I nodded. Before I had a chance to move on my own, he dragged me into the room and held me facing toward the windows looking out onto the forest for a second before he pulled me to the floor.

The demon had laughed and grown to ten feet tall.

'Which direction?' he demanded.

I pointed. 'About twenty yards.'

He nodded crisply, stood up for about a second and ducked down again. 'Yep. I couldn't see any demon but I could sure as Hell see a gun barrel.'

'An interesting metaphor,' I said dryly.

He dragged me back into the hallway. 'I'm assuming it's your housemate,' he said to Puck. 'Wait for five minutes then call out to her. Make sure she knows it's you calling. Keep her talking for at least twenty minutes. Keep her focussed on you. Okay?'

Puck nodded.

He continued down the hallway and paused as he opened the door. 'Everyone stay here. Don't go near any windows, not even out the back. And stay down. Okay?'

I nodded.

As Sam entered the room at the back I could see pots and pans and an ancient cooker. It was obviously a kitchen.

I felt more moisture trickling down my face. I looked up. A tiny demon was spitting on us from above. Oh no, was I going insane again? I had to explain everything to the others before I lost my mind completely. They should at least know what Bella was planning.

'Did you all know that Megiddon Hill means Armageddon?' I said. 'Armageddon is a joining of the name of the city of Megiddo and the Hebrew word for hill. Bella must have renamed it on her map just for us. She's going to create a battle site here.'

'So she really does think this is the Apocalypse,' said Puck. 'The final battle between Good and Evil, where the losing side dies for eternity.'

'Yep,' I said. 'This is it for her. She thinks she's on God's side and we're all going to die.'

'We have to help Sam!' shouted Del. 'Tell him. Go out there.'

'He already knows he's in danger,' said Joe.

'What?' said Del. She was panicky and looking towards the kitchen door.

'That's why he said to stay here,' added Joe. 'We're probably surrounded by her followers. I suppose he took a risk going out the back way. I guess he decided the gun at the front was the greater danger. Let's hope that the others are unarmed.'

'Oh, Sam,' moaned Del with her knuckles on her lips. Her eyes had become watery.

'What do we do?' said Puck, tears on her cheeks.

'Just like Sam said,' ordered Joe. 'We haven't heard another shot so we have to assume that he's okay.' He held

Puck's arm and looked into her eyes. 'It's time now. You call out to her. Tell her it's you.'

Puck nodded. Joe opened the door a fraction of an inch.

'Balala, it's me,' she shouted. 'Yaldah,'

'What's that?' I whispered urgently. 'What names did you say?'

'Balala and Yaldah,' she whispered back. 'She likes to use those names instead.'

'Yaldah?' called Bella.

Puck frowned at me and shrugged. 'Does it matter?' she whispered to me. 'Yes!' she shouted at Bella.

'I'm so sorry,' called Bella. 'I didn't realise. Are those people your friends?'

'Yes,' answered Puck.

'What even Ra'a?' shouted Bella.

Puck looked at me. 'That's her nickname for you,' she whispered. 'Yes,' she shouted. 'He's not that bad, you know. He's changed a lot.'

'Come on out,' called Bella. 'I won't shoot. I thought you were intruders. I wasn't using the gun. Those plants were rigged with home-made fireworks.'

Joe looked around the edge of the door. 'She's walking into the garden, holding the gun in the air,' he said.

I stared at the demon above the door. Why was it spitting? Demons were my way of seeing danger.

At last I realised the obvious. 'Keep her talking for a minute,' I said. 'I need to get something.' I ran back to the kitchen and threw open drawers until I found a carving knife. It was rusty but it would fulfil my purpose.

'Okay!' shouted Bella. 'It's okay. I won't hurt you. I just use the gun to scare people. It's so isolated out here. You can all go home safely.'

Of course we could go home. She had already achieved her purpose. But it was okay, because she couldn't really create a plague, could she? It was just in her imagination but she really believed that she had done it. This was just a trick to get us to come here and then go away. My purpose was becoming clearer. I had to save Bella and I had to do it now. I pushed past all three of my protectors, pulled the door fully open and ran down the path before any of them could do anything. I heard their voices shouting at me to stop.

I stopped a foot in front of her.

She was slightly shorter than me with brown hair, freckles and a slim, almost tiny frame lost within combat trousers and jacket.

I had met her before. She was the unsmiling woman at the sermon I gave just before Dr Matthews died. I may have seen her many times: in the shopping centre, in church, in a pub, but I guessed that my imagination always supplied a demon to distract me. She was unfazed by my knife.

And the demon was behind her.

It was still huge, horned and red, with six-inch talons and an evil smile; still in the image of a Hollywood Demon; all show and intimidation with no real substance behind it.

Bella threw her head back slightly and looked up at me. Her sneer mocked me.

'Hello, sorceress,' I said.

She almost laughed. 'I hoped that you would understand my Hebrew, even with Miriam's appalling pronunciation.'

'Like you I know a few words. You don't really speak it properly any more than I do, though, do you?'

She frowned.

'I assume that you use the word Ra'a to indicate that I am an evil person,' I added.

'What are you doing?' shouted Joe.

'Please don't hurt him,' called Puck.

'She seems to want to protect you,' said Bella nodding at Puck.

I nodded. 'Yes. It appears that I'm not a threat to anyone.' I raised the knife. 'Not even with this in my hand.'

She shrugged.

I stepped even closer to her. She still didn't flinch. Or stop smiling. I offered the knife up to her, handle first. 'Will you need this?' I asked.

'No,' she said.

Sam appeared behind her at the edge of the forest stealthily coming up behind her on the opposite side to the demon. I had to do it now. I had to show them that I was at least temporarily safe before he interfered. I took Bella's arm and placed the handle of the knife in her palm. I closed her fingers over the hilt and drew both to my neck so that the knife blade was at my throat.

'No!' called Puck. 'Stop!'

Bella stared at me her hand shaking slightly.

'You want to do it but you don't,' I said. 'Why? You've killed others before. You've tried to kill me several times. And humiliate me. You hate me. You could do it now. I'll wait for you. I could be your sacrifice. I'm due to die now, anyway.'

Her head shook slightly. It was an involuntary act.

'You've done your job, now, haven't you? I'm infected. We're all infected. It happened in the house, didn't it? There's a demon above the door. All those pot plants exploding were designed to herd us inside.'

Her eyes widened. Yes. I was right.

'I haven't done anything,' she answered. 'There's nothing wrong with you.'

'Yes. You need us to all go away now and spread the infection.'

Again she said nothing. Finally, I was in charge. I was setting the agenda. 'Did you know that the 'flu you're spreading is no different and no more dangerous than any other 'flu? We'll be fine and so will the world. You haven't started a plague. It doesn't target the cheese intolerant. It was your arrogance that tricked you. You've committed the sin of pride.'

'No!' she shouted. She looked around wildly and rubbed her hands. She bent her arm backwards against the joint. It must have been incredibly painful. She was punishing herself. 'Pride,' she muttered. 'Pride. No. Not pride. I never have pride.'

I needed to distract her. 'Is that your demon I can see or mine?' I pointed at it so she would know where I was looking.

Her eyes widened. 'Can you really see a demon?' She stopped bending her arm.

'Yes,' I answered. 'And your followers?'

She was genuinely surprised now.

'Acolytes,' I suggested. 'You have an army of acolytes?'

'Yes,' she whispered. 'I do, but they're hidden.'

And with those words I realised that I could now see an army of demons surrounding us. 'All around us,' I said.

Bella sneezed and frowned. And then she started to cough, not once but repeatedly. She leaned forward and spat. She stared at her phlegm on the path and drew back horrified. She looked at everyone in turn confused. 'That can't be it,' she said. 'It won't hurt me.'

'You're safe,' I said. It's only the 'flu. You made a mistake. You infected yourself and Miriam a few days ago. It's all right.'

She wasn't listening.

So if Bella wasn't going to kill me how was I going to die?

The time for discussion was over. I had to defeat these demons and heal Bella. I hugged her to me and stepped into the demon's world, ready to fight it for her soul.

Even if it killed me and took my soul.

Demons and Angels

John 7:20
The people answered and said, Thou hast a devil: who goeth about to kill thee?

The demon, Asbeel, roars. Its hot, sulphurous breath blasts Gabriel. The skin on his face burns away, but there is no pain to it. Gabriel sees the soul of Bella held captive behind the demon, but she is blind and lost. Another demon in the guise of her father flays her with a whip of fire.

'I claim that woman's soul,' announces Gabriel.

'And what gives you the right to take her from me?' demands the evil one.

'She has attacked me. She took my life as Dr Gideon Matthews. By right of the ancient texts I claim a tooth for a tooth and an eye for an eye. Her life is mine.'

'No, you cannot have her. She is mine.'

'Then I will destroy you and all your followers.'

The demon sniggers. 'Little man you wish to fight me?' It waves its talons in Gabriel's face.'

' Yes!'

It laughs once more. 'Little girl, my little Yalda, you are too weak.' It turns and points to a huge army of demons to support it.

'The name Yalda, doesn't scare me. And you know I have faith.'

'There is only one of you, a weak human against this mighty army. Prepare for your soul to be eternally destroyed.'

A talon flicks out and cuts Gabriel open from groin to throat, but there is no pain.

'You've already danced on my broken body once and yet here I am.'

It places a red hand around the throat of its challenger and squeezes.

I don't need to speak, thinks Gabriel. You know my every thought.

It roars once more, but releases the hold on the throat.

Gabriel heals his body. 'You can't affect me, you know. God might allow pain and suffering in the world but he never allows a soul to be damaged. So, how can I expel you? How about Matthew 8:32 "And he said unto them, Go."?'

'No that's not it little one,' laughs the demon. 'A few Holy words are not enough! Look!'

Gabriel sees that every demon has a piece of the scripture glowing at its forehead.

'There is our power,' shouts Asbeel. 'We use the scriptures to our own ends. Some of our greatest evil is done using holy words.'

In desperation Gabriel summons his rage and attacks the demon with his body, attempting to wrestle it to the ground. He grabs a clawed arm and is effortlessly tossed aside. He wraps his arms and legs around its body and squeezes.

He feels pain.

The pain grows and strengthens.

He is almost unconscious with agony.

His grip weakens.

The demon pulls him away from its body and holds him in front of its face.

Gabriel casts aside his wrath and shouts to God for help. 'Hallelujah, God is great,' he calls. An army of beautiful white angels appears, one for each demon. The pain diminishes.

Asbeel laughs. 'They will not help you.'

Each demon creates mud, muck and excrement and throws it at the angels. The angels remain calm and pure. For each demon with a Bible quote there is an angel. The angels gather the demons into their arms with love to bring them together into one mass.

Gabriel smiles but then the angels disappear and the massed army of demons remains. At first he is confused and fearful. But then he remembers, he has been eaten by the demon of death and still found love. Finally, he understands the message of the angels. The ego, fear, sin and the intellect all conspire against the pure experience of love.

'You use little phrases from the Bible and so distort the message,' Gabriel explains to Asbeel. 'You control the powerful through their pride. You show them a handful of words and convince them that they are great, more important, more powerful than others. A few words of the Bible are interpreted by an ego that can convince itself of any absurd lie. They create mayhem and suffering believing in their arrogance that they are doing God's work by bringing on the Apocalypse instead of God's love.'

Asbeel thrashes from side to side, shrinking in size and power with every statement as they are controlled by Gabriel's understanding.

'You even had me under control,' continues Gabriel. 'Through my ego, I sinned and turned away from genuine love of all people. I was tricked by your quotes and forgot that the whole Bible contains the message, not just parts of it.'

Asbeel shakes its head in frustration and confusion.

'It was my sin that made you strong.'

The demon is on its knees.

'Now let me have Bella. I can save her. She is mine. Despite her threats to me, I give my life to save hers. For it is through the willing sacrifice of my own ego that I will redeem her. I will teach her that sin is tied to this world. That we cannot escape or stop or even expiate our sin. That God will forgive everything and bring us to him despite our nature. We only need ask.'

Asbeel struggles. 'No. She is mine.'

'And you are me,' explains Gabriel. 'Demon you do not exist except that I do. You are just another aspect of my ego.

Asbeel stands and turns to run, but instantly Gabriel hugs it to him. 'Yes,' cries Gabriel, 'you are me. I love and accept you as a part of myself. I do not need quotes from the Bible. The entire Bible tells me of God's love. You cannot tie me to any group of words, Old or New Testament. I love myself, sinner that I am.'

The demon struggles in his arms but Gabriel is all powerful as he cries out 'I declare that you are a servant of God, an angel not a demon. What should I know demon?'

The demon transforms instantly into a pure white angel.

'Do you know who I am?' asks the angel.

'Yes,' rejoices Gabriel. 'You are the demon. You are the angel. You are Gideon Matthews. You are Gabriel. You are me and I am you, for I am both angel and demon, good and bad.'

Gabriel pauses in simultaneous pain and joy before he continues. 'And your purpose is to provide me with unnatural knowledge. Knowledge that is not accessible through an ego or through words but only through intuition and unconscious awareness. Knowledge that comes to you because God's will is for you to tell me.'

'Yes,' roars the Angel/Demon, finally in harmony with its purpose.

'And am I to die?'

'Yes.' It becomes a gentle, disembodied voice.

'I was doomed to death on the day I appeared, so that is no news. When will I die?'

'Your death is imminent, Gabriel, for the act has already happened. The smallest demon can be as deadly as the largest. Do you want a final purpose?'

'Yes! What is my purpose, angel?'

'It is the purpose of all who can speak and all who know. You are to heal the souls of those around you and to deliver God's message.'

'What message is that?'

'What have you learnt?'

'Of angels, demons and death. Of the Bible and of words.'

'Then heal Bella and pass on your message.'

Finally, my powers were revealed. I knew what they were. I understood Bella and I understood myself.

I took Bella by the hand and showed her God's love. Showed her that her ego will die and then showed her that sin could never be overcome or punished away.

God will take us all, believer or not and save us all from sin through his love, through his power.

She understood at last. She was released from her madness.

I was on the ground surrounded by my friends. Bella was lying on the ground nearby, coughing blood.

'Are you okay?' said Del, on her knees by Bella's side.

'What's wrong with her?' I asked.

'We're all coughing blood,' said Sam. 'Except Del,' he added with a small smile. 'I think that maybe this 'flu really is bad.'

'What? We've only just been infected. How can it be so advanced?'

'I've been sneezing for days,' said Puck.

'I'm going to call for help again,' said Sam. 'But if it works this fast...' he couldn't finish the sentence. 'Come on Joe,' he added.

'Wait,' I called. 'We have a job to do. Joe, I need you and your equipment.'

Joe looked at Sam who shrugged.

'Okay,' said Joe.

I dragged my body over next to Bella. The pain was so intense and my breath so weak that I had to stop every few yards and wait.

'Bella,' I said.

She looked up at me, fear in her eyes. 'Will I go to Hell? Have I missed any deadly sins?'

'Only one,' I said. 'Pride.' I smiled at her and sent her my greatest love so that she would feel at peace. 'But God has already forgiven you,' I said.

She nodded, understanding at last.

'Angels and demons walk among us!' whispers Doctor Gideon Matthews, lay preacher and angel named Gabriel. The camera frames him lying against a tree trunk, hardly visible in the fading light of the sun. A bright new moon appears in the east. 'We are surrounded by demons. But they aren't real demons. They aren't disguised as people.' He tries to breathe deeply, but, for the moment, he can only cough and splutter. The camera view stays focussed on him. 'Have you seen the deplorable actions of our so-called leaders? They are happy to accept war, poverty and death. These are the acts of demons!' A shudder of coughing passes through his weak frame. 'But I tell you, the demons are already within us and so we must all fight against evil inside ourselves first.'

He pauses for breath. The viewer can see that he is reviewing a congregation outside the camera.

'There are people so arrogant that they think that they are God's agents in the world. They are trying to take over the world and to create the Apocalypse now, but this is, once again, that old sin of pride.' For a few seconds the power of God's love energises his body. 'Fundamentalists of all religions will take snatches of words from their holy books, add a few of their own words and interpretations and then accuse, judge and harass people they don't like. Sometimes it's another religion, sometimes it's another race and sometimes it's another sexual preference. You cannot take bits of the Bible or any other holy book and then ignore the rest. God's message is too big for that. God is too great. God is love. God forgives. Even the unbeliever is forgiven.'

'Now let me tell you our story.' And so Gabriel tells the story of Dr Gideon Matthews, Bella, Puck-Sarah-Miriam, Joe, Del, Sam and a demon and an angel.

PRIDE

Matthew 10:28
And fear not them which kill the body, but are not able to kill the soul: but rather fear him which is able to destroy both soul and body in hell.

Bella finally realised that her father never understood the deadly sin of pride. He claimed to be better than everyone and it was his pride that had caused his downfall and hers. Her entire life had been distorted by this one deadly sin.

Gabriel had finally shown to her that making the body suffer did not remove the sin, nor did it stop it. We have bodies and egos and we sin. That is the message of Adam and of Jesus. For it is only through God's love that we go to the timeless realm of Heaven.

The End

---

1 Peter 4:7
But the end of all things is at hand: be ye therefore sober, and watch unto prayer.

Puck was lying in my arms. 'I'm dying, aren't I Mister?' she whispered.

'We all are, Miriam,' I said. 'But you have many more years than me for I will soon be dead but I think you are already getting better.'

She smiled and coughed. 'Call me Puck. I like that name when you use it.'

I was just able to lift my head to smile at her.

My chest was heaving; my lungs were working hard but to little effect.

The scientists who declared our safety had forgotten to allow for the natural mutation of every virus. This one was overdue. It was our bad luck that the flu transmuted at this time into a highly infectious and deadly form. But we had been isolated before we infected other people. Our deaths would be of use, for the scientists and doctors could study the new form of flu. A vaccine was now possible in time to stop an apocalyptic plague created by Nature and not by human hands.

For all his mighty power Sam was the most helpless, cradled in Del's arms. He was in almost exactly the same position that he had fallen into, exhausted on his return from calling for help.

I coughed up phlegm. It tasted of blood. I was grateful I couldn't see it in the dark.

'Please don't die,' Puck whispered to me. A tear dropped to my cheek.

I looked over at Sam. His breathing was barely audible. I could see the irregular rise of his chest, splashed by Del's tears.

His breathing ceased.

Gabriel sees Sam's soul rise from his body.

'He's gone on,' I whispered.

An uncontrolled sob escaped from Del. She gently stroked the big man's face.

Del looked up at me. The crying had washed down through her mascara creating painted tears to match the real ones. 'Why?' she sobbed. 'Why him? He could have done more.'

She collapsed, overwhelmed with grief. She lay sobbing into the ground.

'I don't know,' I gasped, uselessly. She would have to find her own understanding for I did not have time to teach her things I didn't know.

I used my insights to look at each of us. I already knew that Puck would survive. Joe would go soon, but after me. Del was untouched by any illness.

I rolled onto my side, disturbing Puck. She moved and sobbed simultaneously.

'Don't go,' she begged of me.

'I wish I didn't have to,' I wheezed and paused once again as pain shot through my lungs.

She hugged me fiercely, trying desperately to capture my soul within her arms.

I was going to heaven, but a part of me was still going to die. This particular person, Gideon, Gabriel or whoever would end his story here. It was the death of all things for both Gideon and Gabriel.

For a few moments I was terrified of dying. Did I really have an eternal soul? Was I more than just a handful of neurons desperate not to be annihilated?

And then I felt the peace of God's love once more.

My ego ceas...

Lightning Source UK Ltd.
Milton Keynes UK
04 September 2009

143372UK00001B/3/P